MW01199211

UNNÁTURÁL
disasters

UNNATURAL
disasters

RECENT

WRITINGS

FROM THE

GOLDEN

STATE

Edited by

NICOLE PANTER

INCOMMUNICADO PRESS

P.O. BOX 99090 SAN DIEGO CA 92169

©1996 Incommunicado
Contents © the individual artists

ISBN 1-884615-16-3
First Printing

Cover design by Jennifer Moody
Cover photos by Mat Roe
Book design by Gary Hustwit
Editing assistance by Sandra Zane and Gary Hustwit
Transcription by Felicia Crossley

All rights reserved. No part of this book may be reproduced or transmitted in any form or by any means, electronic or mechanical, including photocopying, recording, or any information storage and retrieval system, without permission in writing from the copyright holder.

Printed in the USA.

Contents

NICOLE PANTER

Introduction

UNNATURAL DISASTERS: Recent Writings from the Golden State is a collection of fiction, faction and essays from some of the most interesting writers working in California today. These are the narratives/monologues/inner-landscapes of an over-developed, strip-malled, riot/rebellion-torn, earthquake-stricken, stress-plagued, burnt-out, tapped-out, broken-down, post-disastrous, post-apocalyptic, post-boom locale formerly known as Paradise. Until (relatively) recently, California was considered by many to be the pot of gold at the end of the United States' rainbow, a place whose sun-kissed residents were envied and emulated ("wish they all could be California girls...."), and now all that has changed. Artists are societal mine canaries, the barometers of their environment, and these writers have known for years what the rest of the world is just now finding out—that appearances don't always tell the whole story. *Unnatural Disasters* is not a catalog of the woes which have recently befallen the Golden State—you can turn on any channel's Evening News any night of the week for that. It is a journey into the subtext and psyche of whatever it is that lies beneath and beyond. *Unnatural Disasters* is the work of writers living in a world that is poised for the next aftershock—whatever that may be.

The collection of writers in these pages varies wildly from the well-known and critically acclaimed to several who are seeing their publication debut here. At least one is a fourth generation Californian, others have arrived from points far outside of Stateline in the last few years. Some have found great success in the film industry, others wouldn't know CAA's phone number if they were faced with a firing squad. Efforts span from the comic to the bittersweet to the ironic, the tragic and the downright sarcastic. Some are memory pieces conjured up from other times and places, but even these are filtered through the shaky, disintegrating here and now. On the surface, it would seem that some of these writers have nothing in common with others, but that is not the case. All of them share two things: first, each one is a skilled craftsperson, able to weave a spellbinding narrative. And second—earthquake, fire, riot, flood, xenophobia, and recession notwithstanding—each is directly affected by what is going on wherever they may live in California. In their own way, they are all working under the gun at the end of the 20th century, in a boomtown going spectacularly bust.

Settle back for the ride and remember: duck, cover and hold.

—Nicole Panter

Acknowledgements

The editor wishes to thank all the writers, without whom this book would not have been possible and who were wonderfully accommodating and enthusiastic during all stages of the project. Many thanks to the following: to Jennifer Moody, talented, flexible designer. To Lisa Monti for being such a great friend, take-no-prisoners sounding board and unwavering moral support. To David (as usual), Peanut and Peter (inspiration by example) for friendship and constant encouragement. If I were to choose a spiritual home for this book, it would be California Institute of the Arts, which was almost demolished in the 1994 Northridge earthquake, but is now back and stronger than ever. So, to my tenacious, dedicated, gifted students (past and present) at Cal Arts—thank you for being there every week. I'd also like to thank Sheree Rose Levin for her help and access to Bob Flanagan's work. Many thanks to the staff at Incommunicado. And most of all, to my publisher, Gary Hustwit who didn't take much convincing, didn't ask too many questions and gave me completely free reign on this project.

In memory
of
Bob Flanagan
1952–1996

UNNATURAL *disasters*

DAVE ALVIN

A Prayer for Los Angeles

Our Lady, Queen of the Angels, Queen of the Chumash and Gabrielino Indians, Queen of Gaspar de Portola, Pio Pico, Kit Carson, pueblo of sweating desert winds, oasis of burning canyons, downtown looming above unmarked founders' graves—mestizos, indians, blacks—who trudged from Mexico to Mission San Gabriel then down Mission Boulevard to settle on chaparral river flats. Their ghosts haunt pawnshop storefronts, tits and ass theatre lobbies on Bella Union Main street. Skid row, no longer home for road-weary Woody Guthrie or road-jazzed Kerouac slumming 1940s burlesque houses, just men sleeping in plastic trash bags and cardboard boxes in front of the midnight mission or men with throats slashed beneath artists' lofts or throwing up on the steps of City Hall. Queen of the women silently waiting for buses in front of Mexican bars, Cuban bars, Guatemalan bars, Vietnamese bars, Chinese bars and old white men bars where the old white men play big band on the jukebox so they won't hear the Spanish outside in the dying palm tree streets of Philip Marlowe stucco and heat apartments. Our Lady of limousines, of Hollywood movie and tv stars, dead stars, rock stars, has-beens, hopefuls, directors, producers, their scripts, their lunches, their homes, their tennis courts, their motorcycles, their bodyguards, their Mercedes washed and their lawns mowed by illegals who wait for crumbs on street corners. Our Lady of Musso and Frank's and Graumann's Chinese where Bible belt tourists try to fill the shoes of John Wayne and Shirley Temple. Virgin Mother of Santa Monica Boulevard street corner boys staring numb at passing cars, of heartbroken queens boasting dried blood wrists and negative test results. Hookers, pimps, tricks and some guy working all night behind the counter of an adult book store, someone working all night behind bulletproof glass at a self-service gas station, someone working all night selling lottery tickets at a convenience store, religious cult apostles handing out throwaway pamphlets of throwaway salvation and heavy metal white boys cruising endless, identical suburban streets tempting the wilder side of blonde girls with eternal tans. Our Lady of KRLA lowriders cruising Whittier Boulevard past the Silver Dollar Cafe, past Ruben Salazar's ghost while east side vatos spray paint boundaries on hopeless walls. Queen of a south-central thirteen-year-old armed with an automatic weapon and a desperate heart that can't forget a past that still exists. Our Lady of drive-by shootings, of nervous police trigger fingers and choke holds. Our Lady, Queen of the victims of fires, landslides, earthquakes, of dark freeways. Queen of Native Americans, Hispanics, Asians, Whites from Pacoima to Little Tokyo to Little Seoul, from Torrance to Bell Gardens, from Fairfax to Boyle Heights, trying to get by just one more day underneath the air-conditioned views from the half-empty skyscrapers downtown. The unemployed aerospace workers and steelworkers of glamourless Maywood, Commerce and Gardena. The corporate computer drones of Westwood and Century City. The World War veterans who came here for the good life of sunshine in La Mirada and La Puente next to post card orange groves under snow-capped mountains but found themselves in imitation Spanish colonial tract homes, New England tract homes, imitation French provincial tract homes, imitation Bauhaus tract homes under exhaust-brown skies the same as Chicago or

Detroit. Our Lady of cars. Our Lady of mini-malls. Our Lady of vanished Chumash and Gabrielinos, of vanished hillsides, vanished ranchos, vanished citrus groves, vanished Angel's Flight, vanished Pan Pacific, vanished red cars, vanished Garden of Allah, vanished Bunker Hill, of your vanished river. Our Lady of the Pacific Ocean, that brought Cabrillo and the Yankee whalers, that comes to the sand directed by you, through moon and stars, again and again, forever and ever, Amen.

DIANE SHERRY CASE

Spa-Tel

Billy left me in the smoking hot car in front of this desolate fifties-looking motel, *Spa*-tel the sign says. I wait and wait and finally I decide to look for him. It's real quiet when I get out of the car and listen to the water boiling in the engine. Yep, we're stranded I say out loud, repeating what Billy said ten minutes ago but without the Oh Fucking Great.

I walk into the courtyard and there are yellow "happy faces" painted on the cement, with their mouths wide open, laughing at you. Billy stands at a pay phone while this poodle stares up at him and barks. Billy has his datebook in one hand, he's dialing with the other, the phone's stuck between his ear and shoulder.

"Gas station's closed on Sundays," he tells me. Then he talks into the phone: "Listen, have to cancel lunch, I'm stranded in the desert…Call you when I get back."

Billy kisses me on the ear and pulls the brim of his day-glo baseball cap down to shade his eyes. Then he starts dialing again. "Guess I'll go wait over there," I say, tilting my head toward the pool. He asks if I'm okay and pulls me close. Then he turns back to the phone. "Let me speak to Shana Gold—this is Billy Fire…" He twists the phone away from his mouth. "What are we going to do?" he whispers. "My flight leaves L.A. at three." I pull away because it's hot and Billy's sticky and I don't know what we're going to do. "Why don't you go hang out by the pool," Billy says. "I've got one more call." He licks his lips and throws me a kiss that reminds me of a photo shoot he did where his lips were wet and his shirt fell off his shoulder so you could see one tit. Looked pretty good for a guy in his thirties. Billy's almost as photogenic as me.

The speedy little dog runs backwards in front of me, as I walk toward the pool. "Come here Maurice," a woman yells from the hot tub. There's a shrunken head made out of rubber laying on the ground. I can only hope it's for Maurice. This whole place gives me the willies. Reminds me of a motel I once stayed at in Vegas for some job I would never want Billy to know about. I take off my sandals and dangle my feet in the pool, careful to keep my legs together since I don't have any panties on. Billy likes it when I don't wear panties.

The woman climbs over the short wall that separates the mineral tub from the pool, swims to where I'm sitting and says "Hi, I'm Bea." She's old and tan and wears a bright orange bikini. She acts spacey like a leftover hippy. "You need a room?" "I don't know yet, our car's broke." "Maybe you're meant to be here," she says, and smiles sort of menacingly. Then she swims away.

Billy's got on boots too hot for the desert, his Combats, he calls them, not just boots. He's got his black jeans tucked into them and he has on a white sleeveless t-shirt and his baseball cap's on backwards now and it's got a feather stuck in its hole that he says he got from some Peruvian Indian he met in New York. He's pouring on suntan oil as he walks toward me and his shoulders glow like a weightlifter's sweat and I can't take my eyes off him, I want to marry him. "You going to call that producer or what?" he asks.

He came up with this brilliant idea yesterday when we went to Nevada to get some money. He thinks we can sell this book he wrote to the movies before it gets published, which he says will be soon. Then we'll have thousands of dollars so we can rent a cool house on a hill overlooking the lights of Hollywood. It's a long way from posing for calendars in Vegas. Et cetera. I was always afraid my Grandma would find out. Like maybe she'd go with Grandpa to get his car fixed or something, and look in the mechanic's shed, at the calendar, to see what day it was and there I'd be, staring at her with my tongue on my lips and my legs wide open.

So I'm supposed to call this producer that I went out with once, who said I had a great look, that I should act, but didn't give me any jobs. He just wanted me to come swim in his pool. I never went. I hate to swim.

The operator takes Billy's credit card and the producer takes my call. We already rehearsed what I'm going to say. I tell him I've read this great book, which is a lie because I haven't seen it. I tell him it's a historical novel about New York in the sixties, and that he better jump on the idea now, because when it gets published there'll be a bidding war. The producer says let's have dinner and talk about it, and I say, "How about I send you the book," and hang up.

Billy's pissed. "I told you to take a lunch, pitch him the idea."

"Well I thought you should send it to him first."

"No no no," Billy says. "That's not how it works. Movie people don't read. Two sentences, I'll give you two sentences. That's all you need."

"All right, I'll call him back."

I call back and the guy says, "Colorful, I like the idea, Andy, Edie, all that? How about tomorrow night?" I say not this week, but Billy starts poking me and shaking his head, so I tell the guy okay and slam down the phone.

"I wanted to go to New York with you."

"I thought you wanted to go bigtime," Billy says, "Come on, toughen up." I remember about the house on the hill and getting out of the Midwest forever and never getting stuck in Vegas again. So I shut up. "You're so beautiful," Billy says and cups his hands around my breasts.

We've been together two months already and haven't fought except once, the week after we moved in together. Billy wasn't home and the doorbell rang. It was a real pretty woman with dyed black hair and gorgeous blue eyes and she had on one of those skin tight dresses like I'm wearing now, and not the cheap kind either. She looked like she just stepped out of I don't know where and when she said let me speak to Billy, I felt like I should put some makeup on fast. I looked at her and thought, "Let you speak to Billy, Fat Chance." And then I said, "Who are you, anyway?"

She says, "Cynthia Fire."

My first thought was to get rid of her as quick as possible in case Billy came back and saw how good she looked and starts thinking maybe he made a mistake. But I was curious. Who is this chick? Maybe I could learn more about him. So I let her come in. Billy came home immediately, saw the taxi waiting with all his stuff piled in which she'd dragged out all the way from New York, and took her outside before we even got to sit down. I watched from the window but didn't get to hear a word. Ten minutes later he came back in with a purple linen suit and a pair of Nikes in his hands and she took off with the rest of his stuff.

"Who the hell is that bitch, how come she's keeping your stuff and why didn't you tell me you were married?" I asked him.

"Because there's no room for all that stuff in this crummy little apartment," Billy said. "And she's just someone I married when I was drunk one night. When we get money for a house I'll buy new stuff. Okay?"

"Well, have her change her goddamned name," I said.

Billy's looking in the Yellow Pages, he's hysterical, and I'm hot and bothered because I have to stay here overnight with the damned red car. Billy's going to New York if he has to walk. There's an airport half an hour away, but the cab company doesn't answer their phone. "What the Hell am I going to do???" he says. "If I miss my plane..." I tell him to look up bus station or something, but he decides to go check on Cherry to see if he can fix her himself.

Billy's car's a '57 T-bird, Cherry he calls it, like it was a girl. He says it's because she's red and perfect but that's not exactly true. She's already broke down five times since he bought her four weeks ago. She's still making spitting noises when we get out there. Billy raises the hood and looks at her insides for a while and finally shakes his head and says "I don't know."

I'll ask Bea, I say. Her door's open and she's changed from her bathing suit into some hot pink shorts and hot pink high tops that say Try Me on the tongue. Her skin is leathery from the sun. "Of course I have a room for you," she says. "5C's available, and no I can't take your friend to the airport."

Bea shows me to 5C. There's brown and orange carpet that kind of buckles and a towel with home sweet home written on it. And there's a photograph pasted on wood that has yellow sunlight going through redwood trees. The picture has no middle like most pictures. Just sun rays through the trunks.

"Here's the thermostat," Bea says as she hands me the key. "But you won't need heat, it's warm at night, lots of stars. I'm getting back in the pool. Join me if you like."

"I don't like water," I tell her.

"Oh, it's so good for you, all the minerals. Honey, you need it. It'll calm you down."

"Don't like to sit in water deeper than my pelvic bone," I say. "Certainly not with minerals."

"Well, if you change your mind..." she says and I realize she has a Midwestern accent.

Billy gets his stuff out of the car and we walk past the freeway we coasted off of a few hours ago and down this deserted desert road to a one street town. The sun's setting but it's still ninety degrees so I'm glad it's just a ten minute walk. Billy leans on the pole of a bus stop sign and complains about buses. "It'll take me an hour to get to Palm Springs. I better not miss my plane. Buses suck." He gets on anyway, when the bus finally shows, waves and says "I'll call you tonight."

I buy some Kentucky chicken and carry it back to the motel. "I was going to invite you to stir-fry," Bea yells from the hot tub as I look for my key. "Thanks but I got this," I say and hold up my Kentucky bag. I look through my purse but there's no key. "Wait until I get out and I'll open it for you," Bea says. I go to the pool, where Maurice, the poodle, stands at the edge and looks down at the shrunken rubber head which he's dropped into the water. I sit on a ratty old reclining chair to wait.

There's something that makes me stare at Bea. She sticks her hand out of the water and digs it into the earth beside the tub. She pulls up a purple crystal, a big raw rock, and shakes the dirt off. Then she closes her eyes and moves it in front of her face like it's a blow dryer that gives off wonderful heat. "These give energy," she says. "They're from the earth, but not of it." She sighs deeply, smiles. "Your boyfriend, he's a writer?" she asks, acting normal again.

"Used to be an actor, but he's written a book."

"What's it called?" she wants to know.

It dawns on me that I don't know what it's called. Billy refers to it as The Book. But I'm not going to tell her I don't know. "He's still thinking about it," I say.

At five o'clock I sit by the pool and stare at the cactus. It's already night in New York and Billy hasn't called. I need to know the name of that book or I'm going to look like some dumb blond when I meet with that producer. I decide to call the number Billy gave me, his friend Dan in New York. I don't have Billy's credit card number so I'm pouring in coins.

"Is Billy there yet?" I ask. There's a pause. "Billy Fire?"

"That what he's calling himself now?"

I hesitate, I don't know what to say.

"No, I don't expect him here, he owes me money. Try Cynthia's."

This is not good news. I try to sound casual, not to let it show. "You don't happen to know the name of that book he wrote, do you?"

The guy laughs, big and hearty. "He told you he wrote a book?" he says and it's not really a question. "Listen, honey, when you talk to him, have him call me…"

I stand there and watch Maurice eat some live lizard's tail and Bea comes and hands me the car keys. "You left these in the ignition."

"Thanks," I say.

"I hope you don't mind," Bea says. "It was blocking my sign, so I moved it."

"What?"

"I fixed it. Runs fine," she says and walks toward the pool.

I take a deep breath of warm dry air. "I'd better get it together," I say out loud to myself or the dog or whatever. I go to my room and start brushing my teeth and thinking I've made another big mistake. I'm rinsing out my teeth and Bea comes knocking at the door.

"There's a phone call for you honey," she says and as I pass her to get to the pay phone she says, "It's him." The little poodle is trying to trip me and I say, "Maurice, Cut it the Fuck Out" and kind of add a kick to my trip before I can catch myself because I may do a lot of things but I don't kick dogs on purpose. Bea says, "Oh honey, I sure wish you'd take that mineral bath."

Billy goes "Howdy." He likes to pretend he's a cowboy for some reason. So I just go "Hi." I don't say how's New York or where are you staying or does this fucking book really exist or did you just forget to tell me you haven't written it yet? I just say "Hi." But my hi must tell him something, because there's a two thousand mile silence.

"Did you get the car fixed?" he finally asks and I say, "It's getting late, Billy," with a hard B and I'm about to hang up when he starts telling me about this photo shoot and this white Armani suit and I say, "What are you talking about?" and his voice goes up high when he says, "What do you mean?" and I say, "I gotta go, this dog's humping my leg." Billy doesn't say what's the matter you sound cold and far away, he just says, "Okay, later babe."

I hang up and walk back to my room. So much for that home on a hill and my honest stab at life and what am I going to do without Billy? I sit there and think about it while it gets dark. A hot wind rattles the open window in 5C and the door flies open.

I go to shut the door and see Christmas lights on all the palm trees and Christmas lights around the mineral bath and I walk out into the hot breeze. It's starting to sprinkle which I think is odd, because desert means no water as far as I know.

No one's at the mineral tub, so I take my dress off and put my foot in the water. It's real hot. I slip my leg in slowly and water moves slow around me, bubbles gather on my skin. My body sinks down into it.

The black desert sky is full of tiny white lights and there's water everywhere, water falls on me, water comes out of my eyes... Water presses against my muscles, my thighs...There are faces, men, men before Billy and men before that. Bodies I didn't ask for, men I never knew...There are stars in the desert sky, thousands, lit like fireflies on my Grandma's farm...There are colors, colors in my head, fabrics, colors, costumes I've worn, photos I've taken. Eyes lined black like some Indian princess. Golden shoes with heels pointed sharp. Lips red as a sheep's slit throat...

"This is very special," Bea says in a soft and soothing voice. "Desert rain." She smiles at me and I realize that she's been sitting there, across from me, this entire time. "I like you," she says. "So I will tell you a secret. When the world ends, they are coming to pick us up. There are stations. Only a few of us know. We'll meet them at the stations and they'll take us."

Bea gets out of the hot tub and her body glows, really glows, as in 'glowed in the dark.' Just lights up. "Wow," I say. "From the minerals," she answers. And then she says, "When it happens, you can come, too."

I open my mouth to say "yes, yes, take me take me, please, I love you wonderful, wise lady." But suddenly that's not right anymore. "You're fucking out of your mind insane!" I scream, dripping wet. "Nobody's going to pick you up you stupid broad. I'm outta here."

I go to my room and dry off and put on my dress and stick my birth control pills and toothbrush into my purse and put on a pair of panties. I'm on my own.

It's quiet in the desert. My footsteps sound real cool in the gravel, a sound I never hear in Los Angeles, footsteps, or if I do hear it, I don't notice.

"God bless you," Bea yells after me. I look behind me at Billy's red T-bird and she looks just perfect, like she belongs at the Miracle Spa-Tel. So I toss the keys into the cactus and head towards the bus stop.

JILL ST. JACQUES

Just Another River in Egypt

Never did resolve things with the old man. We hadn't spoken for at least eight maybe ten years before my sex change. Years. That time goes by like fat Brazilian ants, it's stocky but it hustles; pushy, bitchy, undeniable, irrevocable. Well, the old fucker's gone now so I suppose that's that. No good crying over spilled milk, especially milk a wee bit rancid from the start, poisonous milk, asphalt milk, napalm milk, whatever the shit is—it's better when you just get rid of it. Get your kitchen clean. There wasn't ever an initial state of purity anyway, it might not ever've been milk at all. My dad said milk was bad for you after you turned eighteen, that calcium collected in your bones, gave you rheumatism before your time. If you had too much calcium in your bones it'd spill over into other areas; your kidneys, your testicles, your eye. Next thing you know you're paralyzed from the neck up.

When the old man died, it must've been about Christmas. I say must've cuz I found out about his death through my Marmee after the Northridge quake—I hadn't spoken to Marmee for a few, but quakes have a way of changing your heart about a lot of things. Maybe you give up a lot when you look at Death, or at least unglue your fingers from The Pie. Who knows? Marmee told me Dad'd been dead for a while by then—

Throat cancer.

I wonder if they put the fucker in a box, or if they burned him. He always said he'd prefer burning, but you never know what people're gonna do with your corpse once you give it up. We all have our dreams. Candy. Golden foil candy, rooms full of gold, like a Gonzales-Torres Gallery Installation. You get lucky. You get candy. You get lucky candy, maybe a stocking under the tree. After a while the stocking's got holes in it. It looks better that way. It looks different.

My old man could put a bullet in a bull elk's heart from a pickup truck at five hundred paces. Do it in the dawn. Do it in the dark. In the night. Nobody's lookin. My father was a doctor, but his heart wasn't into medicine—dad loved to hunt, that's what he really loved to do. He was a hunter-gatherer, happiest with one clean shot, straight through the heart. I see my father in the way I write the alphabet. Certain perversions of letters; the eye, for example, or the eff. I got the letters from my Marmee. Q, P & J. But I have a habit of rearranging things. Even memories. Even memories of dead animals. You set your feet down tight before you squeeze your trigger. Pop the gun off safety. Red for fire. Red for thirst. You squeeze that trigger tight, pull off a clean shot, you got yourself some dinner.

My dad never did take me hunting for buffalo. We got our buffalo from someplace else. I forget how the old man conned Marmee into going to Kansas alone, while he arranged some affair with my stepmother or one of his patients back in town. Marmee took me and my brother with her, all the way past Kansas City. This was long after the divorce. Marmee drove and drove for hours, days in that white Plymouth station wagon; the wagon she wrecked when I was ten, twelve, fourteen was the last time she wrecked it.

Buffalo are big and brown. They get red when they're frozen. Turn brown again when you cook em. I forgot how the old man conned Marmee into getting the buffalo. He had a way of talking that made you want to do things.

I remember thinking we were nowhere. Back when they had Sinclair gas stations, big green signs with a giant green dinosaur. Marmee pulled into a Sinclair station to get my brother Ethan n me a grape soda. We'd been buggin her to get us a grape soda for miles and miles. And there was green grass all around the teeny white gas station with just one pump dirt packed yard where mechanics tinkered on cannibalized roasted Plymouths and Chryslers. That grass seemed to stretch out to infinity. I can't remember if there were crickets, but it felt like everything was silent, or if it wasn't silent the words spoken between Marmee and the man at the gas station didn't mean much of anything at all, or if they meant anything they meant that the grass and the gigantic green brontosaurus and the silence of the summer was bigger and heavier and meaner'n all get out, and there wasn't a damn thing better that we could make happen between all of us put together—not my Marmee, not my brother, not me, not at all.

My dad made the buffalo into hamburger. I don't remember what Marmee did with her share. She may not have done anything with it. She may have let it spoil. No good crying. Marmee may not have done anything with her buffalo, it might still linger in her freezer, maybe I'll inherit it when she dies.

Back at his house, my dad got my stepmother to bring out the Grinder. She scrubbed it till it shone stainless clean, and he used a small wooden malletpeg to stuff the slab of buffalo in. The maws of the Grinder were fluted and yawning—he'd spent a lot of money on it—the best Grinder he could buy—and this seems odd to me now because the old man never I mean NEVER spent a smiffling smidgen lick of money on anything except shotguns rifles, a good butcher block of thirsty white oak, and a fine set of knives from a catalog cutlery house in Chicago. And that Grinder.

We ate buffalo off and on for a couple of years. We had a big white chest freezer with heavy black rubber seals that'd puff out wisps of frost whenever you hauled the fucker open, and right after you thought that buffalo meat'd be gone for good the old man'd stick on a pair of blanched pigskin gloves he set aside just for freezer retrievals and delve around in there, and trawl up yet another frozen saran wrap slab of buffalo. There were a zillion other dead animals in that freezer, grouse and quails n rabbits smoked trout venison pate riverfrogs a snapper, but that god damned buffalo meat just kept reappearing like a haunting. My old man didn't really like it that much, and Marmee never went to get another, but there were several more times when I felt like I was nowhere again, times when the silence packed tight as the maws of a Grinder, and the sky pressed it down like a wooden peg; small, stiff, and frightened.

My dad gave us haircuts that really pissed us off, but if you whined you got slapped. We never really got beaten per se, cuz my dad was a doctor with a reputation to uphold, so he just took you apart with words. When your father is a twisted psychiatrist scumbag he doesn't really need to use words—after a while just a look in the rearview mirror, or the flick of a cigarette dumb white plastic aquafilter, the threat of the words, winters of words and wooden pegs and the maws of the Grinder.

The haircuts were short, and your neck would hurt after, cuz the old man used this Ronco hairshaving plastic comb device that he got at Walgreen's or Skagg's. It came with a cantilevered razor blade, and that's how he finished the haircut off. Your neck would be blazing red hot, and the kids made fun of the haircut. I took my head with me to school, and Joey Mack and Cheryl Buchalter said I looked like *Dobie Gillis* or *Dennis the Menace* or *Leave It To Beaver*, hair all short crooked tufty cowlicks lasted for years.

That summer there were storm warnings over the Panhandle. Rain thicker'n molasses, thicker'n Mrs. Butterworth's, thicker'n gooseberry jam—purpleredrainlips French toast breakfast honeydrizzle. C'mon, get in the car, we've still got four hundred miles to go. What, Marmee? OK, I'm sorry, I was drying my hair, I'll be out in a sec. Don't forget to brush your teeth before we leave, sweetie. Sure thing, Marmee, I'll be out in a sec. And your ears, don't forget to Q-tip your ears my jewel! Right, Marmee. I'll be out in a sec. I'll be out in a sec. Break it down, take the long way home. My Marmee had daisy blonde hair with bangs, cornflower blue eyes, eyes a little too eager to believe, to suffer, maybe even to die. She took her ten-year-old kid with her to Dallas and sold some painting. That was back when blueberry pancakes had real blueberries in em. Back when they came with real butter, you didn't have to ask for Vermont maple syrup, it came with the breakfast. *Runaway* was the big song on the AM, and Marmee let me choose the songs I liked, little funnel clouds dropping down from the flat gray up above. Dallas catfish motels and pool green turtlekid imagination. Marmee sold most of her paintings that trip, pigment/gouache panels of Greek women with antique instruments, large-eyed blonde women with long precarious limbs and bowls of flowers. This was the sixties. Flowers were big then, some people were even considering sticking your nose in em might be good. Marmee's panels were selling for one or two grand apiece, we felt like we'd made a fortune. All the way back to New Mexico we talked laughed and sang along with that hothead white Plymouth radio. Runaway. Wildfire. Stampede.

She was riding Wild wildfire she was ridin' Wild wildfire she was callin' Wiiiiiiiiiiildfirrre…

I go to a cutting edge art school now, I've learned to do my cutting edge art school things.

My dad taught me how to hunt. When I was six or seven, I had my first gun. When I was fourteen and Marmee chowdered her car for the third time; lost her four front teeth in that one and broke her right hip, she wasn't wearing her seatbelt but lucked out cuz the Plymouth came out of the tailspin in a double endo embankment to embankment and the door opened ping shot her clean out of the driver's seat and into some sweet blue new mexican sagebrushes. A few stitches but she was OK.

I was on the St. Michael's wrestling team that year. We drank hot lime jello in thermos mugs, and I tore the shit out of some poor kid's knee trying to prove to the old man I wasn't a fag but even now that we both know I am a fag (or whatever) I still have a lot of violence rabbit guts back forty bailin wire the guillotine hold the body slam the grapevine left inside. It seldom seems to find its way to the right home. The old man's dead now, and the worst of it is I can't kill him or smash his brains in or better yet, now that I've learned my cutting edge of art school words, I can't use those newfound cutting edges to welcome him and that Freudian Sadist rhetoric to the torture chamber the way I should've a long time ago. We can't fight. We can't fuck. We can't bitch. We can't touch. The old man is in the box now the funnel clouds've pulled him away hammer tongs bailing wire dead rabbit roadkill my dear old man's dead on the Dirty Girl's windowsill. Fuck! I can't summon him up forever just to beat him down—that'd be too similar to the shit he pulled on me when I was a kid. I've got to get away from it somehow, but the bailing wire rabbit skull grinder mawed my widdo wee jackwabbit tail, there ain't much scamper left. I bet I finish it off soon.

The first thing I ever killed with my BB gun was a lady blue jay lived in a mud cliff hole near our yard and that nice lady blue jay had her a nest full of chicks. I pegged her ass good but had to pump BB after BB into her brain to actually kill her, Daisy BB gun Chuck Connors in *The Rifleman* cocking and cocking to build up that BB compression ksssshick ksssshick ksssshick but kikirikee killing something with a BB's harder'n it knocking it back into its little mud housie little chicks screeching and screeching, and I left them there to either starve or get eaten by wild cats, and when I got home with my limp blue feathered trophy, my dad made me eat her.

"Gotta eat what you kill," he said and I fried her up cuz frying's the lump sum total of my culinary expertise at age ten...not even a batterdipped blue jay, blue jay omelette, blue jay flambe, blue jay souffle—just sear its ass up in a pan, garnish with Hormel Chili and Eggo Frozen Waffles. "Gotta eat what you kill!" I choked down each horrible brown morsel, and secretly added to "Gotta Eat What You Kill": "Yeah, unless you don't bring it home with you."
Life's little lessons. Hands and pleasures dead.

My dad had wimpy sandy tow-blonde and green jack mackerel eyes. Flipped his hair over his head with his right hand. Women thought he was handsome, my sadist fuck father. I don't know why. He didn't look like Clint Eastwood. He didn't look like Frank Sinatra. My dad looked like my dad, like an irritable intelligent cruel white charismatic psychologist cocaine addict. Just picture Reverend Jim Jones with tow-blond hair. There were other similarities. I could easily see him making his patients take the cyanide kool-aid test; "Prove how much you love your Father." My dad loved cop movies, *Kojak* and *Mannix* especially. His favorite musical was *Man Of La Mancha*, he'd cry and paw at my stepmother whenever they played that song. My mother was lucky to get rid of him, but unfortunately she never knew just how lucky. My stepmother knew. The gypsies have a saying: "Fickleness has its own rewards." You don't envy the person that kills the blue jay and her chicks. My old man cheated on everyone who ever loved him, cheated more on those who didn't; I remember the time he cried when we were watching *For Whom The Bell Tolls*. The part where Ingrid Bergman cries and the soldier guy dies and the bell goes tolling off its head. I made fun of my dad crying by imitating the bells "Bong Bong Bong."

She had a funny nervous smile. She'd sit on the grass and read mysteries while I caught brook trout with grasshoppers impaled on small barbed hooks. She wired yellow plastic daisies to the radio antenna of the Plymouth. She took me to a carnival once and got stung by a bee on her elbow, and I loved her and it made me cry.

Denial ain't just another river in Egypt.

I don't think I'm really like him, though. I mean, just because them Lacanian Feminists say that when a man wants to be a woman it means he/she/whatever wants to be the Object of Desire for the father that never loved him/her/whatever; the woman stuck in the man's body or whatever. Not to mention the female to male brothers, although I suppose it's the same isn't it? Only do those guys want the dad to desire them cuz of that calfskin Phallus they got droopin the frog's body. What a con job. The Gay Gene. Gay Braincells. One bad frog can spoil the whole bunch girls. The frog princess fluffs up her petticoats and turns to the Church Social; "I was born that way dontcha unnerstand? I was born all fucked up I admit it's freaky but I just can't help it, *it's in my Genes dammit,* now can't I please eat at Pizza Hut with y'all without gettin my nuts kicked down my goddamn throat? I just want to get to the bleu cheese dressing and the garbanzo beans without some plains state housewife gettin her pitbull husband to punch my bags apart!" Born that way. Born that way. You can tell when there's a tornado brewin. They drop down soft n savvy, flirtatious, pluckin curled n swift, 1920s lace opera gloves dippin into the flatiron Panhandle skies, at least four or five a minute, but most of em never hit the ground. Buffalo. There's a point where it all connects, there's stars and stars, but there's only one funnel cloud that counts in the sky, and that's the one that hits the ground. The Egyptian River, I did want him to love me. I do want to fix the broken Marmee. I want to bring back the dead, only not the old man necessarily. Dead rabbits black forest elks venison Egyptian Riverturtles pondchirping frogs mudcliff blue jays barbed grasshoppered trout and buff bobtopped quail. Certainly all of the sides of myself that he wanted me to kill, I'd like to bring all those sides back. Choir boy. Shakespeare. The Hobbit. Mamma's boy. From the dead Insecticide. There's no escape. It gets in those hard to reach corners.

When we got back from Dallas, I went to stay with the old man for a while. He had a way of looking at you over his fried chicken that made you feel like he was chewing on your bones. He smacked me once when I insulted my stepmother's cooking. He said she was the best cook in the world. I said, yeah if you like chicken burned and greasy. He never trusted me much after that. But he still took me hunting, because the truth is, I was good at it. And like I've said, my dad was a cheapskate as well as a sadistic psychiatrist fuck, and he had that enormous banged-up white chest freezer back behind the porch, and he liked to keep that freezer full. I shot and I shot and he butchered and cleaned, and pretty soon we'd not only filled that freezer to the brim, but we'd filled a few other freezers as well. I'm not going to mention the names of all my father's mistresses, even though the sadistic fucker took special pleasure in seducing those of his patients who happened to be lesbians or catholic nuns. He liked making them crawl. I helped him fill their freezers. There's something dreadful about helping your father fill his mistress' icebox with meat. There's something strange in all of this. The buffalo, the violence, the weather.

You know me well enough by now to know that I dream a lot. I'm not lying about it, I have so many dreams that most of the time I can't tell the difference. Between anything. Anthropomorphic funnel shapes, hysterical transsexuals of the wind and clouds, they leave grooves in the ground, spit out barns like cornflakes, whip it all up and leave cross-hatch ditches in the tender furrows of sorghum and beans. Dead winter wheat. The Honey Wind Blows. Mercy killing.

My First Thousand Years in San Bernardino

I. Why I Love The Inland Empire

Brian was a lifeguard. A lifeguard who lives in the San Bernardino mountains and whose doctor still prescribes him Ritalin. He never takes his medication and he drives Betsy crazy. He's bouncing off the walls but he never really gets anything done. But it's great when they do speed together because he gets really quiet and calm. Whenever he acts like an idiot—which is anytime he's sober—Betsy just keeps telling herself that in two years he'll grow up and he'll be really amazing looking. Besides he's been so nice to her. He fills up her gas tank and holds her hand and introduces her to all the snowboarders, and doesn't think she's fat and steals beer for her because she's just turned sixteen. So she could almost overlook the fact that he gets other girls pregnant. One night she's drunk (which could be any night) and they start to make out while watching TV in his parent's living room. She really just wants to get the whole thing over with so she starts groping at his crotch and halfheartedly trying to pull off his pants. She is trying to let him know what she wants without actually saying anything and feeling like a teenage whore. And just as she's thinking, isn't he supposed to touch me or somethin? she feels a gush of blood to her head and it feels like she's being ripped open. She lays completely still trying not to scream and bites her lip until it bleeds and she's quite sure that's not the only part of her that's bleeding. She just keeps telling herself he's going to stop any minute, he's going to get turned off by the fact that she's not moving. Can't he smell the blood? He finally stops, tells her he loves her and she passes out hoping that he doesn't notice that there's blood all over his dick. The next thing she knows, he's gone. Stole her car again and went to some party where some guys got into a fistfight ending with someone landing on the hood of her car. But thank God he's gone. She has time to clean up the large blood stain on the carpet. Thank God she never told him she loved him back. She just screamed "Kill me kill me I want to die" and ripped off her clothes in one of her drunken fits when all her friends were in the next room listening to her.

II. Backyard Keg Party King

He'd really tear her up. Inside, I mean. Bruises of love I guess. They didn't fuck often but when they did it was until they both passed out from exhaustion or she started bleeding and crying out in pain. She'd go to all the fucked up backyard parties with him where they'd try to make them pay $2 to help pay for the kegs. She'd only suffer through these parties because she knew if she hung out all night he'd probably let her come home with him. So she'd be standing there digging in her pockets searching for change that didn't exist when she'd notice he was gone. She'd have to pay attention for his "psssst come this way" or she wouldn't see him again until she somehow sweet-talked her way inside, promising she really didn't drink and she just wanted to find her friends. But it never worked unless the person working the door thought she was cute or felt sorry for her because she was a terrible liar, because she drank a lot and she really didn't have any friends, except for him. She hated climbing people's backyard fences. But it was either that or standing outside the party without a ride until the cops came to break the whole teenage riot up. The good Seventh-Day Adventist kids at school think she's getting beaten and they want to report her to the school counselor because of the bruises all over her so she's always having to explain that it's a long way down from her bathroom window at 10 P.M. and climbing people's fences doesn't help either. Those good kids notice every detail. Even the minuscule pinpoint red marks all over her hands that stayed there for two days because he tied her up too tight and she lost circulation for awhile. She'd get kind of nervous that if she left him alone too long he'd be picking up on girls because that's what all his friends were like. It may be worse what he did. He humiliates girls in public. Not her, he just ignores her. But these poor girls that he ends up picking on calling them whores if they looked at him wrong, telling them they need to go to Jenny Craig, conning then into doing humiliating things. Like the girl he talked into running around the perimeter of the pool which was empty except for the layer of stagnant brown swampy water on the bottom. He told her it was a matter of physics and if she just ran fast enough she could avoid falling into the water, like skateboarding on the side of a pool. Betsy tried to stop her, but he pushed Betsy back into the crowd that had gathered around. Of course, the girl ended up spraining her ankle and smelling like piss and slime but Betsy guessed it ended up OK because she got to leave the party early.

III. My First Thousand Years In San Bernardino

Betsy squirmed self-consciously on the hard wooden bench to alleviate the pain in her crotch. The bailiff eyed her suspiciously. She was glad she didn't wear underwear beneath her jeans. The denim was just rough enough to help the itching. The older man next to her had a hard-on and a droplet of spit had formed in one corner of his mouth. It reminded her of the trees her brothers would cut open with their pocket knives. It would take a bit to chunk away at the gnarled bark, but then they would reach the stringy inside that began oozing out the clear sap. She wondered what else would come out of the man's gnarled old skin if she poked at it. The judge, a pasty white-faced spinster was busy reprimanding a white supremist groupie girl about her courtroom attire: a really short miniskirt with garters and see-through stockings that revealed legs mapped by tattoos that her boyfriend probably did for her with his homemade gun.

Jason was up next. Fucker, he didn't let her know about the arrest until now. He said he didn't want to worry her. And these past few days she just thought he had dumped her because he never returned her calls when she paged him. So she had to find out that he was in jail from Tony who had stolen $50 from her gas card last year when they were at the street races and she was too tired to drive home. Usually she made Jason drive but he couldn't this time because he had to trailer his drag bike out there in the hopes of making enough money to start up his drug empire again.

Her Dad would probably really disapprove of this whole thing. She knew what her parents were thinking: "You're a debutante for Christ Sake." Well, they were sort of right, although she had only gone to one Cotillion and never went to her TickTocker meetings where she was supposed to take the minutes. She had a nervous breakdown and they canceled her coming-out party last year. But compared to this scum she was practically the goddamned Princess of the Inland Empire.

She thought it was funny when she'd see the girls in her dorm peeking out their windows to see what piece of trash was bringing her home each night. She wanted them to think she was bad. Not the kind of bad girl whose big thrill is to sample new frozen dinners while trying to remember the night before and wondering if she had her period that month and reading Danielle Steele books while waiting 45 minutes for the guard to let her visit her boyfriend in Jail every other week, but the kind of bad girl who would tell her professors to fuck off and run away with a motorcycle gang to Manhattan to become a Supermodel.

They can keep their Frosty Freeze slushies and 59-cent tacos on Tuesday and weeks of sipping up the speed that they let float on top of their Diet Coke because they were afraid that it would burn through their perfect noses if they snorted it. All that paranoia and those sleepless nights of cleaning the bathroom for hours and picking up every white piece of fuzz on the carpet to see if it was some speed that they dropped, just so they could stay thin for their asshole boyfriends. She wasn't going to end up like her roommate Sandra, the 1990 Dairy Princess of Hemet, 18 and engaged to a mini-truck club guy. She knew it would be a disaster when she moved in and saw Sandra's stuff. Warrant and Poison tapes. Application to Barbizon, pretend you're a model or just pay a lot of money to act like one. Prom pictures of girls in strapless fluffy metallic dresses and big permed hair proudly displayed. And letters hidden in the desk drawers the truck dick wrote to her about how he wanted to fuck her up the ass in the back of his truck.

Betsy's relationship with Jason had begun to degenerate. It really only became apparent to her when Tony and he were driving her home one night and Jason wouldn't shut up about how most girls were sluts and you could always tell the coal-burning ones. Then he said that this year instead of a kissing booth at the annual fair they should have a feel-up booth and Betsy could run it because that's all anyone would really want to pay her for. So she reached up front and punched him in the eye. She told him that a black eye was a nice accessory to his wardrobe since he had refused to wear any other color but black for the past five years. But at least now he'd have a little more color in his life, fluorescent orange for the next 2 to 4.

NICOLE PANTER

The Comedy Writer

It was hiatus and Timmy Schotz was back on Maui. Eyes closed, a just-right tropical breeze ruffling the palm trees and his blonde hair and the warmth of the sun tickling the bridge of his nose. The elements of paradise combined with the gentle hand shaking his shoulder began to trigger an erection. Any minute now, he'd feel that mouth of hers on him. Down there. He just knew it. A ukulele strummed in the background. "...lovely hula hands, graceful as the wind in motion...." Hello Cocksuckers!!! Life *was* good...

"Señor...Señor Schotz...Señor Schotz..."

Timmy Schotz groaned, a groan from deep, deep within his chest cavity. Transported from that tropical dreamland and onto the grass in his own backyard on the morning after his fortieth birthday, he opened his eyes, or at least he tried to. His head ached, throbbed, pounded, split into a full symphony percussion section The grass he was laying on—next to the pool, his pool, the one he bought with the salary he made, the huge salary writing the show he wasn't particularly proud of—was damp, or was it? Again, he tried to open his eyes, but the sun shone too brightly. Ildefonso, the gardener, repeated his name as he shook his shoulder.

"Señor Schotz...por favor...Señor...wake up..."

Timmy Schotz tried to open his eyes. The upper and lower lids of the right eye stuck together, so he looked through the crack of the left. He could see the blur of a spider on his nose and beyond that, the silhouette of Ildefonso's head leaning over him as he spoke. Timmy Schotz lifted his head for a few seconds and looked down at his feet. One of his shoes was gone. Clutched in his hand was a piece of yellow legal paper. His head dropped back to the grass and he waited for the earth to stop moving. The gardener took hold of his elbow and forced him to sit up. As he sat there, he realized that something between his legs felt bad, cold and stale. He began to lose the erection. He gazed at his crotch, at the dark staining his pants. Christ. He'd peed himself. The odor of boozy urine pervaded everything.

Ildefonso helped him to his feet and into the house. Timmy Schotz went into the bathroom, stepped out of the pants and, supporting himself on the sink, looked in the mirror. The guy who stared back seemed, well, old, and that was a first. Timmy Schotz fancied himself youthful for 40. Although he was originally from the East, at 5'6" on the short side (and decidedly not athletic), he had the healthy good looks of a surfer—he'd always looked younger than he was by about 5 or 6 years, everybody said so, and in this business, that was important—40 was the kiss of death. When a writer turned 40 in this town, his union sent him a packet called "Ageism in The Industry: How to Live With It." In the weeks leading up to his birthday he was determined to prove them wrong. He was, after all, fearless. To show that he was one of them, he liked to tell younger writers, "I am the Kurt Cobain of comedy..."

He looked in the mirror, saw the gray around the edges of the blonde, the rings under his eyes, the rough, unhealthy texture of the skin and his nose—it was beginning to go red and slightly bulbous—there was a name for that, what was it? Gin blossoms...he'd never noticed that before, maybe it was just the way it looked in this light.

Suddenly he was aware of the piece of paper still in his hand. He examined it closely. Although the writing was his own neat, consciously executed script, it took him a minute to make sense of the words. The note read:

The most charming thing about me is my bank account. I drive a big car, I have a small dick.

Oh shit. He wasn't ready to think about how the note came to exist and right this minute, he sure as hell couldn't remember. He made his way toward the kitchen for some bi-carb. Every part of his body hurt.

It didn't surprise him to see Roberta at the kitchen sink washing the huge mountain of dishes and glasses. She was the self-appointed clean-up woman at all of his parties, year in, year out, like Old Faithful. No matter who his current lady-friend might be, Roberta—Bobby—always imperiously took her place as Our Lady of the Clean-Up. She spent her time at all of his parties alternately insulting whoever he might be dating and running around emptying the ashtrays and wiping up watermarks from the end tables. If it was apparent that Bobby was in love with Timmy, he never acknowledged this fact. He figured if he didn't cop to it, he wouldn't have to deal with it.

Bobby was no prize, never really a contender, she was a little too skinny, a little too old and a little too bitter and disappointed looking to do well in this town. To top it all off, she spoke with a pronounced, embarrassing Bronx honk that she hadn't made much of an effort to get rid of and her favorite party patter was the superiority of life in New York over life in Los Angeles. "There's just no culcha here," she was fond of exclaiming. She'd worked her way up as far as line producer for a production company that only made shows for one of the more obscure speciality cable channels—the Food Channel, or was it the Diet Channel? He was never quite clear on that—but she had never been able to parlay it into anything else, despite the fact that she could be a real ball buster—a quality prized in women TV executives. Timmy Schotz had been fucking her on and off for years. It was nothing intense as far as he was concerned, but every few months he'd get a bone for some strange, no-strings-stuff, and she always made herself available to him—it was safer than a hooker virus-wise. Lately though, she was beginning to expound on the subject of diminishing returns and commitment. He thought about hearing that whine every morning, first thing, for the rest of his life and it made him cringe.

He stood there and watched her for a minute, and almost as though she could read his thoughts, she turned around. "What happened to ya pants?"

Timmy, at first not knowing what she meant, looked down, his bare genitals bobbled underneath the hem of the dress shirt. "They got wet. On the grass. I slept there…"

"Yeah, right. Ya mean ya passed out there…"

"Whatever, look, leave the dishes, the maid's coming later."

"It's fine, I don't mind…"

"No, really, leave them. I need to be alone."

She reached out to brush the hair from his face and he jumped back a full step. He snapped at her. "There's soap on your hands...look, just leave, OK? I'm not feeling too great."

"OK, but call me if you need anything. We still on for the movies next week?"

"Yeah, I'll call you."

"Timmy..."

"I'll call you. I will."

She dried off her hands, picked up her purse and walked out the back door without another word of protest. Mercifully, she didn't try to kiss him goodbye.

Timmy Schotz made the hang-over cure and then circled around the kitchen a few more times without much point, finally heading into the darkened living-room. He laid down on one of the couches, closed his eyes and tried to think about absolutely nothing. Now that he was awake though, he couldn't stop thinking how unfair it all was. It was supposed to have been perfect. He'd looked forward to it for months, the way a bride anticipates her wedding day.

It all began to unfold in front of him, like a slow-motion accident. He could see now that things had started to unravel earlier in the week at work. He was a staff writer who had been given a producer's credit (in lieu of a raise one year) on *Shashi's World* a hit comedy about the adventures of an east Indian immigrant during the night shift at his convenience store. Timmy Schotz' speciality, his particular area of responsibility, were the dick jokes—what was the saying? "When in doubt, stick it in…" Aside from Dan, the executive producer who ran the show, Timmy Schotz was a good fifteen years older than any of the other writers. He considered Dan more than just a boss. He thought of him as a friend and a contemporary, the two of them together were teaching these young guys what funny really was. Laying on the couch, eyes closed, a tear rolled down Timmy Schotz' cheek. On Monday, Dan had announced his retirement and told the assembled writers that he would be naming a replacement at the end of the week. Timmy Schotz knew that he would be tapped as show-runner.

His revery was interrupted by the phone. Of course—people wanted to do a postmortem on the party. But he didn't want to talk to anyone. He just let the machine pick it up. He heard his own voice on the tape…"Lordy, lordy I'm turnin' forty…"

"Daddy…daddy…it's me…Are you there? Are you still passed out? I wanted you to be the first to know, the network caved in and my salary is being doubled next season, my agent just called…call me…oh, and happy birthday, the party was a blast."

His stomach turned. God, he'd have to hear all those fucking jokes. Like before, when he was doing stand-up and couldn't even get arrested—a real joke considering the fact that he was also selling blow in the men's toilets at comedy clubs to meet those child support payments—then Corrina, his daughter, got cast in some sitcom as the cute, precocious kid and was pulling down 25 grand a week. He'd had to listen to every coke-addled asshole in town make cracks about "father support" at his expense and now twelve years later, he could see it happening all over again, thanks to that asshole, his boss, his friend, Dan Adler, who didn't even have the decency to take him aside and prepare him privately for the fact that he was being passed over for the promotion. He just called the writing staff into the conference room and let Timmy Schotz sit there with a stupid, expectant smile on his face while he announced that Greg Jennings, twenty-five-year-old fuckface Greg Jennings (nee Janov) would be the show-runner. Well, what did he expect? Those Jew bastards always stuck together when it came down to it—so much for all the back-slapping jokes and hearty assurances that he was an honorary Yid. Dan did pull Timmy Schotz aside later to tell him that not only would he not be the executive in charge, but while he would retain his writer/producer title, he wouldn't be required to spend so much time at the office next season. Dan said he knew Timmy understood and Timmy Schotz knew better than to argue with the boss. He just swallowed it and nodded and smiled while Dan shook his hand.

Dan's betrayal had a couple of days to sink in, so by the time the main event, the big four-oh rolled around, it was really stuck in his craw. He almost cancelled the party a couple of times, but decided he wouldn't let the bastards win. He could always come up with an idea for a series and write the pilot on spec. He'd show them. He was perfectly capable of putting on a suit and running a twenty-million-dollar show. No fucking problem. He jumped up from the couch and began to pace. Timmy Schotz in charge, that was more like it.

He felt antsy and began to straighten up a little. Bobby and the caterers had cleared up the left-over glasses and dishes, but it still looked like a party had taken place. He eyeballed the bookcase and saw in the midst of the chaos that the framed photo of him and his last live-in, Marina, was smeared with something white and goopy. Cheese. Brie. How did that happen? Jesus, people were pigs. Then it came back to him. He, himself had done it. Marina had been his trophy girlfriend, a minor starlet with a pretty face and big store-bought knockers—a Christmas gift from him their first year together. She was no brain surgeon, but she'd lasted two years before he'd had enough—the domesticity, her relentless efforts to please him, the idea that she seemed to live only to make him happy had become too much for him. She was talking marriage and kids and he couldn't stand looking at her anymore. He'd asked her to move out about a year earlier and had been supporting her ever since, to the tune of four grand a month. She had been crushed, but they'd stayed friends. Timmy Schotz prided himself on the fact that all of his ex-girlfriends were still his friends—several were here tonight at this party. She'd come, she'd even brought a date that she introduced to Timmy. As her fiancé. It hit him while he was shaking the guy's hand. He felt sick. He loved this girl. How could she do this to him? For the next hour or so, he went through the motions of having a good time at his party and played the genial host but inside he shook. He drank tequila at a steady clip. Finally, when he couldn't stand it anymore, he went over to Marina and asked if he could see her alone. He took her into the guest bedroom, a bedroom she'd decorated herself when she'd lived there, and closed the door. "Marina…you can't…"

"I can't what?"

"You can't get married."

"Why not Timmy?"

"Because we love each other."

"No, Timmy, I loved you and you got bored with me."

"That's not true. I've always loved you. You know that." He grabbed her and began kissing her along the collar bone. His hands fumbled with her large breasts and he popped one out of her low-cut gown.

His mouth moved down and attached to the nipple. He suckled it and began crying. "Don't leave me, please, don't leave me. I'll marry you. I fucked up, I love you. I've made a mistake, let me make it up to you." He nuzzled her tit. She pulled away from him, tucked herself back in and straightened her clothes.

"It's too late Timmy. I'm in love with someone. He wants to marry me."

"Marina, tell me the truth…it's because…it's because I couldn't satisfy you in bed—that's why you're leaving me, right?"

She looked at him with absolute disbelief. "Jesus Timmy, you just don't get it, do you?"

His face turned red and his tone was cold. "You're not getting another penny from me…I think you and lover-boy had better leave my house now."

"Fine." She opened the bedroom door and looked back at him. "You are such an asshole."

He went into the bathroom and sat on the edge of the tub for a few minutes. How could she fucking do this to him? He checked himself in the mirror and, satisfied that his face gave nothing away, went back out into the party. The first thing that he saw was that fuckface kid writer—Greg Jennings, the one who stole the promotion out from under him. Jennings' back was to him and he was deep into a make-out session with some girly in the hall. He could see Jennings dry humping the girl who was backed into a corner. One of her legs was snaked around Jennings and Timmy Schotz could see that Jennings' hand was moving in and out of her pussy. He held his breath as he watched for a few minutes. The girl giggled, and the sound froze Timmy Schotz' blood. It was Corrina, his daughter. He went into the kitchen before they could see him and cracked open a fresh bottle of tequila. Dispensing with the formality of a glass, he drank straight from the bottle.

Timmy Schotz went outside, back by the pool to attend to his guests. A big band played while people danced. There were tables set up on the lawn with lamps that had skin-flattering pink bulbs shining from beneath the shades. It was meant to look like an outdoor version of "21". There were about two hundred guests in the formal evening attire the invitation had requested. He looked at the faces. He didn't know many of them intimately. They fell into three categories; those who he had hit up for a job, those who had hit him up and the Peanut Gallery—his own entourage of 5 or 6 guys he'd known since his days in stand-up—if he had been a D grade comedian, they were Z grade, and he never let them forget it. They all laughed loudly at his jokes, especially the bad ones, and absorbed his insults—the trade-off was that Timmy Shotz picked up the tab whenever the Peanut Gallery danced attendance—which was almost every night. Aside from those guys, it was wall to wall Industry Scum—if a bomb was dropped on his property tonight, Sit-Com Heaven would have a no-vacancy sign out in front. Bobby was running around collecting dirty plates. Jesus Christ, she was proprietary. Couldn't she just let the caterers do it?

Dan Adler sat at a table next to the dance floor. That bastard had a lot of nerve taking advantage of his hospitality. Sitting next to Dan was his bitch-wife Marguerite. Suddenly, Timmy Schotz realized that it wasn't Dan who had blocked his advancement. It was her. Everyone in town knew that she was the one with the money. She called the shots. If he hadn't been promoted, she was the reason why. A wave of ice-cold rage swept over Timmy Schotz. Putting on his best smile, he bowed in front of Marguerite, extended his hand

and asked her to dance. She plastered that phony aristocratic smile on her face as she allowed Timmy Schotz to sweep her into his arms. He was a fine dancer and he twirled her around the dance floor a few times.

"I was surprised when I didn't get the promotion."

"What?"

"Then I realized, it was you. You don't like me."

"Timmy, I don't think we should be discussing Dan's business…"

"Why not? Everyone knows Dan's business is your business…" Timmy Schotz guided them close to one of the ringside tables. He snatched the shade off of the lamp and in one swift move, plopped it on Marguerite's head. It covered her face. He held her close to him and whirled her around the floor. They bumped into other couples, and she struggled to get away from him. "How does it feel to be humiliated in public Marguerite. Not too great, huh?" Out of the corner of his eye, he saw Dan approaching, coming to rescue his wife. "Hey Dan, Marguerite and I were just talking business."

"Let her go you little prick." With that Dan shoved Timmy Schotz, throwing him off balance long enough for Marguerite to break away and pull the lamp shade off of her head. She took a step toward him and with full force, slapped him across the face.

"Fuck you Timmy."

Dan grabbed Marguerite's elbow and hustled her toward the gate. Halfway there, Dan turned around and, shaking his finger at Timmy Schotz, began yelling at him. "Don't bother coming into work on Monday you little piece of shit. You are finished. When I'm through with you, you won't be able to get a job cleaning up horseshit from the streets of Disneyland, you little fuck."

Timmy Shotz rubbed his face. It really hurt.

Bobby led him inside to the breakfast nook. All the tequila was finally having its effect. She sat him down at the table. "Stay there, see if ya can stay outta trouble for a few minutes." She left and Timmy Schotz picked up a pen and began to write on a piece of yellow legal paper.

As he stood there the next day, the details of his final moments at the party came back to Timmy Schotz and he began to feel sick to his stomach. He scraped dried cheese off of the picture of Marina and him taken during happier times. Not only didn't he have a job to go back to on Monday, most likely, he wouldn't be able to find a job anywhere in the business—ever, bad news because he was over-extended in the financial department. He'd been picking up the tab for so many for so long that he didn't have anything left in the bank. Marina was marrying someone else, and his daughter, who out-earned him and would shortly be supporting him, was fucking his rival. Timmy Schotz began to heave all over the very expensive transitional Navajo rug he was standing on. He sat on the floor and began to sob, but no tears came, just dry, wounded-animal noises.

The doorbell rang. He debated answering it and finally got up and looked out the peephole. A red-lipped, ice-cream blonde in an antique lace slip stood there with a big package. Her right arm was tattooed from the shoulder to the wrist in an intricate Japanese flower pattern. Nadia. He shouted through the door for her to wait a minute and he went into the bedroom to put some pants on. He stopped in the bathroom to wash his face, then went to the front door and let her in.

They'd met when he struck up a conversation with her at a lunch counter in Farmer's Market. He had been wining and dining her for six months, or rather had been trying to, but she consistently refused to go to high-profile industry hang-outs like Morton's or Ava's or the Monkey Bar and had always insisted on paying her own half of the check. She intimidated him. She had that weird post-punk attitude about money, a distaste for it that he just didn't get. She worked on small, labor-of-love projects that were never going to make anyone any money. Although he wanted to, he hadn't been able to make a move on her. He knew the fact that she didn't give a shit how big his paycheck was scared the hell out of him.

She handed him a package. "Sorry I missed the party, but I wanted to finish this. Open it." He carefully tore the wrap from the painting. "It's acrylic. It's almost dry..." she laughed. It was a portrait of him, rendered in the style of John Singer Sargent. His eyes welled up. "It's beautiful." He hugged her tightly leaning his head on her shoulder for a minute, the power of the emotions he suddenly felt scared him. "Let me take you out for a cappy, or some breakfast."

"It's got to be quick. I've got to get back to the beach. I've got work to do."

When they finished breakfast they got in his big black top-of-the-line BMW. "Let's go up to Laurel Canyon, there's a place off Mulholland where you can see all the way to the ocean. I've never showed it to you."

"Timmy, I've got to go."

"Please, it won't take long...please...for my birthday...come on..." he hated the pleading tone in his voice.

"OK, but quickly." He thought she sounded irritated. He drove them toward Laurel Canyon and they were both silent. He began to think about his birthday party, and how fucked-up everything had gotten. He began to get mad at Nadia. For once, he wanted to show her something she hadn't seen. She thought she was so fucking cool and unapproachable. He could buy and sell her and her arty little life and her arty little asshole friends a hundred times over. God, he was slow on the uptake—she was probably after his money too, she was just cagier about it than the others. He was a good catch and they both knew it. He pressed the gas pedal down a bit harder. They were just climbing up Laurel Canyon and it was still early. Traffic was light. The car squealed around a bend.

"Timmy, how fast are you going?"

"I don't know. Are you scared?"

"Slow down."

"I thought you were so fucking cool, don't tell me you're frightened?"

"Timmy, what's with you? Slow down."

With that he pressed the gas pedal harder. He took one hand off the wheel and undid his pants. He began to stroke himself.

"Timmy, what the fuck are you doing?"

He continued to pull at his penis until it was hard. Somewhere inside of himself, he knew that she wasn't the enemy, but he couldn't stop. His small, stiff cock peeked from his lap. "Look at it. Pretty pathetic, huh? Tell me it's pathetic." She said nothing. "Tell me it's pathetic you little whore." Still nothing. In a quick move, he grabbed her hair and pulled her down closer to his exposed part. She was crying, but still not speaking. "Go on you fucking cunt, tell me how little it is. TELL ME I HAVE A SMALL DICK YOU FUCKING CUNT!" He began to slap her. "Tell me my little cock isn't good enough for you."

"Timmy..." Black makeup was smeared all over her cheeks, snot was running out of her nose and into her mouth and her face was red. She didn't look so goddamn cool anymore. "Timmy... please..."

"Tell me my little dick isn't good enough."

"Your little..." she faltered. "Your little..."

"I want to hear you say it, you fucking slut..."

They reached the top of Laurel Canyon and when Timmy Schotz slowed the BMW down to turn onto Mulholland, Nadia jumped out of the car. In the rear view mirror, he could see her dusting herself off and limping down the hill, back toward Los Angeles. When he turned off the road and parked, he could see the ocean. He jerked off until he came in his hand and then leaned onto the steering wheel and wept.

He sat in his car for a half hour or so, then headed back down the canyon toward home. When he got there he saw that Nadia's car was no longer parked in front. Well, good riddance to her anyway. He took the painting she'd done and threw it in the trash. He grabbed the bottle of tequila from the top of the fridge, went into the living room, and laid down on the couch. Fuck them all anyway, each and every one of them.

As he drifted off, he remembered his final act at his birthday party. Standing in front of the band, he spoke into the microphone. He cradled the bottle under one arm. "Hello…testing…hello…testing…" He tapped on the microphone. When he had the attention of everyone in the place, he began to speak. "I have a little speech prepared. Some of you enjoying my hospitality know me, some of you don't. There are a few things you should know about me. My name is Timmy Schotz…I'm 40 years old today." He looked at the piece of paper in his hand. "The most charming thing about me is my bank account. I drive a big car. I have a small dick…" He stretched his arms outward and shrugged a self-effacing shrug and then Timmy Schotz dropped first to his knees and then pitched face forward onto the manicured lawn next to the swimming pool where he slept straight through until morning.

He opened his eyes and looked around the living room. That couldn't have happened, not in front of everyone in the business, could it? He'd really have to leave town now. In a place where having the edge counted for everything, the only thing he knew for sure was that his own name would be the punch line for a lot of jokes for a long, long time. He began to shake. What could he do? Go back to Buffalo and take over the family business? Right, Timmy Schotz— "The Lock Doctor." He'd shoot himself first. Maybe it hadn't happened. Maybe he was making it all up. Maybe…maybe…maybe…

He sat on the couch and stared into space. Although the shades in the living room were down, he could tell from the movement of the light in the house around him that hours were passing. Paralyzed, he finally just buried his face in his hands. The back door opened and he heard footsteps coming toward him. He couldn't see who it was and he didn't really care. With any luck it would be Charles Manson. He felt a hand on his shoulder. "Timmy? Timmy?" The nasal twang was unmistakable—it was Bobby. He looked up at her and opened his mouth to speak, but nothing came out. She sat on the edge of the couch and stroked his hair. "It's okay, baby, Mama's here." He buried his head in her lap and began to cry. She continued to talk to him. "It's okay, baby, it's okay." He sobbed and curled himself around her body. "Help me...I feel so lost." He reached up and put his hand inside her shirt and kneeded her small tit. She moved to the floor, onto her knees and unzipped his pants. He was already hard. As she faced the couch, she leaned over and went down on him. The length of him fit easily into her mouth. She made him feel warm and safe. He grabbed her hair in his hands and guided her motions. Still crying, he began talking as she worked on him, "I hurt...I hurt...help me...please...I hurt...are you my dirty little whore? Tell me you're my dirty little whore..." She stopped sucking him and looked up at his face, "I'm ya dirty little whore, baby." She continued pulling at him with her hand. "I'm ya dirty little whore and I don't want you to give ya big, hard cock away to anyone else. She licked at him like an ice-cream cone. "Tell me it's all mine Timmy baby, go on, tell me it's all mine."

"It's all yours, it's all yours, it's all yours..."

Kill Your Darling

Melinda Sue Martin hated tug o' war. It always got her bent out of shape. She was no fun to be around. For Melinda Sue, it was like getting the ass torn right outta her. The manifesto of confrontation spun and churned her stomach into creamery butter. It drove her mad. It drove her mental. Or was *she* "it"? Not even a psychoanalyst could decide on either, but to the doctor, the insurance money was good and a problem was created. The hilltop luxury home and the sport sedan wasn't enough for this high-priced head doctor. Its fangs lodged right into her neck and all her insecure blood showered the shrink. Bad enough to drain a person of life every week for at least 50 minutes at a time. But poor Melinda Sue. What a nutcase. Her peers deemed her wacko. Her elders wore blinders and called it creativity. Maybe it was because she could see every red, blue, and green dot in the television because she always sat so damn close to the set as a child. Electrical vibes with ill effects? Quite possible, that was the '80s, you know. Her I.Q. tests scored high with "gifted" attributes, but she was also sick with the flu both times, and you can fluke twice. Melinda Sue can prove that in any circumstance.

Melinda Sue hated tug o' war. She couldn't climb her way out of her doldrums. She snagged her only claw trying to scrub nail polish out of the carpet. It snapped backwards, leaving poor Melinda Sue with a carpet smothered in nail polish. Fresh blood, and a broken, yellow nail on top. At least that carpet (nail polish and blood stain or not) was better than the *carpet padding* that remained, the only thing separating cold concrete from her bare tootsies for a few weeks. The carpet people fucked up three times and Melinda Sue suffered. Hard. Her feet were constantly cold.

Melinda Sue Martin hated tug o' war. Her body longed to be warm, but something always conflicted with her wishes and blanketed them with a chilly frost. It all starts with one fingertip, one little toe and then slowly engulfs her entire body. Until completely numb. It's not really a "burrr...get a blanket cold," it's a "death cold." A slowly depreciating cold. And it's scary. What if not enough blood is getting to parts of her body? What if her heart implodes? She'd slump over, eyes rolled back in her head, mouth gaping, and she'd probably drool. This is in no way an uncommon look for Melinda Sue, this time, it would just be fatal. Fatality. Something people Melinda Sue's age don't think about. But Melinda Sue does. Everyday. She didn't think she would live to see 18, and three years later, she doesn't look at 22 too optimistically either. Ah, Melinda Sue...stylish, witty, and optimistically pessimistic. Cynical. Beaten. Slapped by sarcasm, kicked by misunderstanding, whipped violently by manipulation, and scarred with insecurity. Nothing good. Ever. Always a catch. Maybe if Melinda Sue didn't play tug o' war so often, she'd think differently.

Melinda Sue Martin always thought differently.

Melinda Sue loved *Win, Lose or Draw*. It had nothing to do with drawing, it had everything to do with guessing. She was quite talented in the act of guessing, it was the answer department that she fell a little short in. Maybe that's why she was never asked to be in the school academic decathlon. Her gift of guessing all started right around the second grade spelling bee where her spelling of the word "train" sparked some confusion amongst the judges, spell-check attendant, and auditorium of onlookers. Melinda Sue loved *Win, Lose or Draw*. The fact that she could watch a program where the people seemed more pathetic than she thought she was pleased her. Richard Simmons, the entire cast of *Dallas* and other washed-out celebrities teamed up with Overzealous Average Joe Blow Greedy. Now put them on an oversized couch facing each other and time them as they attempt to draw phrases that end up looking like genitalia. What entertainment! Melinda Sue felt proud she could draw non-genitalia scenes and with out the help of Harvey Korman. Melinda Sue loved *Win, Lose, or Draw*. She could see the red, blue, green of it all.

Melinda Sue Martin was disgusted with the 12 Steps. 1. She wasn't particularly talented in leaving a safe spot. 2. She thought solving a problem shouldn't take as many as twelve steps. 3. She went through that AA bullshit before. 4. She shouldn't have to deal with it again. 5. Besides, they always ran out of coffee. 6. It was brainwashing anyway. 7. She always had more "bads" than "goods." 8. At meetings, people didn't want to help themselves—they wanted the problem solving fairy. 9. That fairy needed to whack them in the heads a couple times with a stick. 10. O.K. a few times. 11. The meeting chaperone needed to be bludgeoned to death with that stick. 12. Her name was Melinda, too.

Insomnia was Melinda Sue Martin. She was afraid to sleep. Afraid to let her guard down. No dreams of sugar plum waltzing, no rainbows or pots o' gold. No daisies or midgets singing *A Chorus Line*. These were nightmares, baby. Big ones. None of this "going to school naked" or pink squishy guy with a razor glove—real Macoy. When the curtains closed, the show began. Giant frogs underneath circular boats, Yoda painfully moaning under cracked floorboards, Lee Marvin terrorizing Heather Locklear. Why be vulnerable to those bizarre not-so-commonplace images? Horizon= Vulnerable=Bad. All awake and no siesta make Melinda Sue a whacked girl.

And pretty soon Melinda Sue didn't exist anymore. It was sad, really. It happened real slow-like, ya see. Drawn out. Suffering. Heavy Suffering. It could have been much quicker, you know, but she struggled. She struggled with the dominative grip that was constantly around her neck, and because she constantly thrashed, shifted, twisted, swung, and hit, it made her weaker and weaker. Pretty soon there wasn't a lot left. It had to kill her…really it did. It needed to put her out of her misery. She just didn't know its weak points. She could've kicked it in the groin, so it fell on the ground, overpowered, breathless, feeling like it was gonna puke, leaving her to just walk away, not dealing with it, not putting up with it, not taking it anymore. But it wasn't her fault. She had grown up knowing a *certain way*. Maybe it wasn't right. Maybe it wasn't wrong. Maybe it wasn't the "General Public consensus"—the same conflict that serial killers have with the public that it's *not* okay to kill when you get upset. But cops do it all the time. How are serial killers supposed to not try to mimic the most law abiding citizens? The killers were twisted in their youths. How are they supposed to know better? And how was Melinda Sue supposed to know better either? Everybody reacted the same way. Everybody took the same things from her. Everybody told her so. And she gazed in understanding like a small infant does to new information, soaking it up like a Bounty paper towel. Melinda Sue Martin, always the quicker, picker upper.

She always was the quicker, picker upper—soaking up surroundings, conversations, reactions, situations, and many other factors of human nature that end in "S"—she just wasn't the quick learning upper, learning by ouch. Actual learning. Like babies do, the hard way, touching the Christmas light, naive to the idea that they have been on for the last 12 hours and how long that actually is in non-baby time. Or if you pull its tail enough, or push it over enough, or poke it enough in the eyes, a dog *will* snap at you. Burned fingers, knocked over baby, wet diapers—crying babies.

And yet, you do those things and learn you sure as hell don't do it again. Melinda Sue learned from them, she just didn't follow suit with the "Babies' theory of single mistake making." Besides, the more the merrier, they always say.

Maybe "they," whoever that might be, talk too much. Melinda Sue had never spoken to them, she came up with that one on her own. Pretty good, eh? Melinda Sue always was the inventive one. She invented a new level of lack of feeling. An accumulated effort—fully self-created, fully contained—contained unit. A result of society. Like the misguided Rambo. Except Melinda Sue didn't own a gun, sneer, or hold resentment to the government that left her in a foreign country to fight an army alone. But then again, Melinda Sue Martin didn't get to repeatedly star in movies with Burgess Meredith *and* get paid for it. Although Melinda Sue always was the inventive one. She had a particular talent for inventing understanding. Understanding in a being, an understanding that was unsurpassed. Too bad that understanding was in a clump of stuffed fabric. In simpler terms—Melinda Sue Martin had invented an invisible friend as a child. True, it is a well known fact that most children do in fact create imaginary friends during adolescence, but little Melinda Sue let her friend take shape in a material object—a doll. Okay okay, *lots* of little girls have dolls when they're young, but big Melinda Sue knew no matter how much abuse was relayed to it, no matter how long she babbled to it, stuck it in a freezer and then stuck it in the microwave to defrost it, it would always be there to relieve, listen, freeze and reheat—it would always be there and once in a while laugh at her stupid jokes. And always *love* her, and for that, she will never ever leave it. That is why 21-year-old Melinda Sue Martin still has a doll. Doll, yes. But Tonto to her Ranger, a Starsky to her Hutch, a Butch Cassidy to her Sundance Kid. Two Outlaws riding into sunset after sunset after sunset. Just the two of them, each of them in their existence, each a creation of each other. A two-for-one deal. Yes it's a two two

two-for-one deal! Yessss, Crazy Larry is letting it all go! How can he do it? How can he offer two personalities for one low price? He's craaaaaaazy Larry! And if he was any more crazy, we'd have to put him away! Hurry, these models have a limited time warranty. So after a certain time, you break, you pay.

VAGINAL DAVIS

Dead President's Son

no i didn't steal him away from the sea horse. he never belonged to her, they were just over-extended summer lovers like in that movie she made with Peter Gallagher.

i fell in love with Peter Gallagher when he starred in *The Idolmaker*, his dark hair and blue eyes, but he had a hairy back and that i can do without.

she should go back to jackson browne,

runnin' on empty
runnin' round, runnin' round
runnin' into the sun
but i'm runnin' behind

they made the perfect hippie couple until he caught her with his fragile teenage son, the boy, all young male & angsty, with mothers milk on his breath except for the fact that his mother committed suicide while he was a baby.

everywhere i go
everyone i know
people need some reason to believe
i don't care about anyone but me
if it takes all night, that'll be all right
as long as I get you to smile before i leave

with a country rock cocaine daddy and a movie star step-girlfriend who gets in your pajamas, the boy had no choice but to become a model and hip hop dj, but the point i'm trying to make is that she had no right to let her crust come between a father & his son. not only did she give her cooties to the both of them, but the son passed the nasties on to his then actor boyfriend who starred in that movie *Reality Bites.*

how do i know this for a fact? Well it's somewhat embarrassing, though i shouldn't be embarrassed or ashamed, as a black wo-man i have no shame. i knew the risks involved when i embarked on my little journey, no sad songs for me baby, no woes for the misbegotten. i graciously volunteered to be a pitiful victim.

so now he's telling me the entire story over what i was hoping was going to be a romantic dinner.

get tested, get treated, i know you will hate me forever. the thought of green discharge oozing from my cootchee.

i wasn't listening to anything he was saying to me. all i could hear was that she gave it to the dead president's son but…and…maybe he had given it to me.

i've always prided myself in never getting anything with my initials on it. even back in the '70s when everyone had herpes & hepatitis

& these nasty little amoeba infections and don't forget anal warts, i always managed to avoid those annoyances, not even a pair of crabs or scabies. i always figured it had something to do with why mosquitoes would never bite me—a natural immunity.

sometimes when men wanted to plow me i would tell then that they were nefarious babymakers that could even do the impossible, and make a girl like me preggers, and i wasn't about to give up my illustrious career...my art...to be having anyone's little baby christ child in the manger.

i'll let you titty pluck me and leave me with a purlie mae necklace, but that's as far as i go.

that's what makes the situation with j 'n' j so difficult, here i convince myself to go against my bitter judgement and every ounce of my immoral immortality justifies that a dead president's son couldn't possibly have any diseases, perversious, abstractions or abnormalities.

they wouldn't let the one and only manchild of the promised land be with leprosy, forsaken, barren in the wastelands, a nomad—he the most desirable man in the known world.

i wanted so badly to experience his ecoli fluids, his manly sucreations in all their rabid form / come on just take a chance, and throw caution to the break wind, lay an egg fart, make me swoon / and let him do unto me as he thou thusly see fitteth without making him use a barrier reef.

and at that moment the heavens opened

...let the heavens rejoice let the earth joyful be for jehovah god has become the king...

and a little black dove flies out, this the moment of reckoning:

dead president's son j 'n' j of massachusetts & ports wyannismouth takes the nuptial of her militant dinge transagressive lover vaginal davis jr. formerly of watts & compton slauson & normandie manchester and dr. martin luther king jr. blvd de la avenida real.

and then he commences to mount me, his peterkus maximus and all the property it contains and i'm saying to myself this is not a good thing, those kennedy men have bad reputations, they drink, they don't age well, but sweetheart you have a bad reputation as well and you can hide quarters in those bags under your eyes.

i'm a little annoyed at our lack of foreplay, it takes me a good period of time to fully get warmed up and sufficiently wet and sloshy, his vested interest only in devout penetration uninterruptus, is that all i'm good for? and here i am with the sexiest man alive, all America is envious of me and i should be more than satiated, i should be *chieta*.

honestly did i really expect romance? philip shriver's walkup on the upper west side isn't exactly the kennedy compound in palm beach, but it ain't shabby either, and he is making some pretty righteous moves with his buttsticle muscles reacting to the tender flap of my childbearing thigh.

now the inner voices are calling me out as the scrapa that i am. i feel dirty, stinky, but i can't get over the fact that from the day this man was conceived, weaned, and first communed before the great eyes god's roman apostelic catholic church we were desecrated to be lovers, hi-tailed and bushy-eyed lovers.

yes we are in bed, a water bed, and look it's a sight! my ebony nudeness and his high snow.

does he know that what he is doing is wrong? and that society, cafe society discourages sin.

does he care anything about what his skinny dead mother thinks? or the legacy of his father? well, if he doesn't, i do. where could this relationship possibly go? he isn't going to marry me. even if he did what would i do in musty old camelot? what are my options? i'd make an awkward mistress.

i bite at his knees and calves, i'm slap sucking, nipping and tucking the stretch of his body. i pound him in the chest with all the weight of my fist, i pull his leg hairs, and the skin around his scrotum. i kick him, and he is hurt, he screams, i stab him with my elbow, he thinks i'm being kinky so he reacts by spitting in my mouth, and i let him get away with it, then i teach him, and hack a french cut loogy right on his tongue and plant some residue up his nostrils and in his ears, he curses me and i stab him with my elbow again and again, then i start jumping up and down on his chest, i'm wearing 6 inch spike heels. he is a trampoline, the lady is a tramp, he's become part of my sick opportunity, and it makes him happy.

RON ATHEY

*Gifts of
the Spirit*

The Holy Woman

From the time I was a baby, my Grandma and Aunt Vena repeatedly informed me, "you've been born with the Calling on your life, Ronnie Lee." I was just becoming aware of what that prophecy meant—how being chosen for a ministry made me different from everyone else. According to this message from the holiest of holies, I was to sacrifice the playthings of the world, in order to fulfill the plans of God.

Throughout the course of my religious training, I encountered many great prophets, faith healers, mystics and savers of souls. In church I would close my eyes and absorb the rambling vibrations given from the gift of tongues, mixed in with the sounds of foot-stomping, and bodies hitting the floor hard as they went out in the spirit. I would listen intently as people testified to physical healings, the exorcism of demons and the detailed arrival of Armageddon. My childhood was spent among adults who believed that their lives read like the book of Job. It mystified me, that as a mere test of faith, God unleashed hideous disease and allowed actual demon possession. Later the diseases and demons could be removed, pro-viding the laying on of hands was executed by a powerful Reverend Minister.

The rarest and least talked about miracle is Stigmata, wherein the gifted would spontaneously bleed from the same parts of the body that Christ bled. Because the only two living examples with stigmata were women, there seemed to be some indication that women were more open to receiving the gift. I believed with all my heart it could be given to me.

One day Aunt Vena received a promotional flyer announcing "Sister Linda's Miraculous Gift of Stigmata: A Three Day Visit to the Indio Area." It described how sometimes she bled pure blood, and other times she bled a clear, scented healing oil.

With the sweetest, holiest look on my face I could muster, I expressed my interest in attending. "Aunt Vena, I'd like to see this miracle." My family drove into the desert to let me witness Linda bleed.

That first night, after sitting through an uninspiring sermon delivered by the local Pentecostal minister, it became apparent that Linda was not going to bleed. I was disappointed, but still anxious to return.

On the second visit, the air was so still outside, I just knew she was going to bleed that night. Sister Linda had dark circles under her eyes, and her face was all shiny with sweat. She sure looked like she had the holy spirit rattling around inside of her. I joined in the hymn singing, a chorus of twangy hillbilly voices belting out, "when we all get to heaven, what a day of rejoicing that will be, when we see Jesus, we will sing and shout with victory." Again, the minister tried for—but did not achieve—inspiration. Towards the end of the service, when she still had not bled, I wanted to have a temper tantrum. I thought, "she's just a big fat faker." I couldn't understand why everyone else was so patient waiting for her gift to reveal itself. All she had shown us were pictures, cheap snapshots of her blood-stained clothes, as if that were sufficient evidence of a miracle. She also told the congregation that impressions in blood would appear in her Bible, but I didn't want to hear stories of psychic phenomena, I wanted her to bleed. I had gone there with the desire to be anointed in the blood seeping directly from her palms.

I wondered if she'd bleed from the place where the spear had been inserted in Christ's side. I pondered on whether or not she'd expose the hole. Would she be modest like my Aunt Vena, or was a stigmata wound different? I imagined what the blood would look like seeping through her clothes. But she hadn't bled at all on those two nights.

The Catholic Envy of Vena Mae

The grandparents that raised my brother and sisters and I were from Texas. They were vague about specifying exactly where from in Texas, they constantly moved around during the Depression. Grandma had stories of living in a car and surviving off of the squirrel meat her brothers killed and cleaned. She seemed resentful that my Grandpa and his mother, an Apache Indian, had lived on a small farm and had the "easy life." They never told me how they met and married, just that they'd moved to San Jacinto, California, because my grandfather could get construction work there. They settled down in Hemet long enough to raise their two daughters, Joyce and Vena. Eventually he landed a job doing construction on the Claremont Colleges, and bought a house in the city of Pomona, the farthest suburb east in L.A. county before you hit the small farm/milk dairy/state prison community of Chino, and the San

Bernardino County line. When they purchased the house, Pomona was a racially mixed area. In the late '60s, due largely to race riots and the rise of Chicano gang violence, white flight occurred, except for my family. We were the only white family for a square mile. My family was somewhat racist and we were completely isolated.

In Texas, my grandma and her mother had been devout Pentecostalists. My grandpa protested that it was extremist and seemed to take over my grandmother's life. Her religion made him uncomfortable, so she vowed upon leaving Texas to leave Pentecostalism behind her. And perhaps on her part she'd had enough of the scandals and gossip that seem to plague spirit-filled churches.

Raising children and enjoying a better quality of life in the '40s and the '50s, she was able to leave the Pentecostal Church for about 15 years. My grandmother had been attending a Lutheran Church with her family, but found it unbearably lukewarm. She was just going through the motions, teaching her daughter about the Bible, but her heart wasn't in it. One day she and her youngest daughter Vena, a mama's girl who was now teen-aged, saw a Revival tent meeting. They went inside, and my grandmother felt shame for ever abandoning the spirit. Revivals were spontaneous and loud-miracles happened. She was re-ignited with the fire of the holy spirit and filled the gifts of tongues and prophecy. Vena felt that this was also her future, and together they committed to the Pentecostal way. My grandfather wasn't too happy about this, but eventually they broke him down some. He went to meetings with them and studied his Bible, but to his dying day, he was never born again. He would never admit to having received Christ. My mother Joyce had no problem with the showy gifts of the spirit, though to me, her tongues were indistinguishable from her epileptic mumblings.

I called my mother Joyce because she didn't raise me, but still, Joyce was my real mother. She was diagnosed paranoid schizophrenic, manic depressive, and on top of all that, she suffered frequently from grand mal epileptic seizures. I wondered if Joyce's body was trying to destroy her: she often convulsed face forward into the street. One time, she went right through the dining room window into the back garden. That particular day was the only time I ever remember her cooking. This is one of my earliest memories. She made silver-dollar-sized pancakes, which we smothered with margarine and Karo maple-flavored syrup. After making her last trip from the stove to the table she just started staring straight ahead, then mumbling, then trembling, then there was a crash and she went through the window. Joyce was face down in the garden, still convulsing. I remember there being blood and glass everywhere, an especially thick paste of it forming in her hair. My grandma and Aunt Vena came running out to help her, shooing us kids aside, and an ambulance was called. I asked about the thick blood coming out of her head and my aunt told me it was strawberry jam, which I didn't believe. Joyce never functioned as part of the household after that.

The only thing Joyce seemed to care about, or ever talk about, was how beautiful she was. Her exceptional looks could best be described as a mannish Marlo Thomas. She spent hours poised in her California Girl skirt suits and big hair, almost picture perfect, except that with rigid motions she would take her big strong hands and smooth out the front and sides of her jacket, then move down the length of her skirt, continually fighting non-existent creasing and bunching.

Joyce's final downfall was physical violence: she had hideous temper tantrums, usually directed towards her younger sister, Vena. For no apparent reason, she would beat Vena down to the floor, or begin throwing dishes at her from across the room. Probably the most extreme occurrence was when she tried to shove Vena into the hot oven while Vena was bent over, removing an apple pie. Joyce claimed she heard Vena saying terrible things about her, and refused to apologize. For this she was sent to Camarillo, the state mental institution. A few months later she got out, only to be returned. She only stayed out of institutions four years, long enough to have two husbands and four children. She was finally "placed" in a private "board and care." As one father was missing and the other denied visitation rights, my grandparents and Vena were left to raise us.

Although Vena had only ever been involved in Pentecostal churches, she had an intense obsession with the Catholic Church. She found herself truly moved by stories of the lives of saints, and found immense strength in the way Catholics glorified the Virgin Mary, almost as an equal to Christ. This worship of the Virgin was definitely not included in her previous Lutheran lifestyle. But as Vena proceeded with her exploration of "holy roller" revival meetings, she found less rules, less structure, and an entire spirit world to draw off. She knew better than to straight-out bring it to a church meeting, but she justified bringing Catholic rituals and icons into her daily life. Vena may have felt cheated out of the Catholic God-given right to publicly pray to a vast array of suffering idols, but she made up for it at home.

In any church she had ever been to, this form of worship was not only frowned upon, it was considered praying to false idols. She followed her conviction that without the idol, it wasn't. The graphic depictions of martyrdom and the high-drama rituals were spirit-state and vision-inducing. Devout Catholics, she knew, with the help of saints, would experience spiritual ecstasy through imagining the suffering of Christ during the exact moment of crucifixion. In contrast, the altar pieces in Protestant churches, the stylized crosses with no body, paled beside Catholic grandiosity. She could have converted, I suppose, but all of this representation of bloody spectacle still placed second to the Pentecostal's receiving of the Baptism in the fire of the Holy Ghost. She stood by her conviction that in her spiritual life, she could have the fire of the holy spirit, and guidance from the holy Virgin and the bloody martyr saints.

The 18-year-old Vena became so deeply involved in her Charismatic Pentecostal spiritual practices, that she began to question her lifestyle. She was engaged to an artist, and she wore her hair in platinum waves, and dressed "of the world," in clear high heels and skin-tight clothes. She wanted to become a proper church lady. She began to develop her new, more appropriate presentation. For revival church wear, she began dressing in outlandish fashions only worn by gospel singers in poor, small Pentecostal churches. Her favorite outfit to wear was a floor-length powder-blue dress with white side-panels, puffed sleeves, and a matching floor-length vest. Though it seemed to clash, on special occasions she wore a black mantilla, like the Chicanas in our neighborhood wore to funerals and weddings. She would carefully pin the large black lace square over her frosted beehive hairdo, and wrap a matching black lace shawl around her shoulders.

Even when Vena spoke in tongues, Latin would slip in. She would constantly insert "oh christo christo" into her babalogue of "she-kund-dera-mah-see-kee-yuh," thinking she was speaking in Spanish tongues. The Pentecostals explain the gibber-jabbery tongues to be a channeled spirit language, which differs from the gift of zenolalia, a gift of speaking an actual foreign language missionaries were supposed to have been miraculously given in order to communicate with the natives. I certainly didn't know the difference between the two as a child, and apparently, neither did Vena.

There was no practical explanation for Vena's quasi-español, except for her never-ending obsession with details from the Catholic Church, and Mexicans in L.A. being her main reference point.

In the summer of 1959, a sign came that Vena had made the right decision in remaining true to her instincts. She received a vision from the Virgin Mary, which was to be the first in a series of visions. In this vision, she said that Mary had come to her and told her that she was going to have a great ministry. But in order for this to happen, she and her family were to be tested by God. She was to break off her engagement and remain a virgin, she would be given bone cancer, but later be healed as long as she went to no medical doctors. She was to live as a nun until this deliverance. Deliverance was the day our family was to be released from spiritual oppression. On that day Vena would miraculously, via Immaculate Conception, bear the second coming of Christ.

My grandma not only believed her, but encouraged her to pursue the visions. Shortly thereafter my grandmother prophesied, directly through the voice of God (this was her style of prophecy), that she was being called on to join her daughter in this journey. In order to become chaste as a nun—minus the virginity but forgiven by God—she would have to stop having sexual relations with my grandpa. After this revelation, Grandpa didn't know what to do but move into the spare room. A few days later, she moved Vena into her bedroom, and they slept in the bed that my grandpa had once shared with my grandma. They would stay up late at night, praying, and doing holy women things like going on fasts together. Basically, I was raised by two self-appointed, self-styled Pentecostal nuns.

To say the least, Vena and her mother had a strange relationship, but they shared that bed before I was born, so it never seemed odd to me. When our lot came along, it was us two boys and our grandpa in one room, my two sisters in the other, and the church ladies in the third. It made perfect sense to me.

What made me suspect the holiness, or even the normalcy of their relationship was the enduring tradition they had of betadine douches. Vena had "female" problems, and for reasons that were not to be questioned, her mother needed to give her a betadine douche once a week. Vena and her mother would go into the bathroom wearing bathrobes, and disappear for at least an hour. At first I thought these troubles were legitimate, as my aunt had a dresser drawer in the bedroom full of prescription vaginal medications with plastic inserters, various douching equipment, a large container of betadine solution, vaginal suppositories, and mysterious items such as FDS feminine deodorant spray. I had figured out early that Kotex weren't for wiping your ass with, though I always figured they had something to do with the toilet. In the bathroom, Vena needed her mother to repeatedly rinse her out with a betadine/hot water solution until she was clean. Apparently it took quite a few rinses. I tried innocently walking in on them in the bathroom, but the door was always locked, and when I pressed my ear against the door, all I could hear was the shower running full blast.

Later, when the door would finally open, Vena would walk straight to her bedroom, and close the door. My grandma would clean up the bathroom, then meet her in the room. Though I was curious, I knew better than to enter their bedroom or get caught listening at the door. Eventually my grandma emerged from the bedroom, closed the door and washed her hands in the bathroom. She'd say to be quiet because Vena was taking a nap, and she would go lay on the couch and read her dream interpretation book.

As soon as she was gone, I would go straight to the bathroom and inspect every inch of it, looking for a clue to what exactly had gone on. The walls were so steamed up they were dripping, and the room had a vague, medicinal smell. I inspected the drain, the toilet, the used Kotex bucket, the empty douche bag and inserter, but I never even found a pubic hair. I had no idea what I was looking for, I was being nosy because there was something extraordinary going on that I wasn't a part of.

Later on, my younger sister was also cursed with "vaginal problems." Grandma didn't go as far as douching her, LeeAnne would be taken to their bedroom, where she would be made to kneel doggy-style on the bed, rear end hunched up, head down. First my grandma would squirt inside of her with the vaginal inserter, then she would mix it in deeper with her finger. I knew about this because one day LeeAnne confided in me about how my grandmother had hurt her insides with her long fingernails. I asked her why she didn't put the medication in herself, but she seemed too ashamed to talk any more about it. A few months later, my sister had to undergo corrective surgery because something was wrong in her vagina. I'm not sure if she had even started menstruating yet. This was told to me in such a way that I knew not to pursue the subject, and my sister never talked abut it afterwards. Ever. She also never went into their bedroom again.

Patiently waiting for Deliverance, Vena began channeling Saints through one of her most important spirit gifts, automatic writing. she also began channeling her dead grandmother Audrey. Her mother's mother was the one who first brought the Pentecostal tradition to our family, and was held in high regard. Vena "officially" canonized Audrey, and had a psychic sketch a portrait with colored chalks, which was framed and placed above the automatic writing table.

Though the task of bestowing sainthood seemed a bit grand for a nun to decide on, Vena was prone to do anything the spirit compelled her to do, which, aside from the Catholic influence, seemed to include an array of mystic tools. I found nothing strange about her channeling the dead through writing, and was intrigued during the brief period she tried using a crystal ball, but the prophecies starting sounding outrageous. As prophesied, Vena suffered from undiagnosed bone cancer, and was healed after three years of suffering and massive weight gain. During the weight loss period, she developed a stomach ulcer, also from God. After the cancer healing, she received word from Mother Audrey that after she bore the second coming of Christ, she would be wed to Elvis Presley, and would bear twin sons. Then Grandma and Vena received word that whenever a celebrity on television placed their forefinger on their nose in a straight line, it was a sign that they would support their ministry when Deliverance came.

One night my whole family was in the living room watching TV. It was the first time the movie *Sybil* was being shown, and I remember having unbearable feelings of embarrassment and shame: because my mother was schizophrenic and heard voices, because my sister's female organs were damaged, because Vena's mother was still giving her weekly, closed-door, betadine douches in a red-hot, drippy, steamy bathroom. All I had known up to that point was that we were the most important family in the world, chosen by God to kick off Armageddon.

CAROL TREADWELL

Suzanne

We park at the top of a cul-de-sac in El Cerrito. The black asphalt is just one shade darker than the sky. I shut the cardboard-thin door of Suzanne's car, leaning against it momentarily to balance on my high-heels. Laughing, I ask her, "Hey, Suzanne, are you sure we brushed this wig out enough? It feels like steel wool." My hand catches in its dry snarls.

"Oh God, Carol, it's cool." She puts her arm through my elbows and shrugs me closer in reassurance. "Your head looks so big...and your face is so small, it's hilarious."

Suzanne and I work at Zachary's, a yuppified pizza place, and we're going to a Christmas party. Julie decided to "give" a formal dinner party and she got in trouble with the boss for not inviting everyone she thought she should have. "Is Tracey being socially shunned?" were Barbara's words on the matter, which was outrageous, considering that she'd just finished explaining how generous she'd been to give us all the night off.

When I first started at Zachary's, Suzanne was already a big personality there. She hugged people when she got to work, yelled and joked like an eccentric proprietress in a novel set far away. I was intimidated by her confidence. I've never felt comfortable acting normal at work, I always act sort of proper, you could call it. She can still make me feel awkward, which I'm pretty sure I could never do to her. It's new to me, this whole being on the lower-rung in a friendship, kind of thrilling.

Suzanne is pretty mostly because her skin is translucent like a pearl and her eyes are a clear, uncomplicated dark brown, without all those mossy weavings like mine have. Her body is a little goofy and I think she likes it that way. She wears long, ill-fitting plaid shorts and her old Catholic school skirts with her Zachary's t-shirts at work.

Julie lives with her older brother and his evil girlfriend in their mother's old house. Their mom moved out when she got remarried. Walking up the tiled entryway, I notice that it's one of those crown-of-the-cul-de-sac houses: set at the end, with the widest driveway, the oldest trees and the least obvious front door. The levels of it overlap and open up into taller and shorter spaces. I bet the kitchen and bathroom are hard to find.

We sit down on the manicured sofa and Julie generously pours us pre-mixed cocktails from a pitcher. Her black ponytail flowing high and smooth like Jeannie's, she makes the necessary introductions. "This is Carol," she fastens her eyes on my wig. "A girl from work nobody quite knows what to do with. And this is Suzanne," she looks her up and down, shaking her head. "She's a bitch." Julie reaches down and pinches Suzanne's cheek hard, lit cigarette in hand. "But we forgive her because she's just so good at it."

"And this is Julie," Suzanne counters. "I'll let you make the call."

I hoist my glass in a half-assed tribute.

A large poinsettia sits on the low coffee table in front of me, the requisite gold foil covering its pot. I've never understood poinsettias, I think, looking at the leaves and petals, different only in color. What do you have to offer? I ask it.

Lifting my drink and remembering to put it back down on the coaster requires a mid-motion adjustment each time. When I have people over, we sit on the floor and spill whatever we want onto my beautiful beige wall-to-wall carpeting. Oh well, I breath in peacefully, let there be rules.

I exchange witticisms with various people, and, as I drink more, become passingly intrigued with a tall skinny guy named Chris. Even though I know I'll regret it later, I begin to stare at him. I guess I feel a little desperate for something to focus on. We glance wooingly back and forth but do not talk.

I get up to go to the bathroom, striding up the two steps, turning left down the wallpapered hall. I find the right door and click it locked behind me. It must be comforting, I think, living in such a fatherly house: the matched towels and the faux-crystal fixtures, the arc made in the carpet by the closing of the door.

I slide back in and onto the couch, smoothing my dress behind me as I sit down, and bounce my legs crossed. Raising my glass to my lips, I sense everyone looking at me funny, but swallow the thought and try to move on. I rest the glass against my bottom lip for a moment and take another drink then glance down at myself furtively, inconclusively, and offer up a winning smile. Everyone's still staring at me though now they're pretending not to, and I turn to Suzanne with question marks in my eyes. "Calm down," her look gently begs me. "We'll talk later on."

By the time we take our name-plated places at the dinner table, I'm drunk enough to be interested in watching my hands move from napkin to drink and find satisfaction in studying their resting positions carefully. Seeing one person's mouth speak, I guess whose will be next; I get good at predicting. Whenever laughter becomes the table-wide consensus, I laugh as well. I take up gazing at the Chris guy again, lazily now though, between bites and sips. If this were high school, I think, we could've already made out and been done with it.

Suzanne looks at her watch and tells Julie that we have to get going now, that we're expected at the other party, at our other job.

See, Suzanne and I also work together at Westside, a yuppified breakfast place—you know, banana oatbran muffins and chilaquiles. In fact, I guess I got her the job there, even though I don't think of myself as someone who can do things like that; I just told her they needed someone, and told them she was nice, anyway, they're having a party there tonight, too.

Even though we told Julie ahead of time, she gets mad, incensed even, says she would've invited someone else instead if she'd known we weren't staying. She lights a cigarette and tosses her lighter down on the tablecloth, then picks it back up and points at us, her fist wrapped around its pink plastic. She says nothing, just takes a drag and thinks, analyzing our betrayal at 90 miles per hour.

I try to let sincerity seep into my eyes as I apologize. Julie stares at me. Little piles of words come out of my mouth and melt instantly; "C'mon Carol," Suzanne says finally, seeing me drowning in them, "let's just go."

Keys out, she heads straight for the door. I follow less decisively, scattering well-meaning waves behind me, fishing for a friendly face as I go.

"She'll get over it," Suzanne tells me. "I've known her longer than you have. Believe me, she will." Her heels click importantly as she strides up the driveway.

"Alright…hey," I try to walk tidily like she is, "and besides, it's not our fault we have two parties to go to."

"So true," she sighs as we reach the street, slowly twirling across the wide circle of asphalt, arms rising naturally out from her sides.

"Hey Suzanne," I ask through the window as she reaches over to unlock my door and I open it, "was something going on in there?"

"Something going on?" She starts the car and glances at me, hands on the wheel. Goofy-harsh rock blares from the speaker at my calf. Primus? I wonder, hoping it won't come up.

"Yeah, yeah, when I got out of the bathroom I could swear—"

"Oh my," she said grandly, eyes sweeping over me as she releases the emergency break. "Yes there was." She glides out into the street, "And I'll tell you what it was. Julie was trying to convince everyone that you were really a guy in drag."

"What—?"

"Well, you are wearing a wig—"

"Hey—" My hands go to my head, fingering its wiry encasement underneath the big curls. "But I love my wig." I poke through and feel a cold fingertip on my scalp, my fantasy of being Loretta Lynn crumpled up and blown away from me like trash in the wind.

"I know, I know, me too! It wasn't really that anyway," she laughs. "She told everyone to look at your hands—"

"My hands?" We're cascading down the hill now, bouncing around curves. "Excuse me, what about 'em? Last time I checked, I wasn't hanging around a bunch of bitches with manicures!"

"Oh my goodness. Chill, doll, chill." She pressed down on my leg. I'm studying my hands, imagining them growing out of the ends of a man's arms; my fingers look as distant as plastic, as lifeless as wax. "She's just a freak tryin' to be freaky."

I cross my arms quickly, tuck my hands up under my armpits. "But did anyone believe her?"

"Well..."

"Suzanne!" I've got to stop her now, my chest is breathing inside this dress and I don't know it. I press my arms into my body and can't tell whether I feel them or whether they feel...I shake my head, slow then fast, but it stays silent on its stem. I see myself walking across Julie's living room, laughably confident, with my legs as thick as tree trunks and my feet shoved into shoes too small to hold them.

"Hey, Carol, chill, nobody believed her. She tried hard to get 'em going, you know how she is." She stops at a red light and looks at me intently, waiting for my eyes to join hers. "Anyway," the light goes green and she puts the car into first, "she's just jealous."

Jealous, I let the word float, try to keep it airborne, slapping the rearview mirror toward me, maneuvering my face into view. "Yeah, you look hot," Suzanne says, bouncing a curl up off my shoulder. She pulls up to the curb. Eyes, nose, mouth—all there, believable? And my mole suddenly seems right, as if someone'd drawn it on.

Across the street, people are inside. Heads bob past the windows at different speeds, talking, dancing, drinking. We leave our coats in the car and rush through the wet winter air. "It's weird being here at night," I say, tripping over the old train tracks in the road, parallel streaks that curve off down the block and disappear into the grass of a vacant lot.

"Thank God we got out of Julie's, Carol. Oops!" She slides between two parked cars, lifting her arms in pretend prissiness. "I've just never been able to take dinner all that seriously."

"Oooh! I knew you wanted to leave. I know, though, dinner as an event?" I follow her through the cars. "I don't know."

"Yeah, at least maybe here we'll get some action."

She pulls open the door, letting a giant swirl of music escape past us into the night. It's hot inside, as the door closes, sweaty. All the tables are gone, so for once we're free to dart across the room at any angle. As we're pouring ourselves some beer, our boss Janice glides up, her dress plunges and her cleavage convinces. Her eyes are slightly slurred behind a thick veil of mascara and liner, her teeth darkened by red wine.

"Whoa, you look hot!" Suzanne exclaims.

"Why, thank you. You kids look pretty queenly yourselves." She puts an arm around me, this woman for whom I can never seem to make cappuccinos quite fast enough. All's forgiven, I think, smiling as she mussed my false curls.

All around the place, everyone looks, I don't know, fancy-free. I've never seen them dressed as they choose, all dolled up with no fear of coffee, syrup or grease to contain them. Boyfriends and girlfriends radiate out from people's sides, let me in on their secrets. I realize I've never realized they all have actual lives. I gulp my beer, lick the foam off my lip. Janice dances off, runs into someone, and hugs him. Suzanne yells that she's going to go say hi to Belinda. I follow her part-way with my eyes, then collapse them down onto my beer. I sip it, leaving it close to my face, breathing its beer smell. How many times I've drunk beer from a keg, I think, bending the cup in and out and waiting. The buzzing of the B-52's has given way to the scrapings of The Clash.

"Hey, Carol," I hear behind me, and turn stiffly, like someone in a neck-brace. Who's that? It's Alex? Then he's upon me, flanked by three friends. Do I recognize them? I don't know. Overgrown skater boys with their lanky bodies and tough eyes.

Wait-a-minute what's Alex doing talking to me? "Yeah, hey." I greet him shyly at first, then let myself go. "These cups are semi-solids," I enthuse, squeezing my cup until the beer threatens to spill over the top, feeling zany in a science teacher kind of way.

"Yeah, hey," he moves quickly past this. "You been here long?" He's taller than me, his hair a black crewcut, his eyes a ways away.

"Um, just around five minutes." I take a little sip.

"Hey, well," he pulls the keg's black tube toward him, fills his cup one-handed, and lets the tap fall. "I've got some weed, if you wanna smoke it," he winks lazily, cool. "Let's go in back."

I ease myself away from the keg, pulling a bottle of wine along with me as I go. I glance up at the friends, see nothing in their faces, guess they see nothing in mine.

It's darker in back, quieter. We pass by the boxes of dates I eat all the time, those chalky sweet pellets that rest in my mouth taste-lessly till I bite through 'em. Oh, to untwist the plastic and take a mouthful, I wish, a sticky brown blob—but we've already gone by. The time clock's greedy dial and vacant slit leer out at me. "Maybe I'll stick my card in now!" I yell, stooping to look through the rack. My arm goes slack as the wine bottle plants itself on the concrete.

Into the tight metal pockets are tucked rows of same-looking beige cards. "I can't find mine!" I wail. "They all look alike—"

"Hey, Carol, c'mon. Let me get that for you." Alex reaches down and takes the bottle by its middle. As he lifts it, I feel my fingers uncurling one by one off the neck.

"Okay," I smile forlornly, staring down at my empty hand, its big, flat palm. He motions me toward the back office, a wedge of bright yellow light, an open door.

Blinking heavily to fend off the fluorescence, I grasp the door-knob, let it pull my arm behind me as I enter the room. They're all sitting on the desktops and counters, smoking, splayed out every which way. I roll Janice's chair out from under her desk and lower myself into it, first clasping my hands in my lap, then grabbing onto the padded armrests. I cross my ankles. They're talking about going out after, maybe to a dive bar on San Pablo. Do I want to come, they pass the joint to me. "OK, maybe, sure." I bend down into the joint, like an old lady sipping tea too warm for her taste. Their legs dangle, jeans and bulky techno-sneakers surround me like vines. I look up at the cabinets, the order sheets and clipboards, all that bother.

"Yeah, that's cool," they're saying. "We could hit the Ivy or the Office…" The wine bottle's in my lap now, the joint making its second round. I heft the jug up and drink, filling my mouth till it bulges. I need three swallows to down it all, and a wipe of my hand to finish. I'm drying my hands on each other, spreading the wine thin so it'll soak into my skin.

"Yeah," I take the joint between fingertip and thumb, adjust it to make room for my lips. "But remind me to get Suzanne."

Alex smiles slyly, "Hey, Bontempo's here?"

"Yeah," I answer, keeping my mouth closed over the smoke, swallowing and sucking it ever deeper into myself, waiting for the cough, which comes. "She drove us." I wave randomly, eyes watering "She's out there."

"Cool," says the blond friend. "She's a cool gal." He nods to himself, eyes closed.

What? I wonder, Suzanne's been palling around with these guys? Oh yeah, I drift toward a thought, she said something about Alex once…

"Hey Carol, babe, what's up with the wig?" Alex asks, laughing down at me not unkindly.

"What?" I'd forgotten all about it, now feel its vague digging at my scalp. "Oh yeah," I stick a finger underneath and scratch the skin behind my ear till it's red hot. "Y'know, Halloween…I mean, I know it's more Christmas now…" They're all staring and I flood my mouth with wine again. A stream flows from the corner of my mouth. I stop it with a finger, swallowing, feel warm splats dripping onto my neck. "I guess I just wanted to dress up as a girl…you know, a girl girl." I wait. They don't know. "But it didn't work. Julie told everyone I was a guy in drag!" I slump over the wine bottle, propping myself on it, letting it stab into my chest.

"Huh?"

"Earlier!" I implore, throwing myself against the back of the chair. "At her party!"

"A guy in drag?" Alex laughs again, curious underneath it. "What do you mean?"

"I mean would you believe her?" I stare at him, at each of them "Would you?" I beg, "I mean I know I'm flat-chested, and my hands…" I raise one, spread my fingers for inspection.

"Well, there's one way to find out." I hear these words and turn to find them: he's smirking over there, the shorter, brown-haired friend, his arms crossed over a wrinkly plaid shirt, back against the bulletin board, blocking the official poster on workers' rights. I smile up at him thankfully.

"That's right," I say, taking the ends of my wig hair in opposite hands and crossing the strands under my chin, pulling them tight like the drawstring of a hood. "Who wants to know?" I demand, letting my hair go. "Does anyone care?"

"Yes, we care," Alex says calmly.

"OK then!" I yell. "Let's find out." I begin pulling apart the snaps of my dress, slowly, hearing each small pop. That dumb camisole is underneath, beige and too big, a Christmas present maybe from my mom, I can't remember. The straps had already fallen from my shoulders and it drops easily with my dress, leaving my chest...alone. I stare down at my white skin, focus on the small pink mole in the exact center. "I'm not convinced," I whisper, feel the breath waft down my body. "I'm not convinced," I say louder, a cold wind.

Lifting my shoulders first, then my hand, I ask, "Are you?"

They say nothing, don't move.

"Well, then," I stare back at them, their softened faces, their muted mouths. "Come check!" I scream, trying to awaken them. "I want someone to tell me. You," I address the brown-haired one, place the wine bottle on the floor by me feet. "Your idea, you come here." His pale eyes question me but I am strong and unyielding. "Yes," I say. "You." He appeals to his friends who shrug or run hands through their hair, He sits up slowly, pausing over his knees, then lifts himself one half at a time down off the desk. He walks into my stare and my stare directs him to stand in front of me, to drop down onto his knees. My stare tells him to reach out, to touch my chest, to pull at my nipples, each one. I feel the other guys crowding closer. "What do you think?" I ask, as he reaches around behind me, pulls me toward him. His wet lips suck at my tit. "Don't you want to bite it?"

"What the fuck is going on in here?" I hear. Suzanne is at the door yelling, stopped, blocking it, pointing. Her mouth is tense with disgust, her knees locked like a soldier's. I let him fall off of me, my friend, try to pull the hair back around my chin. "What the fuck are you guys doing?" Her eyes burn wickedly at Alex, then throw him right away. "Get the fuck off my friend!" She pulls the brown-haired one by the back of his collar and he falls over toward her. "Get the fuck out!" She yells, kicking his shoulder as he scrambles up.

"I'm sorry," I say, watching him disappear through the doorway, the last one to go.

"No, she's not!" Suzanne yells, wiping tears from my face. Her warm hands fix my camisole straps, place them back, heavy and silky on my shoulders. She snaps my dress now, starting at the bottom, like a mom and a winter coat.

"It's not their fault, Suzanne," I tell her. I tell her big brown eyes. I taste my salty lips, my happy salty lips.

"Now listen," she whispers. She moves the wine bottle aside and it sounds hollowly across the rough concrete floor. "That's the small part." She takes my shoulders gently and holds them in place. "The big part, and the only part I care about you knowing, is that it's not your fault."

The hushed seriousness of her voice stays in my brain, sounds like the Caldecott Tunnel on a rainy day, with all the cars bringing water in along with them. She wipes beneath my eyes with the backs of her thumbs as I run a finger along the hairline of my wig, tucking stray hairs back inside.

DANIEL CANO

Giving Up the Ghost

I.

When Manny Cardoza's forehead hit the steering wheel, he saw a bright flash, a cameo, an imprint: Beto's face, brown, wavy hair, perfectly combed, his dark skin powdered and pale, eyes closed, lips and nose pressed flat, hands folded across his chest, and a dark, neat hole in the center of his forehead. Manny threw open the car door, and in the light of a street lamp, hopped up the curb and ran down the sidewalk. When he reached the Highland Nursery, he scrambled over the chain-link fence and jumped to the ground. He felt his way in the dark, dodging trees and plants, moving deeper into the nursery. He heard the screeching tires and dove into a dark space between two palm trees. He lay still. Red lights shone against the trees, reflecting into the dark sky. There was cursing. A chain-link fence rattled.

Manny's mouth was dry. He gulped air, heaved and moaned, desperate to keep quiet. The sirens wailed and the tires skidded. Voices called, echoing. His chest pounded. He pressed his cheek to the ground and the smell of fertilizer rushed through his nostrils.

The ground in front of him brightened, brilliant, as a flash-light searched, leaping from earth to trees. He closed his eyes and dropped his head. The voices neared, getting louder, the boots crunching gravel. His legs shook. He raised his head and saw shadows and lights and night. He rose to his elbows and looked around, waiting. He thought of making a run for it, jumping the fence, and disappearing down the sidewalk. Two men moved past. He hesitated. A blunt instrument struck the back of his head. His side exploded in pain as a crunching blow split his ribs, lifting him from the ground. He coughed, spit out, but said nothing. He tried to raise his head, but a weight pressed against his neck, a shoe shoved his face into the gravel, pebbles scratching his face.

"Move!...Move," said the voice, quivering, "you dirty shit, so I can blow you away."

"Put up the gun," said another, a strong, gruff voice.

Manny closed his eyes tightly.

"We could do it," the shaky voice said, overanxious. "Right here, Mick. We could do it."

Manny recognized the rookie's voice.

"Not tonight Goddamn it. I ain't dealing with all that shit tonight." Cigar smoke filled the air. "Load his sad ass up. Let's get outta here."

They cuffed Manny, hands behind him, and walked him past the squad cars scattered about the street, red lights flashing, officers standing around, shotguns in their hands, voices buzzing over the radios.

Some people came out of their clapboard homes. They stepped to the sidewalk and porches. It was past midnight. They stood in pajamas, pants, and t-shirts.

The police searched Manny's car, ripping out seats and yanking at the hubcaps.

Mick, a veteran detective, butch haircut, dark suit and tie, huge belly, looked into Manny's eyes, flashlight shining, cigar smoke filling the air. "High as a DC-7. Under the influence," he said. "Told you last time I didn't want to see you around here again, Cardoza. Can't keep that shit out of your body, huh?"

They slammed Manny against the police car's side panel. His knee hit a blunt edge, and he slid to the ground.

"You don't have to be so rough," a woman's voice called from the crowd.

"G'won, you all get the hell to bed. Let us do our jobs here," said a helmeted officer, who stood beside his motorcycle.

"*Siesta* time...*siesta* time," said another officer, gripping his night stick.

The rookie grabbed Manny by the throat. He squeezed and lifted him to his toes, then shoved him into the back seat. He sat there, dazed, looking down at his shoes, at the clumps of mud. He thought about jail and his knees began to tremble, but he kept his eyes hard, defiant.

A tow truck backed out of the shadows, jacked up Manny's sports car and lifted the front tires off the ground. Manny turned away, as if unconcerned. The tow-truck driver gunned his engine. The heavy auto bucked, lunged forward, and moved slowly up the street.

Manny knew Sharon, his wife, would be sitting at home in front of the television, waiting, her eyes on the screen, seeing nothing but the reflections. The baby would be asleep in her crib.

Sharon's father had told her that Manny was lost and that she should forget him.

Three years earlier, after meeting Manny at Cal State Northridge, Sharon had invited him to her parents' home in Granada Hills. They had all sat down to a nice family dinner.

The Foster family listened to the handsome, intelligent veteran who had recently returned from Vietnam excitedly talking about college, about his future. But a year later, Manny had changed.

"He's not the same person, Shari," her dad had said. "Manuel's sick. He needs help, and until you realize it, he'll drag you down with him. Leave him, honey."

"But, Daddy, he's trying."

Her father made a sarcastic expression, twisting the corner of his mouth, narrowing his eyes.

"Okay," she said. "So he quit school. He's still got a good job."

"For how long, Sharon? Don't fool yourself. He's a junkie. He doesn't want help. You took him to the Veterans Administration. He quit the program. Bring the baby and come home, Shari."

"He's my husband."

"He'll end up in jail...again. Next time I won't help, and he won't get off so easy."

After a year's marriage, she had tired. She didn't understand Manny's life, and she was afraid of his friends. They came around at all hours, hard-gang-looking guys, hippies, bikers, and students, always anxious, tense, peering over their shoulders. She knew he tried keeping them away from his home, but they came anyway.

In the back seat of the police car, Manny pushed the thoughts away. He twisted his hands, feeling the hard metal around his wrists.

The rookie sat behind the steering wheel. He took off his hat, placed it on the seat, slid his hands over his thigh, and said, "Shit, wetback bastard made me tear my pants." He reeled around and slammed his fist into Manny's face, just below the cheekbone. There was a crack, a sharp pain, as if someone had driven a nail into his skull.

"Hey! There ain't no need for that," said Mick.

"Ah, who gives a shit."

Manny sat up straight.

II.

The patrol car pulled slowly form the curb. People peeked into the back window. A little boy about ten, hair in his eyes, held up his thumb.

They cruised Sunset Boulevard, driving past brick storefronts, the local high school—Hollywood High—and the drive-in restaurant at the corner of La Brea. Neon lights flickered from marquees at the tops of buildings, advertising movies and record albums. Slowly, the cops turned down Cherokee, a smaller, darker street. Manny's arm muscles tightened, his head throbbed. They cruised past his aunt's house, her front yard over grown with weeds, an old boat on a broken down trailer parked next to a hedge. He looked to see if any of the guys were out front. At a brightly lighted intersection, they made a U-turn and headed towards the police station on Wilcox.

They passed the brick Baptist church, its three-story bell tower rising higher than the old concrete apartment buildings. They moved past lawns, gardens, flowers, white fences, sidewalks, concrete curbs, hedges, telephone poles, and electric wires. Manny saw a white Victorian home, long wood porch, steep roof, Mr. Martinelli's place, the one with the corn field next to it, the corn tall, spread out over an acre of land, the last field remaining in Hollywood. Manny thought that if he could have reached the corn field instead of the nursery, the cops would have never caught him.

*   *   *

Earlier that evening, he'd been parked across from the Catholic elementary school in front of Junior's apartment. Junior had told him not to leave the house, not until he'd come down some, was feeling *tranquilo*. *"¿Sabes qué,* Manny?" he had said. *"Te lo juro, ese. Espérate hasta que estés bien suave. Porque si te vas,* you know, you split now, an' the 'man' swoops, *te van a chingar,* bust yer ass, *y* you couldn't fool a nun right now, brother. *Te digo, no ajuantaras otra vez en el bote. Casi muriste las otras veces…*you don' wanna be pullin' no hard time, *carnal.* It ain't your style. They been lettin' you off easy 'cuz you was a Vietnam vet an all, but those days are gone with the wind, *ese.* You're just a hype now," he said, sitting at the kitchen table, leaning back in a chair, wearing his dark Ray Charles sunglasses, nodding his head.

"Hey, Junior, I'm cool man. I got it together, especially now. I feel good, can't nobody touch me, dude."

"You're still a cherry, Manny. Take it easy, that's all, *¿tú sabes?* You ain't a veteran of the streets like the rest of us."

"Yeah, cool."

"Cool, my ass, *ese,*" Junior said with a smirk. Then he said, as Manny walked to the door, "Hey, why don't you bring over one of them fine hippie broads next time you come over? There was some fine ones over at the last party you and your old lady had at your *chante.* I'll turn you on to some free *carga,* man."

Manny laughed. "Those white broads don't dig this scene. Chicanos like you scare them."

"Hey-y-y, man. I can grow my hair long, *ese.* I can look dirty and stinky like those hippie *vatos.* I can even talk like them. 'Out of sight, dudes. Dig what's happening.'"

Manny laughed as he walked down the stairs.

Outside Junior's apartment, Manny had sat in his car, a green 1967 MG Midget hardtop. He had bought it with the money he'd saved in Vietnam. His mom and dad wanted him to invest in a house. He had enough for the down payment. He bought a car instead. All he wanted was to drive around and get high.

The first time he stuck a needle into his arm was in Phan Rhang, two months after Beto's death. Back then, Manny hadn't been able to get the fatal image out of his head. He'd drunk whiskey, smoked weed, dropped Darvon…anything to forget, but nothing helped. He'd see Beto's face, then Charley's face. He had memorized each scene. In the rear area, he had talked about it to whomever would listen. He was obsessed with it. In a bar, a secret back room, away from the drunks and prostitutes, a place the M.P.s didn't know, a white dude, Mingus, had shown Manny a different world.

"Stuff will cool you out, Manny. Mellow you, keep you low and slow, man."

He had been offered heroin before. Manny had always declined, even telling Mingus once to go to hell. But there came a time when Manny was willing to try anything, anything to keep the dogs away, to keep Beto's face out of his head. On that day, Mingus had happened along. He had taken Manny to the back room. The place was filled with paratroopers. They sat on couched that lined the four walls. Lou Rawls' deep voice rose above the dense silence, "Move on black snake, stay away from my baby's door."

Manny saw beautiful Vietnamese women moving about the room. One woman, not a girl, but a lady, in her thirties, voluptuous, mature, was fixing a guy who looked like he was already nodding off. She stuck the needle into the young, blond soldier's arm. His bangs fell to his forehead. He looked like an Indiana farm boy. She withdrew the syringe, opened her blouse, placed his hand on her breast, and kissed him deeply on the mouth. The soldier didn't respond. He was somewhere else, somewhere far away. Manny couldn't decline. He sat down and waited his turn. He made the woman open her blouse first, kiss him deeply, and when he could barely breathe, his heart pounding, she slid the needle in.

He returned a few more times. The place had scared him: the drugs and the women, the music and the smoke, the decadent environment.

He arrived home two months later. From Cam Rhan Bay to Los Angeles, just like that, no buffer, no debriefing, just a new uniform, a steak dinner, and an airline ticket.

Manny had been anxious to get home to his family, to taste his mom's cooking, hear his dad's voice, be in the security of their house. Yet, he was also hesitant, guilty. His sins ran deep. How could he face them? Would they ever suspect, ever believe, ever imagine the things he had done and seen?

At the airport his first night in L.A., a taxi had pulled up to the crowded terminal. It was night, and the lights were a blur.

"Come on, soldier, hop in," the cabbie had said. He looked and sounded like Woody Allen, thick glasses, thin hair, melancholic eyes.

"Thanks," Manny said.

It was December. Manny had gotten used to the tropical climate. The concrete beneath his feet was ice. The voices around him, although American, sounded foreign, neurotic, frenetic. He had wanted to plug his ears, close his eyes.

He bent down to pick up his duffel bag, but the cabbie grabbed it first. "Let me get that for you."

A man, dressed in an expensive three-piece suit, walked past the two and placed a suitcase in the trunk.

"I've got to be in Century City in twenty minutes. Let's go," he'd said, and moved towards the back seat.

"Hold on, sir. This soldier was here first."

"I don't have time for this..." the man said. He looked at Manny, who stood in his green winter uniform, ribbons and jump wings over his left breast pocket, his trousers bloused, the bottoms tucked into his jump boots. "You don't mind soldier, huh? There're plenty of other cabs."

Before Manny could respond, the taxi driver said, "No, sir," his voice rising, an excited New York accent.

Manny was about to tell him to go ahead. He was in no hurry.

"The soldier was here first. This is his cab," said the driver, who then turned to Manny and said, "Where to?"

"Who the hell do you think you are?" the man in the suit growled. He moved close to the cabbie.

They argued. Manny watched. A crowd formed.

"You mind if I take this cab?" the man asked Manny.

"Yeah, mister, I do. It's my cab. I was here first."

"There! You hear that? Hear!" said the cabbie.

"I want your driver's number!" the man shouted.

"It's on the dash. Get it yourself," the driver said, and walked to the trunk with Manny's duffel bag in hand. He took out the man's luggage and replaced it with Manny's bag.

"Let's go, soldier."

"You won't hear the end of this, you!…"

"What?" said the driver, "Say it…what?"

"Bastard."

The driver laughed out loud as he opened the car door and got in.

The man in the suit looked into the car and sneered at Manny, who was sitting uncomfortably in the back seat weary and silent.

* * *

He never thought he'd get addicted. The first times he did it back home, he told himself, it was to take away the pain, the memories. Maybe that was true. Then one day, the memories were extinguished, burned from his mind, and Manny realized the truth. All he cared about was the high. He craved it again and again. Each time the tip of the needle touched his arm, his mind raced back to Phan Rhang, the woman's open blouse, her bare breast, her lips on his, and the needle entering his skin.

Family no longer meant anything to him. Sharon was a body he lived with. He stopped going to school. He began to miss work.

Then the baby was born. He swore to Sharon that he'd work hard, go back to college and get his degree, but each night after work, he'd drive through Hollywood, buy the stuff, and party.

III.

The rookie chewed a toothpick and hummed an Okie song, *Jambalaya*. He drove past the streets where Manny had played as a kid.

"Turn here," Mick said.

The rookie turned.

"Stop."

The car halted abruptly. They were in front of Manny's parents' home, a long stucco house on a tree-lined street. At first, Manny turned away.

"Take me to jail, man!" he yelled. The rookie smiled, but he wouldn't move the car.

Manny looked out the window towards his house.

He saw his dad's new Buick parked in the driveway, and beside it, his mom's car, a Nova station wagon. Along the curb was his dad's old truck, the front fender dented where Manny had driven it into the tree when he was fourteen. His father kept the truck as a reminder of the years he had worked delivering plants while he put himself through college, finally earning a doctorate in education. He'd gone from a classroom teacher to a principal, and was now a deputy superintendent teacher for the Los Angeles Unified School District. He urged his children to do the same. The others had all graduated college and were settled in their careers.

There was a light shining in the living room. Manny knew his parents were asleep. They always left one light on.

Above the roof, like a shadowy giant, was the avocado tree, the branches stretching out over the house and sidewalk. Manny saw himself and his older brothers as kids, sliding and swinging from the branches, laughing and calling out, "Be careful, Manuel. Don't fall, ya might break something and Mom'll shit."

He smiled and remembered his first girlfriend, Connie Fujimoto. It was in the fifth grade. He never should have told his brothers that Connie was coming over to visit him. Manny had taken a bath, put on clean Levi's, a blue and green checkered shirt, and combed his hair, parted to one side. A half-hour later when Connie came to the back gate and called out for Manny, his oldest brother had yelled for her to come into the backyard. His three other brothers were in the garage, watching and giggling from behind the door, as the gate creaked open, Connie peeked through. She didn't hear Manny yelling, the tape was too tight on his mouth. She pushed the gate open and stepped inside. She wore red shorts, a white top, and white tennis shoes. When she finally saw Manny, she screamed, stood for a second, turned and ran home, her feet slapping the sidewalk. Except for a pair of oversized work boots, Manny was in his underwear, hanging upside-down, hands bound with a cord, one end of a rope tied to his ankles, the other tied to a branch. He swung back and forth, shaking and struggling to get loose. He never trusted his brothers after that.

Manny slumped back against the seat.

The rookie, fidgety, ran his hands over the steering wheel. He put his head down, then raised it and looked out the window. "Come on, Mick. We've been here ten minutes."

"Wait."

"It's getting late."

"I said wait, damn it!"

Mick was also looking at the house. He'd been on the force a long time, and he knew Manny's father, who was active on boards and committees.

The burly officer looked into his side mirror, studying Manny's face.

Manny dropped his head.

"Let's go," said Mick.

It was after one in the morning when they pulled into the police station. They made Manny wait two hours before he could call anybody. Sharon cried. She said that she couldn't post bail. They didn't have the money and she wasn't about to ask her parents.

He panicked. She'd gotten him out before, somehow. He slumped against the wall. The heat rose to his head. He sweated, and at the same time his hands were cold, frigid. He begged. Still crying, she hung up.

He made another call.

"No more," his mom said, choking. Both of his parents were on the line. He pleaded, like a boy, "Please, Ma…Dad, please come and get me. I'll pay you back every cent. Just post the bail this one last time. I can't stay here. It'll kill me."

"Manny, we can't talk to you anymore," his father said in a soft voice. "This is it, son. We've tried everything. You're destroying us and Sharon, and your son. If you want to keep playing in the sandbox, you start cleaning your own socks and shoes. Goodbye," he said just like a high school principal, and the phone clicked.

Manny held the phone in his hand, at waist level. "Clean my own socks and shoes," he blurted, laughing, tears clouding his eyes. He stared at the ceiling and saw a fly buzzing around a light. He thought about Lincoln, a biker from Venice who had some good stuff.

The rookie came to take him back to his cell. Manny hollered and tried to pull away. The rookie shoved him, forcing him against the wall. "Fucker!" Manny cried as he threw a wild punch and missed. More cops came. They struggled. Manny hit the floor, and they dragged him back to his cell.

"He couldn't fight his way through cotton candy," one officer chuckled.

"Look here, these bell-bottoms are good for something," said the rookie, taking hold of the baggy pants and pulling as the others laughed.

They dragged him along the smooth floor. Manny could smell the polish. He knew the procedure: the isolation, the sickness, the trial. This time there would be a jail sentence. He was sure of it.

When he reached the cell, he got to his knees, then to his feet and stood up straight. "You shit," Manny said, to no one in particular.

The rookie hit him, the fist catching Manny under the jaw. He bit down, his teeth slicing through his tongue. As he reeled backwards, he saw the Vietnamese woman, her white *ao dai* open above the waist, her breasts exposed. He saw Beto and Charley. They stood beside a tree.

Manny dropped to the ground, his head hitting the corner of a metal bunk bed. He lay still on the floor, sat up, and touched the back of his head. There was a deep gash. He looked at his blood-stained fingers and fell back, his head hitting the floor where a pool of blood formed. He closed his eyes. The officers moved in closer. Blood dripped from the corner of Manny's mouth. A cop stooped down and reached to feel his pulse. The officer squinted. "Somebody get a doctor, fast."

Vaguely, like a lost echo, Manny heard a sound, decreasing in volume with each utter, "Cardoza, ardoza, doza," until it stopped.

"He faking it?" asked one of the cops, looking around nervously.

"No," responded the one who held Manny's wrist.

"Screw him! Bastard! No big loss," said the rookie, half-smiling.

"You don't know shit about nothing, asshole," said Mick as he approached. He pushed the rookie aside and knelt on one knee beside Manny.

"It was an accident?" one of them said.

"Did anyone get a doctor?" another said, angrily.

"Why waste the taxpayers' money?" said the rookie.

"Too late?" asked the cop, still trying to feel a pulse.

"Too late," Mick said, taking a blanket from the bunk and covering Manny.

Highway 1

I came down the stairs with my little dog to answer the door at six in the morning, wearing only a long black and orange bathrobe. I was excited about seeing the man who was waiting there because I didn't get to see him very often, and then only at his whim.

He had called at 5:30, drug-crazed, belligerent and exciting, demanding that I throw out whoever was in my bed, which I did. His name was Artie Mitchell and I had met him when I worked on my first porno film. He had continued to call after the work was through. Being addicted to bizarre sex, he was the only person I'd ever met who had no fear of the physical or chemical edge.

There was an air of chaos and sleazy glamour that permeated his life, now confirmed by the silver limo at the curb driven by his hunky blonde cousin who smiled as I was pulled without resisting into the backseat littered with children's toys. I'd heard his wife was fertile.

I complained to him that I hadn't locked my apartment door and he told me with drunken gallantry that he would replace whatever was stolen. There wasn't much there anyway.

He had an uncommon ability for calling when I was on my period, but it wasn't really that hard because I was bleeding more often than not. We did some cocaine and soon were humping like mink on the approach to the Golden Gate Bridge. Being concerned about the nice gray velour seats I told him I was bleeding heavily. He told me he didn't care. We had hot, wet, mad menstrual sex on the bridge at sunrise, filling the back seat with orgasms while my little dog slept peacefully on the floor.

We took a break on the road to Mount Tam, where he pulled out a wad of money and wiped the blood off me and himself. He threw the bloody money on the floor with the dog and lit a joint.

Heading north on Highway 1, we picked up a suntanned girl hitchhiker with tangled blonde hair like the morning after. She was happy to be picked up by a limousine but after we'd started up again she saw the puppy and the bloody money and got nervous. He teased her for being squeamish, and asked me to recite some poems. After she heard them, she asked to get out. We pulled over and left her by the roadside. We accelerated our intake of drugs.

We drove another hour up the perfect California coastline, then turned off on a dirt road that led to a little trailer with a small group of people standing around and sitting in lawn chairs drinking beer. We got out of the car and he told me they were his relatives. There was a sweet comfortable woman in her fifties who he said was his aunt. I was in my bathrobe with no shoes on. She was nice to me anyway.

The men had just been abalone diving. They were telling extravagant stories with their hands. I was astounded that my friend would ask anyone to meet relatives in my condition, but they took it well. They joked that they thought someone had died when they saw the limo in the driveway.

We stayed too long and he renewed his drunkenness with beer and hot sun well into the afternoon. When we finally left, we stood up in the open sunroof and made bird noises, calling to the crows.

We resumed our passionate fucking as we returned to the city. The tinted windows amplified the darkness, smudging the edges of things. It was late when we arrived and he wanted to eat, so we went to Japantown where they didn't care that I had no shoes. I ate sushi for the first time, and being so high it seemed to slither down my throat.

A week later I got a card from him: the ace of spades folded in a dollar bill covered with dried blood. I framed it and hung it on the wall.

BENJAMIN WEISSMAN

Twins

This page is written from the never before attempted first-person-twin point of view, which means everything here is from our mutual identical beings. We this, we that, blinking, breathing, blushing—twin plurality talking directly to you, O hot honorable reader, who we hope finds our words a pleasure and cerebral stimulus. Our thoughts are spontaneous and unrehearsed. People (not just guys) have sex fantasies about us because we're twins, and we model lingerie.

Since we were created in the same package guys believe they're entitled to the double set. They start out with one, and then beg for two. We say, *uh uh, sorry, no good, not moral,* because we believe in YOU KNOW *WHO* above the apartment, clouds, and planets, and we never use *his* name in vain, so let's just call him HIM—the inspiration for everything on earth, from a hymnal to the Himalayas (affectionate exaggerations of our asymmetrical breasts.) Guy swaggering is a cover-up for the yawning need for giant spoonfuls of reassurance, mommy stuff, and little rubby-rubs on the head. We strip and the boy-bull stops breathing. What is inside us exactly besides cells, organs, and gunk? Since we were born with perfect exteriors and we're professional models guys want to get inside us and rummage around, explore out little caves (mouth, vagina, and anus, ouch) not very echoey. Our Jeeps each have a bumper sticker that says, I (heart) MY VAGINA, because it's true, we do love them. We shaved them into the most petite little stingers so our labby lips are bare like a newborn babe's. Just because we model bustiers and teddies everyone thinks we are sex experts, like porn stars. Shatter that myth. We're sexual fumblers. A guy will say harder or faster and we do it too hard or too fast or not hard or fast enough and when he says suck or jerk we always lick too softly or hold it wrong or stab the urethra with our nails. When referring to more than one urethra you say ure*thrae*. When the guy says, flip over girls (okay, so we do fuck the same guys) we usually kick him in the head with our high heels. We apologize, we say, we're sorry, how embarrassing, but there's no recovery. It's like who brought in the bad comedians? Their head hurts, they want to go home. Since you asked, our favorite movie is *Shoah*. A gentleman of the Jewish persuasion took us to it. Eight hours long, one movie, the tickets were $20 each, took us two days to watch it. We got a terrible feeling looking at the popcorn machine. Very morbid. Cooking, confinement, bursting kernels. We bought a large, but out of respect for the dead (& our date) we didn't eat a single morsel. Popcorn used to be our favorite food. Now we throw up when we see a forested landscape. When we see beauty we want to know what's hidden. When the war ended the clergy removed portraits of Hitler and put up the almighty *HIM*, but the walls had discolored, the frames were smaller, and no one could forget the previous face. Women can be nazis too, but it's men who cut off heads, gloat, and experiment on flesh. A woman's offensive is economic, non-violent. We isolate the enemy, boycott businesses, distribute literature. We fight with our minds. It's strange what you have to do to a penis, the same thing all the time. Jerk and suck. We want something less abrupt, less piston-like, something unbroken. Maybe we're lesbians. *Maybe* we're not. Our favorite sexual position is 69ing each other while the guy is loving us doggie, that way we can see the guy's balls going *clang-clang* like hairy tea bags. And if his *iguana* comes out we can kiss it before *escorting* it back in.

SANDRA ZANE

Traveling

The riverbed's fine sand coated the open purse of her mouth. Her cheek to the ground, the 6:45 Southern Pacific rolled towards Barstow, its low rumbling vibrated in her ear. The day's sun had burned her shoulders, the pale skin on the back of her knees. Only a thin sundress covered her and the orange and pink glow of the early night failed to help her eyes. Her opened face couldn't remember the dry heat or how she got here, but her outstretched arms seemed to swim down the wash towards the distant sea. This place gave her nothing and she gave nothing back. She was put here for all the wrong reasons. A way to make a living, a familiar face, another chance. Somehow it took this long for her to move on. As each kick of hot wind pitted the crevices of her nostrils, a sticky odor from between her legs passed through the valley, but no one caught the scent.

Leaving herself behind, she roamed down the dirt road towards buckling asphalt, tract homes, commercial parks. The warehouses all looked the same, uniform glass windows with slogans, figures, and discounts painted in neon. They had never attracted her before, they didn't move her now. She recognized the pool hall they went to, sometimes watching the activity outside through the painted windows. Next door the fitness club with its leotard-clad women and sweating men, across the lot, the Midnight Cowboy where every Friday night, couples stepped out in ruffled skirts and shirts with matching piping. Somehow she wandered out to Waterman, the intersection between bad and worse. The street stretched into the San Gorgonio mountains but nothing grew along the way. She used to wonder who forgot this valley. In between here and there and on the way to somewhere else. One hour to the ocean, one hour to the desert, one hour to the snow. But now she saw a basin of smog and people who would never get out.

She knew the names of the towns but couldn't tell the difference between populations. Loma Linda—elev. 1189 pop. 13000, San Bernardino—elev. 1254 pop. 49000, Highland—elev. 1300 pop. 24000, Riverside—elev. 1150 pop. 67900. Her father lived in Colton, just another elev. 1198 pop. 35400. The people all looked the same to her. Auntie Tranh had brought her here. *Many good jobs. Good school for Lin.* But she didn't recognize herself here. She couldn't see the color of her hair, the width of her thighs, how tall she was. Mirrors confused the impression. She'd sometimes see a girl who seemed to replicate her body but when she tried to walk alongside her, the fit was all wrong.

The night air soothed her. She suddenly felt relief from her body, the weight of legs, as she continued towards the place of origin. There was In-N-Out Burger, the first meal she and her father had had in this valley. She didn't order, her cousin Tracy handed her a hamburger wrapped in paper and french fries dribbled with ketchup. She was perplexed by its appearance, examining it from all sides before taking a small bite. It was rich, a combination of hot and cold. Her father ate with a big smile as he agreed with Auntie Tranh that the price was good, the food ample. She thought about how every day her father told her to take note of those around her, do what they do, listen to the language. When he found a job at the Sunshine gas station he always came back with a new product from the shelves, a different gesture or greeting. *Chile lime corn nuts,*

Super Bubblicious, Hiya bub, waving from the hip. He seemed to enjoy the rules of the game. She watched him join in and become one of them, amazed at how quickly he picked it up. Her mother would not have approved. The stories she told her long ago were almost forgotten, but what Lin could remember had nothing in common with this place. The tumbleweeds were so sharp, her father moved in jerking motions, the food had no origin. She missed the slippery tones, the moisture of every day, she could barely hear the coconut milk of her mother's voice.

As she continued past the mini-markets and used car lots, she noticed an ease in her movements. The difficulty of when to say, where to wear, how to do, and who was who, dropped off like pellets of rain on a window. She moved straight through every time her father reminded her *it sounds like tack, watch how they match it, no like this.* The coolness began to take over, clearing her thoughts. Yet, she felt compelled by something flashing. A metal blade catching a headlight, the short spikes of gelled hair. She followed the continuous stream of lights from the cars below and fell closer. A white sports car with chrome mag wheels and inky-tinted windows led her to a cul-de-sac. She remembered Kimmie. The color of their arms and how everyday they would compare the depth of their tans. She almost found her reflection in the darkly kohled eyes of her new friend. Though Kimmie was taller, Lin felt she could have grown into her with a late spurt or higher heels. She didn't have to worry about the clothes, Kimmie gave her baggie jeans and tight tank tops to wear. Kimmie also gave her a name, Lucky, because she needed more of it and things were going to change.

She couldn't remember where they met, but could feel the first time Kimmie grabbed her arm, she couldn't help but follow. It was the first time she felt a part of someone. There were more like Kimmie, but boys. Their arms were thin and sinewy and when they took off their shirts the tightness of their bellies barely held up their voluminous pants. The Lil' Rascals moved fast, like river snakes in her mother's stories. Giggles, because he always ended everything with a laugh, Choo Choo, because he barely made it past the train when his back wheel got caught on the tracks and Banger, because he beat the door like a deep kettle drum to announce their breaking in. The first time she saw them all together she thought they were the siblings she dreamt she'd always had. She took every chance to be in their presence, to listen to their voices and walk through a crowd as one body. Auntie Tranh was happy to let her take the bus to the library. *That's good. See? It doesn't take long. Tracy had a hard time at first too. Go get good grades.* Her father worked nights and never knew when she came home. The night they told her that she was theirs, she drank every bottle they handed her and inhaled each bong load like a credo of intimacy. They knew her now and she no longer had to look for a clearer mirror. She forgot what the reflection was and who was making it. For a moment they came together. She was one. It was Choo Choo who had sealed the union. Every time he touched her body she felt a wave of moisture. It was damp sand between her toes, yellow curry with potatoes, mother stroking her hair. Each reach for her body felt like knowledge and when his fingers thrust inside her she felt the warm waters taking over.

But the smog brought change. It got harder to find the wetness. Banger wanted more of everything. Money, respect, place. When they entered the pool hall, they scanned the smoky room and flew into a tight rage at the sight of Vipers at the back snooker. Suddenly their lanky movements became restricted, stiff. She never knew what happened that night, but remembered Banger's glare and the quick cock of his head. When Banger said they needed cash to get another Glock, she barely thought twice about him showing up with Choo Choo to pick her up. Her father had already left for work, Auntie Tranh was out shopping at sales. Straddled over Choo Choo she only thought about his tongue against her teeth, the smoothness. She didn't see Banger scoping things out, but when she heard Tracy complain about thieves taking cash, all of Auntie's gold and her only jade earrings, she knew Banger had gotten more.

It began to tear at her. Though she remembered her mother telling her how robbers in the village would pound the doors before entering to give the occupants a chance to flee, it was something about the glares. The coldness. The last night she was herself, they drank Boones Farm and 151, passing around Thai stick that Giggles had gotten from his brother. Kimmie couldn't be kept down, writhing to the music while Lucky watched Banger and Giggles both fuck her. Kimmie didn't seem to mind, but she was barely there. When Banger pulled up his pants and looked her way, Lucky knew he would take her too. It was too late to fight it and she knew that Choo Choo would do nothing. She was once again outside. A sign of where she really belonged. Each jab of Banger's penis in between her arid thighs pushed her further and further away until she knew how she would get out. The thought of it was the only thing that kept her here. She didn't resist, but as Banger stumbled off her, she spit at his hardened eyes.

When Banger said he would drive her home because Choo Choo was too sick, she gladly went along. With bass thumping in her ears, she began to lose feeling in her neck. She didn't watch the road but knew where she was headed. She stepped out of the car and when they followed her to the bottom of the wash, she turned around to see Giggles laughing and Banger's glare. She counted 16 rapid-fire shots in slow motion, below her eyes, through her shoulders and at the center of her thighs. The heat began to leave her, and the dust broke her fall. Each shot pushed her towards the sea, towards the moisture she knew was there.

JERRY STAHL

The Age of Love

Her husband invented panty shields.

"They're going to be very big," she told me. "Bob used to say, 'Create a need, then push the solution.'"

The subject came up because I had my hand up her wash 'n' wear dress. Clamped between her warm, thin thighs, my fingers jammed against what felt like a moist slice of toast. Toast wrapped in nylon.

This was 1969. I was fourteen years old. We were sitting next to each other on a plane from Pittsburgh to San Francisco. I had no idea what she was talking about.

Doris later told me she was forty. But I couldn't tell. When I first saw her, in the airport lounge, it was from the back. She was bent over a lady in a wheelchair, giving her a good-bye kiss. By chance I gazed over at this tableau. I was instantly entranced by the view under her rising hem. My eyes followed hungrily up over the backs of her thighs, under her girdle to a thrilling darkness the mere thought of which had me craning my head right and left to see if any other passengers saw me peeking.

At fourteen, a virgin and chronic masturbator, I knew I could file away this glimpse and call up the memory of those mysterious creamy thighs for unlimited sessions of self-abuse in the months and years to come. At that age, I don't know that I expected to ever even have sex. It was enough, really, just to have actually, almost, gotten a peek of the exalted area. Which may explain my alarm when the woman stood up, looked my way, and turned out to be my mother's age.

I wasn't sure whether I should still be excited. Or if the lines in her face should somehow cancel out the thrill I felt at nearly seeing between her legs. She wore butterfly glasses, another Mom-like detail, and a neck-scarf printed over with little penguins. It was all very confusing. I felt my face flush into hot red blotches. For the first time in my life I wondered if I might be perverted. Though I wasn't entirely sure what a pervert was.

To disguise my discomfort, I pretended to read my hardback copy of *Call Of The Wild.* It was a Bar Mitzvah gift from my grandmother. By now I was convinced the entire waiting room was staring at me, that everyone in the immediate vicinity was whispering about the young boy who got a boner looking up a skirt that might have been his mom's.

It would not have surprised me, at that moment, if some kind of Erection Police swooped into Gate Number Four, guns drawn, led by some burly old veteran with a bullhorn who broadcast the situation to the folks on hand. "It's all right, ladies and gentlemen. It's all right…We've got a lad here who seems to be aroused by the sight of a hiney that could belong to his mother…We'll take care of it, folks. We've seen a thousand punks like him."

When I ventured to glance up again, I noticed that she'd been joined by a couple her age. I knew at once that the woman was her sister, and the man probably her brother-in-law. Both ladies wore their reddish hair brushed up in the back and down in the front, like Lucille Ball. The husband, who seemed to be a real joker, sported a short-sleeve Steelers shirt and arms so dense with hair I could see it from my seat. I wondered, for the millionth time, when *my* arms would start sprouting such a crop. Until recently, I hadn't been hairy anywhere, and it tormented me.

The husband leaned down to the old lady and made a face—bug-eyed, tongue-wagging—and both his wife and the lady I'd peeked at broke into gales of helpless, showy laughter. Except that my lady, as I'd already begun to call her, did not really seem to be enjoying herself. She chain-smoked, she kept looking all over the place, and her two hands never stopped touching, as if the one had constantly to remind the other that it was not alone.

When our glances met, for the briefest second, there was a nervous, almost hysterical quality to her grin. Her lips made a show of mirth, but her eyes glimmered with a desperation I could recognize. It was all so clear.

She's not married. They're sorry for her. She's joking around to hide how bad she feels.

Of course, I knew that feeling. That's how I felt all the time. As I sat there, pretending to read Jack London, spying on Mr. and Mrs. Hairy Arms, on old Moms in the wheelchair, on my secret soul mate, the Unhappy Girdle Woman, this sense of knowing exactly how she felt—how different, how ashamed, how uncomfortable—was absolutely overwhelming.

I didn't even realize I was staring until *Call of the Wild* clattered to the floor.

There were a few reasons my parents wanted to send me to California. But only one that the three of us could actually speak about. My sister Trudy had moved to Berkeley the previous year with her husband, Vance, and everybody thought it would be nice if I went for a couple of weeks to visit.

The truth behind this sentiment was not so nice. My parents hated their son-in-law. "Vance!" my mother had spit right up to the minute of their wedding. "What kind of name is Vance?"

It was her habit, when she loathed someone—which she did with alarming frequency—to find some innocuous detail and rant about that as the source of her boundless repulsion. "Forget that the boy looks like a sneak-thief with those little eyes of his," she'd holler from the bedroom. "Forget that he said *from day one* that he had no intention of getting a job. Forget that it broke your father's heart the day *that thing* married your sister...*What kind of a name is Vance?*"

My sister had upped and married him, at twenty, after a two year engagement to Larry, a brilliant, suitwearing pre-law student from Syracuse my parents both adored. Larry was perfect son-in-law material.

In my twelve-year-old naiveté, even I did not understand what Trudy was thinking. Until one day, during one of our long-distance chats, she told me she broke it off when she realized Larry's hair was thinning. "I just didn't want to wake up beside a bald man in a suit," she said. "Would you?" I said that I wouldn't. Vance wore a Che Guevara tee-shirt and holey elephant bells every day. He also supported an enormous ball of frizzy hair he called his "Jew-fro," and refused to cut it off for their wedding until my father gave him five hundred dollars. Over the years, the "haircut deal" proved another perennial in my mother's boudoir shouting repertoire.

The truth is, my mother's bedroom habits were one reason I'd ended up on a plane fondling a forty-year-old. Along with the reconnaissance aspect—my parents refused to visit my sister now that she'd married Vance, and wanted to send me out to check up on them—there was the fact that my mother had started "staying in" again.

"Staying in" was family code for not getting out of bed. For not washing up or getting dressed or doing much of anything but staying horizontal and shouting out peculiar comments or requests for food. My mother would lay in the dark for days at a time. After a while the room grew thick with her scent, a close, private muskiness that drove my father, if he were in town, to sleep down-stairs on a couch. When he was on the road—he sold novelty items, supplying "Joke & Gag" stores as far away as Duluth or Buffalo—it was just me and Mom.

No matter what, during daylight hours, it fell to me to do bed-room duty. "Bring me a peach!" she'd croak from the pungent dark. If I had a friend over after school, I'd smart from embarrassment at having to stop playing and hop to for this creepy, disembodied voice. Upstairs, with the drapes shut against the afternoon sun, she would throw back the blankets, instantly filling the air with great gusts of Momness. "Wanna cuddle? Wanna play Mommy's little boy like we used to?"

"I didn't know anybody else was home," the friend would say when I came back down. Then he'd look at me in that way people look at you when something's off, when something's wrong in a way you don't want to talk about. "Is that your mother? Is she sick?" And whatever I'd say, whatever I'd try to come up with to try and cover, they'd always treat me a little differently the next day in school. I didn't have a lot of friends.

Sometimes a whole year went by without my mother "staying in." But now she was doing it again. And it was worse than ever. My father told me she'd be going "on vacation" soon. Which meant another visit to Western Psychiatric.

This seemed like a good time to get on a plane and visit Trudy in California.

When we finally boarded, it didn't even surprise me that she was 21-F and I was 21-E. She had the window and I had the aisle. Long before we took off, the heat from her leg was so intense that I leaned her way, feigning boyish fascination in the weedy runway, just to see if I was imagining the oven-like warmth or if she were really burning. What I felt, when I let my right thigh graze acci-dentally against her left, was an even higher centigrade than I imagined.

My seatmate pressed back at once. As possessed as I was by sudden interest in runway activities, she edged against me and craned her neck to take in the cart piled high with Samsonite. Still not speaking, we both pretended utter absorption in the sluggish hand-to-hand loading of each suitcase into the hold.

I could hardly believe what was happening. My whole body shook with excitement. I had to clamp my jaw shut to keep my teeth from chattering. Drawing on some heretofore undreamed of reservoir of nerve, a reserve of untested manliness, I risked still more pressure.

This time my maneuver was blatant. I not only jammed my limb lengthwise against hers, I let my hand dip casually off the armrest, until my little finger dangled against her thigh. To my astonishment, her response was just as bold. The flesh of her hip under her drip-dry dress seemed to stream right through my stiff white Levi's. But that was nothing. Still facing the porthole—baggage-handling was just so fascinating!—she settled her left hand atop my right, pushing downward, so that my initial, timid exploration was hurtled instantly into another dimension.

For a moment, I had to hold my breath to fight off the excited tremors that threatened to slide me out of my seat in a complete swoon. My neck was so stiff I thought it would snap.

To counter this dizzy arousal, I drew back from the window and studied the unlikely object of my desire. Up close, I noticed, her scalp was visible through her auburn hair. I didn't think that women could go bald, yet had to wonder if she might be even older than I suspected. Her hands, too, were less than pretty, the backs showing raised veins that looked puffy and a little blue. Yet even if there was something old ladyish about her, it didn't matter. I'd never been so close to touching a girl—let alone a grown woman—"down there" as I was now. A state of affairs made all the more tempestuous by the fact neither of us acknowledged what we were doing.

Our limbs now jammed together from flank to ankle, I took

the liberty of canting my face still nearer, until I could breathe her heat, the way you would a humidifier placed in the room to fend off croup. She smelled vaguely of camphor, an odor I recognized from having to rub Bag Balm on my schnauzer's teats after she'd suckled puppies. Camphor was Bag Balm's main ingredient, and I found myself stirred anew at the prospect of rubbing the pungent emollient on my neighbor at first sign of a flare-up. If the truth be told, I'd even been a little aroused at rubbing the stuff on Queenie. But this was better. This was a thousand times better, and we haven't even taken off yet.

By takeoff, I'd managed to hook a finger over the elastic lip of her girdle, somewhere in the waist area, engaging a patch of skin that felt taut and fiery.

It was then I noticed that I had an audience.

One row up, across the aisle, a heavyset old man in bifocals was twisted completely around in his seat. He stared back at us, horrified. Unable to peel his eyes from my seatmate's parted knees. You could tell he wanted to say something, but didn't know what. He kept opening his mouth, then closing it again, like a goldfish.

I decided to look nonchalant. As nonchalant as any 14-year-old with half his arm up the dress of a woman old enough to be his mother could. This just made the old guy more furious. He tore off his glasses and scowled. He began clearing his throat, very loudly, all the while keeping his irate gaze fixed on my offending paw. I began to fear someone else would notice. I imagined how they'd turn around, somebody would see them, then they'd start staring, and so on, until finally the whole plane was shouting and pointing in our direction. For all I knew the stewardess could arrest me, the captain drag me off to some secret airplane cell, maybe behind the toilet, where I'd stay locked up until we landed in San Francisco and the FBI scooped me up to ship me back to Pittsburgh. I could already hear my mother, barking down from the bedroom to my

Dad when she saw me on the news. *"Herman, I always knew that boy was sick…!"*

To my infinite relief, the gaping senior finally turned away. But no sooner did I relax than he spun back around, this time accompanied by the apple-cheeked crone to his right. Side by side, they looked like the Wilsons, next-door neighbors on *Dennis the Menace*. If Mr. and Mrs. Wilson caught Dennis the Menace masturbating, I was sure, they'd have worn the same looks of shock and disappointment.

As I stared back, I felt like two different people—cracked by the opposing entities that had slugged it out inside me my whole life. The split was clearest in school. From first grade on, straight A's were matched by straight F's in Discipline. Watching the shocked old man and his wife, the A-making half of me was mortified. But the F-half would have liked nothing better than causing a couple of heart attacks.

"Bob never cared," she said.

"What?"

I was so stunned to hear her speak that my hand popped out of her girdle. For a second I just sat there, staring at the thin red band where the elastic had bit into my wrist. Then I eased under her dress again, like a small animal heading for its burrow.

She turned from the window with a little smile. Her tone had been matter of fact. But when she looked at me she seemed to get nervous again. Her face broke into the expression she wore with the people at the airport, like she was just about to laugh or scream and had no idea herself which it would be.

"Oh sorry," she said. "Bob was the husband. I'm Doris."

"Doris," I repeated, like a man mouthing an unfamiliar language. Up close her eyes were a startling blue. "I'm, uh, Larry," I added, and for some reason her face relaxed.

I glanced back at the fuming seniors, but, to my relief, they'd turned toward the front again.

Doris checked, too, then aimed those strange eyes back at me. "What I'm saying, Bob never cared," she began again, "About people, whatever, what they thought. Like when he went into his project supervisor, at Johnson & Johnson, to pitch them on shields. Bob invented them, you know. Panty Shields were his baby all the way."

She stopped, awaiting my reaction, though I was still fuzzy on the particulars. I pictured something like gladiators used to fend off spears, only smaller, and lodged somewhere south of the border. Then my fingers made their way back to the toast-barrier, and Doris smiled.

"That's right. That's one of the originals. I still have all the prototypes. It's my way of keeping him here, with me. I think he would have wanted it that way."

Again she awaited my reaction, again I was afraid I came up short. "That's...that's beautiful," I said. It seemed like the right time to quote Rod McKuen or something. My sister'd given me one of his books for my last birthday, but all I could remember was the title. "Listen to the Warm," I said.

It was the most grownup thing I'd ever uttered. Doris shook her head and smiled gratefully. She was old, maybe older than my mother, but at the same time there was something young about her. I noticed for the first time the way her lipstick formed a kind of ready-made kiss on her mouth, like Betty Boop.

Doris pressed her legs together, and once again I was shocked by the heat against my flattened palm, and that faint whiff of camphor. I got an erection again, but there was something different about it. I felt all kinds of things at once. For all I knew I was falling in love. My face blotched up red again, but she didn't say anything.

"The J&J guys looked at him like he was nuts." Her voice had gone a little husky. "Some of them were actually mad. *Off-ended.*"

She paused, resting her head of Lucille Ball hair against the airplane window, and I ventured an exploratory probe in an untried direction, towards her thigh, away from Bob's prototype. I soon found myself plucking back the rim of her girdle and feeling something I'd never felt before. Something I'd only dreamed about feeling. Feeling hair.

"Mmmph," sighed Doris, shifting slightly, guiding my arm with her thighs. "Ten little men in pinstripe suits at a teak table the size of Guam. And you know what he said? 'If you boys don't know why this product is gonna make you a million dollars, I feel sorry for you. You've obviously got some very unhappy gals back at the ranch.' Do you believe it?"

I said I did, though this wasn't exactly true. I'd missed something, even though I'd heard everything she said. I felt fourteen again. On top of which I was getting really turned on from where she'd steered my hand—and the fact that she was the one who steered it there. Try as I might, I could only picture the shield as a kind of sewer lid, and I knew that wasn't right either. I wondered if they were handpainted, maybe even tie-dyed. As I was thinking, I felt my way along the side of the shield, past that tingly patch of fur, to what felt like a ridge of warm meringue.

I'd never done this before. I didn't know what happened to women when they got aroused. I'd never aroused one. I didn't know they got wet. Or if that was some kind of a problem. My fourteen-year-old mind was trying to wrap itself around things it pretended to comprehend and didn't.

As I listened for clues, I kept my fingers moving. I felt like a guy doing an appendectomy out of a textbook.

Doris got a dreamy look as she talked. The plane had hit some kind of turbulence but I barely noticed. "It was important to Bob, see, that this was a positive product. Not, you know, something girls are going to buy because they've got some discharge. That's what the Board didn't get. They thought it was just for girls to handle their flow. Girls who didn't want the bulk of a heavy napkin. Girls with some condition that requires insulation!"

"Insulation," I repeated, when I realized she was waiting for a reply. My father, the novelty marketeer, had been passing along tips on What Makes A Top Salesman since I was three. One of his favorites was, "If you don't know what to say next, repeat what the other guy just said." Until this, I'd never had occasion to use any of his advice. We weren't very close. But now that I'd taken a tip, and it worked, I wished I could call him up and thank him. "Insulation," I marched out again, adding *"huh!"* this time, Doris ate it up.

"Exactly!" she cried, absolutely beaming. When she beamed she didn't look old at all. It was confusing. "Exactly," she yelped again, pronouncing it "egg-ZACK-ly" this time. Her voice was getting louder, and I had to fight the urge to shush her. I had a thing about public scenes, since my mother was always making them. The first emotion I remember having is embarrassment—if that's an emotion. But Doris preached on, oblivious. "Arousal is not some kind of condition a girl has to treat—it's a treat a girl has to condition! That's what Bob said. That's what Panty Shields are all about!"

In the middle of this, I caught the head of the man in front of us tilt to the side. I already knew he was a priest. I'd discovered this when I first sat down. As I hitched my seat belt, the *Call of the Wild* slipped off my lap and landed up the aisle, beside his brogans. This was before Doris had plunked down. He made a show of reading the title, then smacked a thick red hand off the cover. "Good book, son. Good clean book." That's when I saw the collar.

The priest's face, I noticed, was almost as red as his hand. Especially the nose, which close-up was pocked and dotted with tiny hairs, like a large strawberry. I said I like the book, too, though in fact I hadn't got past Page One. *That* I read about forty times, unable to concentrate after my secret girdle-peek.

"More young people your age should read good books like this."

"Yes, Father," I said. I'd never called anybody "Father" in my life, including my own father, who was always "Dad." But I wanted the priest to think I was Catholic. I wanted him to like me, though I wasn't sure why.

"And you," he announced, as if he'd given the matter serious thought and come to this lofty conclusion, "are a fine young boy. A fine young boy." He gave my hand a little squeeze and handed over the book. "Aren't you?"

"Well, yeah. I mean SURE!" I blurted, half-shouting though he was only inches away. I did not feel like a fine boy. I felt like some kind of sex criminal. But I didn't tell that to the priest.

He nodded, despite my sputtering response, and tapped me on the head, gently mussing my Princeton. Now here I was, a mere hour or so later, shattering my good-boy image chatting about panty apparatus with a strange female.

I watched the priest's skull rotate slowly to the right, like some hairy radar device, until his ear was aimed at us.

I don't know how I fell asleep. I had a dream that Queenie gave birth to pups on my lap. Except that the puppies kept sneaking back in. I had to search around inside her to try and find them. My hand was soaking. I was scared. But whenever I looked down, there was Queenie, gazing up at me with her grateful Schnauzer eyes, her little pink tongue hanging out, panting away. Instead of a collar, she had a penguin scarf around her neck. I remember thinking, in the dream, *I really love this dog. I love her more than my parents.* But then something happened. I couldn't get in. There was a shield, but it was invisible, like in the Johnson's Wax commercials. "Bullets bounce off!" said the announcer. And suddenly my arms were empty.

I woke up hugging Doris. More than hugging, holding onto her. Squeezing, the way my mother used to squeeze when she wanted me to play "cuddle boy." When she was "staying in," and it was afternoon forever, and I had to lay in her seething bed, my face in the hollow of her throat, cheek mashed to her bosom, gulping hot, under-the-blanket fumes until my eyes watered and I pretended I had to go to the bathroom and ran away.

"I'm going to call you 'Dreamy,'" Doris laughed when I blinked up at her. Something was different. I tried to disengage myself but she said she wouldn't let me. She wrapped her arms around mine, so that I looked up at her at an angle, from under her chin.

Finally I realized. "You did something. Your hair….It's—"

"Step aside Judy Collins!"

"Judy Collins," I repeated dumbly, eyeing the glossy tresses that now fell over her shoulders. When you don't know what to say, say the last thing they said.

"Like it?" she asked.

"Well…yeah! I really do!" Of course, I would have lied to make her feel good. But I didn't have to. Even though I remembered my mother once carping that women should not have long hair after forty unless they were witches. Mom was full of these "rules," just like Dad had a million "tips." But Mom had never met Doris—the mere thought made me shrink. The Judy Collins look was perfect.

I had to lean back and rub my eyes. For a second or two I couldn't take her in. Along with the folksinger hairdo, she'd managed to slip on a flower-print peasant dress, granny glasses and love beads. There was even a peace sign decal on her forearm. She looked like she could be her own freaky daughter. The wash 'n' wear housewife look was out the window.

"Wow!" was all I could say. Somewhere under there was the nervous, unhappy, chain-smoking woman I'd spotted bent over a wheelchair at the Greater Pittsburgh Airport. But she was buried pretty far down.

"Are you, like, from San Francisco?" I asked.

"I am now," she said, a little loopily. This was when I noticed the trio of mini-Southern Comfort bottles peeking out of the magazine slot in front of her. "Bob would have wanted it that way." A chiffon hanky appeared in her hand, dabbing away tears. "I swear"—she pronounced it, lurching toward me for emphasis, "shwear"—"that man died of a broken spirit."

Doris, it turned out, had just come from her husband's funeral. The woman with the matching Lucille Ball hair was indeed her sister. But more than that, the jokey guy was Bob's baby brother, Bo. Bob and Bo had married Doris and Dot in a ceremony that got them national attention. Allen Funt, of *Candid Camera*, actually filmed the ceremony for an episode of his own short-lived *Candid* spin-off, *You Won't Believe This!* But the show, she said, was canceled before their double wedding made it on the air.

"Story of our life," she sighed, reaching for the third of her Southern Comforts to pour into her glass of Coke. "I used to tease Bob that we should change out last name to 'Almost,' 'cause of all the stuff that almost happened. And all the stuff that did happen that almost didn't."

She stopped talking then and looked at me a little tearily. Everybody else on the plane seemed to be asleep or numb. The only overhead lights left on were hers and mine. Even the priest appeared to have given up his eavesdropping, having nodded off with his head still askew, his hairy ear positioned for maximum intake.

There was no sound but the hum of the engines that carried us through the night. The plastic glass was in her hand but she wasn't drinking any.

"Could I have some of that?" I asked, before I knew I was going to.

Doris gave a chuckle. "Why you naughty boy!" Even her laugh seemed different in her hippie get-up. "How old are you?"

"Almost old enough."

"Well why not?" she said, offering the drink with two hands, to keep it steady. "What I've just been through, I should get everybody on this tin trap drunk. Including the pilot!"

With this she grabbed the glass back and took a swig.

"First the bastards didn't want the thing, then they stole the patent. They made him jump through hoops, then they shot him in mid-air. Murder in the boardroom, baby. If old Bob had a shield over his heart, he might still be alive."

Doris let out a long sigh and handed me the drink again. There was almost enough left for a whole gulp.

"I thought it was 'The Summer of Love,'" I said. "That's what they called it in *Newsweek*."

"Don't think small," said Doris. "It's the whole damn age. Howzabout I teach you how to love right now so you'll be ready for it? So you won't have to do any catching up later?"

"That sounds all right."

"Well don't fall off your seat or anything."

"It sounds great, really. I think everybody else is asleep."

"Pretending," she mumbled, and slowly raised her arms for me to come closer. "Everybody's probably watching right now and wishing they were you."

"Well, jeez…"

I felt my throat go dry and couldn't think of anything else to say. I hoped it was too dark for her to see my face flush up. I was already beginning to shake a little. I wondered if my whole life I'd start to twitch whenever things got exciting with a woman. But then, I figured, they'd probably never get this exciting again.

Pain Journal

January

Back in New York, the Gramercy Park Hotel. Back in bed. Forget what time it is—I mean who cares? It's been an awful Christmas and an even worse birthday. Me, my whiny, wheezy, grumbling self, scaring the shit out of everyone, acting like I'm going to die at any moment. Still depressed. All I want to do is die—I mean cry—I meant to write *cry* and I wrote *die*. How Freudian can you get?

•

Birthday party over—thank God. Success from the looks of it. People. Presents. Cake. But me? Where the hell was I? Laid out naked on the Gurney of Nails, big marzipan penis on my stomach, candles blazing. Everybody impressed at the sight of me, I guess— but I wasn't *really* on the nails—not all of me—too chicken shit to let go. Couldn't breathe. My idiot's lament. Terrified at the sight of Sheree with her big knife, slicing into the marzipan penis—afraid she'd go too far—afraid of accidents, always afraid, so I can't get into it, like I can't get into anything these days. Always on the peripheral. Always terrified, exhausted, annoyed, pissed, anxious, out of it—out of the loop, out of my mind, out of time.

•

Horrible stomach aches and nausea. Heavy little shits. Is it the new antidepressant, the Wellbutrin? Don't know if I'm sick or crazy. Short of breath everywhere I go. Making like I'm dying. Am I exaggerating? Why would I? Who am I trying to impress? All the time thinking I'm going to die, talking myself into a frenzy of phlegm and fatigue. Maybe I'm getting better. Maybe I'm not. Now they say I should exercise. First they say use the wheelchair and conserve your energy. Now they say "exercise." Exercise/wheelchair. Exercise/wheelchair. Hard to know what to do or who I am in it all. And while I'm dwelling on death—Preston, 23-year-old from cystic fibrosis summer camp, died a couple of days ago. Funeral tomorrow but I'm not going. Should have called him last week, but what would I have done, wished him luck?

•

Depressed. In the hospital. Taking big red Wellbutrin pills but still depressed. Mom and Dad's 45th anniversary—I made the call—no I didn't—they called me cause I'm the sick one in the hospital. Their sick child. Their dying boy. When my mother calls and tells me I sound like I'm getting better I tell her no, not really, not yet. I'm almost rude to her about it. No, I'm not. I'm not better. I'm not ready to be better, so stop making me better already. And of course I spend the whole day feeling guilty about cutting her off because she was feeling so good that I might be feeling better, but I'll make it up to her—tomorrow I *will* be better, even though I just now spit up a big wad of blood—I'll still be better, just you wait and see.

February

Again by the dim light of the television, dim Bob whines as Sheree snores, but I can't hear the tv cause I don't want to hear Sheree, so I've got earplugs in, which is frustrating because I'd like to hear bald Dennis Hopper talking to Tom Snyder, but I can't stand the sound of Sheree's snoring—I mean I *really* can't stand it. It unnerves me. I'm the worst snorer in the world, but she doesn't know it cause she's out and I'm up—always up. A nervous wreck. Anti-depressants. Anti-anxiety. Vicodin. Steroids. Feel like crying all the time. I don't want to go on this trip to Boston and Berlin. Gave every last ounce of energy to   in New York. Can't give any more. But I'm doing it. I'm hating it, and I'm doing it. I took the earplugs out—one earplug so I could hear the tv with one ear, but all I can hear is Sheree—I love her, I want to be with her, but that sound! Argh! It makes me want to scream.

•

I don't know when the last time was that we had sex. I say that because I'm watching two people fuck on tv. Sheree and I are close, yeah—closer than ever, in some ways—but physically we don't know where to start. Anti-depressants? Maybe. Good excuse. But I still can't shake my depression. This time Sheree's doing great and I'm the one wallowing in darkness—now *that's* true role reversal. I stopped taking Paxil because I couldn't come. Now I can come, but I don't care. Lately I don't even get hard. I come, but I don't get hard. No help from Sheree. She's dead asleep. And when she does try to help, I run. Last night I snapped her head off because she wanted me to hold her. What kind of jerk am I becoming? Mr. Artist. We get news today of Art Matters grants. $2000 for me, and $1500 each for Sheree and Kirby. But it doesn't lighten my mental load. I'm still full of shit.

March

My irritability and depression is amok. I feel like crying all the time. My computer keeps crashing, which is exactly how I feel. I've been off anti-depressants since Christmas. Time to go back? I guess. Will it help? Is all this oxygen related? I've got it up to 3 liters. Too much? Not enough? Who knows. The tv is on but I can't hear it because I've got earplugs in my ears to block out Sheree's snoring. I want to run upstairs and fiddle with the computer to get it working again so at least something's back on track, but it's too late (4 A.M.). I *was* asleep but I woke an hour ago with an awful stomach ache and the usual heart ache. Don't know what to do with myself. Took a couple of anti-anxiety pills, Oxazepams, but they only make me sleepy, so now I'm sleepy *and* anxious. I guess I'm really into the pills now. The age old quest for happy pills. But there ain't none. My body throbs with unhappiness. It's like a big weight, a giant distraction all the time. So I'm always annoyed by it, antagonized from the minute I wake up, till the time I finally go to sleep—doesn't leave room for much of anything else.

•

Up again at 3 A.M.—what gives? Sound asleep since 11. Up at 3, no matter what. Thought I'd escape writing tonight, but found myself mulling over why it is I don't like pain anymore. I have this performance to do on April 1st, and I'm shying away from doing or having S&M stuff done to me because pain and the thought of pain mostly just irritates and annoys me rather than turns me on. But I miss my masochistic self. I hate this person I've become. And what about my reputation? Everything I say to people is all a lie, or at least two years too late—what the...? It's not 3 A.M. It's only 1:30. Can't even tell time. I knew it had to be earlier because the tv shows were all wrong.

April

Hotel performance done. The audience gathered together in one hotel room and peered through telescopes and binoculars while I performed supposedly auto-erotic activities in my own room, across the courtyard, all alone. Don't know who saw what, or what anyone thought, or what it all meant. I'm just glad it's over. Wine enema, butt plug, alligator clips, ball whacking, piss drinking, masturbating, bondage—they wanted a show, I gave them a show. Felt disoriented and depressed through most of it, as I feel disoriented and depressed through most everything these days.

•

The hospital—finally. Seems like I've been talking about coming here ever since the last time I left. Haven't been breathing or feeling well the whole time and will probably never breathe well or feel well again. I'm not being pessimistic when I say it's only going to get worse. That's the reality. My blood gasses are much worse: PO2 81, PCO2 57. Don't know if that's forever, but it's fucked.

•

Here I am tippy-de-typing on the couch cause I'm still on drugs, nothing interesting just antibiotics. Lately I've been longing for Demerol. Flashbacks to those days of post-op—sinus surgery, pericarditus, pneumothorax—when I got it when I wanted it and I liked it—perhaps a little too much. But, ho hum, nothing tonight but Tobramycin, Piperacillin and Ceftazidime in my veins and a couple of Vicodin in my mouth, but that doesn't do much anymore beyond dulling the headache, which is fine I suppose. Sheree's here on the couch too. Not sleeping cause she slept till noon today. She's out on stress leave so she has no schedule. She's waving her naked legs in the air. She's reading about gardening, her new hobby. I want her to put dozens of alligator clips on my dick and balls, but I don't know if I'd freak out or not. I can put a couple on myself. It hurts like hell but most of the time I can hold on until the pain subsides and I get kind of a rush. But can I take it when she's in control? The ultimate question.

•

Getting hard to breathe again. Thought I was doing much better, but it never lasts. My mood has been improving, though. And I've got a renewed interest in sex, mostly fantasizing about this alligator clip thing, and trying it out a little bit with a couple of clips here and there, those jagged little teeth biting into my tender spots as I grab hold of something like the bed rail and squeeze until the pain floats off a little, turns sweet almost, until it's time for another clip. It's almost like eating hot chili peppers, except that the taste buds for this delicacy are in my balls, not my mouth.

May

I had a great hard-on, but now it's gone, and now that I'm writing and not masturbating, it's coming back. That fucker. I was sound asleep, several times. Sheree and I went to bed early, tuckered out after Mother's Day lunch at Barney's in Beverly Hills. A worm crawling along the rim of my plate after an incredible dish of sturgeon got everyone grossed out and me a free lunch. Came home and fell asleep watching *X-Files* with Sheree, but I woke up just in time to catch her video taping me as I lay naked and snoring. I made my penis talk for the camera. Drunken bar penis: "All right, all right, I'm comin' goddamn you, you prick." Then it was sleep, cough, wake up; sleep, cough, wake up, until now, where it's 2:30 A.M., Sheree's snoring and I can't stop her, even if I shake her, even if I pinch her nose. So it's ear plugs in, which makes it impossible to hear *Perry Mason* on tv. Before Sheree plunged into the sawmill, earlier on, after my little penis show, she wanted me to suck her nipple while she masturbated with the vibrator. Not that I didn't want to, but I was still tired and ready to go back to sleep, and it usually takes her such a long time to come (we Paxil pals), that I just didn't want to get involved, but it would have been awful to deny her, so I went forth and commenced my sucking. I felt just like I did earlier this afternoon when I went out to the car to wait for her while she shopped at Barney's after lunch. I was too out of breath to walk around and shop with her, so I sat in the car listening to the radio and waited for her to finish, knowing full well it could take forever. But lo and behold she came out relatively quickly, and what do you know, she came fast too, here in bed, with a nice little shudder of completion, and before we knew it we're both fast asleep, until now, for me anyway. Some weird dream I just had, too. I had a pet parakeet, maybe two of them. I kept trying to play with it in its cage: giving it food, toys, playing with it with my hand. But somehow I was fucking it up. Suddenly the cage was a plastic bag, and I tried to shift the bird around so it could breathe. At some point the cage was like an oven, and I could see the parakeet getting singed and burnt, but it was too hot to put my hand in. Finally I managed to coax him out. He was alive still, but kind of crispy. One of his feet was melted. When I put him back in his cage I could see that he wasn't going to live. He was tiny and stiff. I felt guilty. I thought, since this was the second bird in one day that I had killed, did I do it on purpose, under the guise of "play?" Then I woke up and wrote all this stuff. Now it's back to sleep, and maybe a hard-on if I'm lucky. And look, another *Perry Mason* episode that I won't be able to hear.

•

Saw Dr. Riker today. He said I looked good. "Must be the haircut," he said. I tried to tell him that I was slowly starting downhill again. Feeling like shit whenever I try to do anything, but there's not much to do about it. It's CF. I've got several strains of pseudomonis, but what am I going to do about it unless I want to go back into the hospital and start the IVs again? Not ready for that. Too much to do, or try to do, on the outside. Sheree's depressed again, first time in a long time, mostly about art. I tell her it's not unusual to have doubts about your work, it's part of the process. I think something else is going on. Menopause. She's all sweaty and clammy and tossing and turning in bed all night. Whining and moaning. I like squeezing her big butt. I should go down on her or something. But any kind of sex is too much of an effort, especially where I have to lie down and go down and not come up for air. I panic when I think of it. It's not sex I'm afraid of, it's breathing. I think of sex the way I think of walking up the stairs: I go out of my way to avoid it. Except that I don't miss walking up the stairs.

June

Fun and frustration with the computer. First, I added some photographs to the January journal, which I just finished transcribing last night. But mostly the computer's given me nothing but trouble today. I was trying to do more scanning and cropping but the damn thing kept bombing and freezing and crashing. There are a few things I can try tomorrow, but I'm not sure what's going on. We're taking it into the shop anyway to add a couple of gigabits, so maybe Les can fix whatever's wrong. I sound like a real computer geek, I know, but all my projects are on it now. I'd rather be in front of the computer than anywhere else. Something to do with getting my life in order. My command post. A place where I can get a lot done without doing a lot (physically). I get depressed when it starts giving me trouble. The waste of time. The confusion. The disarray. My life, which is all computerized and digitized by now, feels like it's crashing around me when the system dies. A little melodramatic, yeah, but I'm only human.

•

After all the complaining, of course I'm in the hospital again. Headaches, chest aches, phlegm and all the rest of the shit, the boring shit, my mean mantra. Can I get some other kind of pain relievers maybe, like Demerol or morphine? Don't know if I really need something that heavy, the pain's not excruciating, it's just constant and annoying, to say the least. But why shouldn't I be able to zone out a little? Where am I going? What else do I have to do?

•

Vicodin kicking in. Not much of a kick anymore. More like a tap on the shoulder. And when I turn around there ain't nobody there. And then the headache's back. Who's this nurse I've got tonight? Never saw a porta cath before? I hate new nurses that don't know me at night. I want *them* taking care of *me*, not me them. What a whiner. Looks like I'll be here till next Monday. Sheree none too happy 'bout that, but that's the way it goes. Maybe I'll actually use the time wisely and do some serious writing while I'm here, now that I've got this new laptop computer. Almost finished transcribing the handwritten part of this year's journal, up to the point where I started using this here laptop with a lip. I call it a laptop with a lip because it has this software that lets it talk back to me. It reads my stuff in this real sad disembodied voice that I find quite compelling. This is nuts, but it reminds me of when I was a kid and used to have puppets with me to keep me company in the hospital. Now instead of making a puppet talk I can make this machine my alter ego. I think my Vicodin wave has passed. I prayed for Demerol, not because I needed it, but because my body keeps flashing on it, how fucking good it felt, for a few minutes anyway. But there's no real justification for it now. I keep looking for one, but no. I'm feeling better and breathing better, but I'm not doing anything but sitting here in bed. I'm remarkably well-adjusted to being here. Sheree wants me home though. She sounded very lonely on the phone. It's harder on her than it is on me. It always will be. I'm the center of attention, even at the worst of it. But for her, she'll always be alone. I just called her back and had the computer say, "I forgot to tell you I love you." And I do.

•

Tonight's notes, before I slip off into my pharmaceutical soup: more aches and pains from the aches and pains department. No Demerol. Some Vicodin. The names of these drugs are capitalized as if they were gods. St. Vicodin. Lord Demerol. Our Lady of Cephtazidime. Let's not forget the great and powerful Zoloft, son of Prozac. And now we're trying Percocet to melt the headaches—which are real, make no mistake about it. I'm not just looking for a cheap buzz. I want relief. The Percocet works a bit I s'pose, but the "buzz" aspects of Demerol are sorely missed. I was supposed to try this stupid bipap thing again tonight. It's a respirator designed for snorers that was supposed to give me relief during the night, and maybe alleviate the headaches and chest pain the next day. But it only made the headaches worse, which is too bad because I was looking forward to incorporating the stupid looking face mask into a leather hood, so at least the humiliation of it all would have a more erotic component, and I wouldn't look so much like a geek wearing a jock strap on his head all night.

July

What's with my siblings? Is it survivor's guilt? They hate me for all the attention I've gotten over the years due to the CF, and they feel guilty for that and for being the healthy ones, the bad ones, the survivors. But fuck it, it's time to grow up. Time is running out. If they want survivor's guilt, I'll give them a whole shit load of survivor's guilt real soon. A lot sooner than they realize. As far as details of the day and the life go: I'm dirty, need a shower and a shave. Finally brushed my teeth. I think they're rotting, but I don't want to do anything about it. Carl was here cleaning up while the painters and roofers were patching up and I was spitting up, as usual. Congested, bad bad, dizzying headache this morning, but better now, thanks to Mr. P. No real buzz anymore, but it still quells the spells. And speaking of pain, I again promised Cathy Busby an article on pain in her book. That was last Friday, and still no article. All I am is a pain in the ass with my false promises and procrastination. I took all the '95 journal references to pain and wove them into an 11 page massive tumor. Now I've got to operate on it to see if it's benign or cancerous. And the final detail of the day is I got commissioned by someone at MGM to write ad copy for a film about a guy dying of AIDS who throws himself one last going-away party. Am I the right guy for this job or what?

•

I wuz asleep. But now I'm not. Drugged. Groggy. Headache. Sweats. The Prednisone. The Percocet. The Oxazepam. Distracted as I write because I'm watching Jack Nicholson in *Wolf* on tv. Strangely flat and compelling, possibly completely stupid, but queer as hell. Good tv, none the less, for 5 in the morning. As I said, I wuz asleep after returning home exhausted from Dana Duff's birthday party in Culver City. Exhausted from dealing with Sheree, stoned and creative and panicking over her "reading" at some leather lesbian soiree. I got real exasperated, fucking nasty with her. The Prednisone. Spent the whole day in Photoshop putting a birthday cake into a 10-year-old photo of Dana and me, and then smack dab in the middle of the cake is my big dick (what else) with a candle in it. I think I'm obsessed with these cyber penises of mine because sex in the real world is so much more difficult these days. We did manage to fuck this morning, if that's what you call it. I tweaked a hard-on for the camera and Sheree stuffed it in and rode it a while as she choked me, and snapped a few photos for Aura Rosenberg's book of men's faces in the throes of orgasm, but there was no orgasm here, thanks to the almighty Zoloft. Afterward Sheree did get off a get off with the assistance of the vibrator on her clit and my teeth on her tit. But later that day it was my fangs in her jugular while trying to help edit her damn lesbian piss tape while she raved and yammered and drove me nuts. I didn't want to be mean. Didn't want to say "Shut up!" But I'm just as out of it on my drugs (Prednisone) as she is on hers (pot). It all just made me feel shittier and more anxious, so I took more pills, Oxazepam. Sheree's pretty understanding about the whole thing, or so stoned she doesn't give a shit. So all's right with the world. The sun's coming up. The headache's subsiding (Percocet). And we're watching *Wolf.* The new day awaits. Grrrrrr.

•

We thought we could sit forever in fun, but our chances really were a million to one. Home from the last night of CF summer camp, the last campfire, the last roundup for me, and somehow I pulled it off. I sang at the campfire, I went around to the cabins and sang goodnight songs to the kids, and I sang dirty improvs at the counselor meeting afterwards. Considering all I could do during the day was lie around wondering how it was I was going to do anything ever again, it's a miracle I dragged my ass down there and slipped into the groove again, singing the old songs like I'd never been gone. I'm amazed I had any reserve left at all. Suddenly I could not only breathe, but I could shape that breathing into some decent singing, not like it used to be, but what I now lack in physical ability I make up with experience and a sense of showmanship that I've picked up along the way. If I wanted to I could really do something with the singing, even now, even with the oxygen. I'd be unique, that's for sure. Who wouldn't give the pathetic oxygen boy a chance? Not that it wasn't work for me, it was. It took every ounce of oxygen to get those songs out, but I did it and I did it well. I even introduced my *Supermasochistic Bob* song and they loved it, both the clean version and the real version. I feel kind of weird about the last *Jenny* improv and the *Suck My Jesus* song that I sang for the counselor meeting. A little over-the-top perhaps, but that's what they asked for. After a long week of hard work, and the sadness of the last campfire where the kids remember all their dead friends, I perform kind of a service by singing these ridiculous over the top songs. I relieve the tension of the week. I'm as close as they get to getting drunk and tearing the place apart. But I still feel kind of weird about it. But fuck it, I'm home. Obligations done. Naked now. TV. My own work. Fucking Sheree. My life and what's left of it.

August

New month, same old body, feeling older than it is or will ever have the chance to be. I'm afraid my heart's starting to give out. My ankles have been swelling up since last week when I was Mr. Troubadour at camp. In contrast to the great burst of energy I had "way" back then, today I can barely move without being severely short of breath and can barely stay awake when I'm not moving. While trying to help Sheree with the Pee Boy fountain this morning I couldn't help stepping outside myself to catch the irony of me huffing and puffing trying to get our naked white nasty dick-holding boy to pee in the bowl properly, working up a sweat trying to get the pump connected the right way, frustrated as hell cause my own pump felt so fucked, my connections all kinked and haywire, and even my dick not much good or much use to anyone. Feeling sorry for myself I guess. But if not me, then who? What bothers me most is that it's so hard to do work. I just want to lay around all day and watch tv. I have 20 or 30 different projects or commitments to work on, not to mention the IV antibiotics, the breathing treatments, the physical therapist, pharmacies, doctor's appointments— how can I resist just curling up on the couch, watching the OJ trial, and saying, "Fuck it?"

•

Ants are crawling in and out of my teeth and around my eye sockets and my nostrils. The moisture is draining out of me and I'm starting to shrivel up. My little apple head effigy looks great, almost as good as the real thing, the real thing being me, when I'm dead, buried with a video camera to document my ongoing "deconstruction," but Sheree's having second thoughts. Now she wants me cremated so she can keep my ashes. Of course Kirby's rooting for plan A, the video burial as a ready-made ending to his "Bobumentary." So to placate Kirby and to sell Sheree I came up with this apple head prototype. Who knows, maybe I'll be able to interest a collector or two. I also did a pretty good drawing today for the "Bobumentary": it's a drawing/montage of "me" with a big hard on, standing at a darkroom enlarger to which I've attached a needle, something I did 20 years ago because I couldn't get up the nerve to stick a needle in my dick without automating it this way. Now, at Kirby's request, I'm in the process of illustrating this and other auto erotic "torture" machines I've designed over the years. And they're working out real well, despite the fact that the computer kept giving hell. Sheree had to take the external drive in for repairs. It's ok, and so is my stuff. Not only is the computer fucking up (Photoshop was also a real stubborn bitch today, too) but my body is still on the fritz, even though I'm feeling better and doing more. I'm all filled up with fluids, from my right arm pit, to my ankles, with a large protruding abdomen in between. Looks like I'm pregnant. Feels like I've had an enema. More to worry about. But now I've got to sleep.

•

I feel like Superman, Underdog, Popeye—not the macho heroes, the bloated Thanksgiving day balloons. I feel like I'm walking on the moon. One small step for man, one giant leap closer to the grave. I'm the Pillsbury Doughboy, overdone, crumbling. *Nothin' says lovin' like somethin' in a coffin. Heh, heh!* I'm really feeling the pressure of having to get my life in order before my body gives out entirely. The dying part will be easy (for me), but the constant interruptions, the drives down to the doctor's in Long Beach (even Kirby's had it with that), the drug deliveries that don't come, the oxygen which runs out in the middle of a movie, assuming I have enough energy to drag my ass out of the house to go to a movie, the true humiliation of having to watch Sheree work like a dog to take care of me who used to get so hot being her slave, sickness or no sickness, what a whining wimp I've become, "no" is the first word out of my mouth, it's part of my breathing now, *no...no...no...* I see it like a knife in Sheree's back every time she hears it, and she's getting tired of it, too, but I'm doing the best I can, that's my mantra these days, but so what? It doesn't take the sadness away, and maybe I'm not always doing the best I can. I ain't no super hero, that's for sure, and this is no fucking holiday.

BERNARD COOPER

Burl's

I loved the restaurant's name, a compact curve of a word. Its sign, five big letters rimmed in neon, hovered above the roof. I almost never saw the sign with its neon lit; my parents took me there for early summer dinners, and even by the time we left—Father cleaning his teeth with a toothpick, Mother carrying steak bones in a doggie-bag—the sky was still bright. Heat rippled off the cars parked along Hollywood boulevard, the asphalt gummy from hours of sun.

With its sleek architecture, chrome appliances, and arctic temperature, Burl's offered a refuge from the street. We usually sat at one of the booths in front of the plate glass windows. During our dinner, people came to a halt before the news-vending machine on the corner and burrowed in their pockets and purses for change.

The waitresses at Burl's wore brown uniforms edged in checked gingham. From their breast pockets frothed white lace handkerchiefs. In between reconnaissance missions to the tables, they busied themselves behind the counter and shouted *Tuna to travel* or *Scorch that patty* to a harried short-order cook who manned the grill. Miniature pitchers of cream and individual pats of butter were extracted from an industrial refrigerator. Coca-Cola shot from a glinting spigot. Waitresses dodged and bumped one another, frantic as atoms.

My parents usually lingered after the meal, nursing cups of coffee while I played with the beads of condensation on my glass of ice-water, tasted Tabasco sauce, or twisted pieces of my paper napkin into mangled animals. One evening, annoyed with my restlessness, my father gave me a dime and asked me to buy him a *Herald Examiner* from the vending machine in front of the restaurant.

Shouldering open the heavy glass door, I was seared by a sudden gust of heat. Traffic roared past me and stirred the air. Walking toward the newspaper machine, I held the dime so tightly, it seemed to melt in my palm. Duty made me feel large and important. I inserted the dime and opened the box, yanking a *Herald* from the spring contraption that held it tight as a mousetrap. When I turned around, paper in hand, I saw two women walking toward me.

Their high heels clicked on the sun-baked pavement. They were tall, broad-shouldered women who moved with a mixture of haste and defiance. They'd teased their hair into nearly identical black bee-hives. Dangling earrings flashed in the sun, brilliant as prisms. Each of them wore the kind of clinging, strapless outfit my mother referred to as a cocktail dress. The silky fabric—one dress was purple, the other pink—accentuated their breasts and hips, and rippled with insolent highlights. The dresses exposed their bare arms, the slope of their shoulders, and the smooth, powdered plane of flesh where their cleavage began.

I owned at the time a book called *Things For Boys And Girls To Do*. There were pages to color, intricate mazes, and connect-the-dots. But another type of puzzle came to mind as I watched those women walking toward me: What's Wrong With This Picture? Say the drawing of a dining room looked normal at first glance, on closer inspection, a chair was missing it's leg and the man who sat atop it wore half a pair of glasses.

The women had Adam's apples.

The closer they came, the shallower my breathing. I blocked

the sidewalk, an incredulous child stalled in their path. When they saw me staring, they shifted their purses and linked their arms. There was something sisterly and conspiratorial about their sudden closeness. Though their mouths didn't move, I thought they might have been communicating without moving their lips, so telepathic did they seem as they joined arms and pressed together, synchronizing their heavy steps. The pages of the *Herald* fluttered in the wind; I felt them against my arm, light as batted lashes.

The woman in pink shot me a haughty glance, and yet she seemed pleased that I'd taken notice, hungry to be admired by a man, or even an awestruck eight-year-old boy. She tried to stifle a grin, her red lipstick more voluptuous than the lips it painted. Rouge deepened her cheekbones. Eye shadow dusted her lids, a clumsy abundance of blue. Her face was like a page in *Things For Boys And Girls To Do* colored by a kid who went outside the lines.

At close range, I saw that her wig was slightly askew. I was certain it was a wig because my mother owned several; three Styrofoam heads lined a shelf in my mother's closet; upon them were perched a Page-Boy, an Empress, and a Baby-Doll, all in shades of auburn. The woman in the pink dress wore her wig like a crown of glory.

But it was the woman in the purple dress who passed nearest me, and I saw that her jaw was heavily powdered, a half-successful attempt to disguise the tell-tale shadow of a beard. Just as I noticed this, her heel caught on a crack in the pavement and she reeled on her stilettos. It was then I witnessed a rift in her composure, a window through which I could glimpse the shades of maleness that her dress and wig and make-up obscured. She shifted her shoulders and threw out her hands like a surfer riding a curl. The instant she regained her balance, she smoothed her dress, patted her hair, and sauntered onward.

Any woman might be a man; the fact of it clanged through the chambers of my brain. In broad day, in the midst of traffic, with my parent's drinking coffee a few feet away, I felt as if everything I understood, everything I had taken for granted up to that moment—the curve of the earth, the heat of the sun, the reliability of my own eyes—had been squeezed out of me. Who were those men? Did they help each other get inside those dresses? How many other people and things were not what they seemed? From the back, the imposters looked like women once again, slinky and curvaceous, purple and pink. I watched them disappear into the distance, their disguises so convincing that other people on the street seemed to take no notice, and for a moment wondered if I had imagined the whole encounter, a visitation by two unlikely muses.

Frozen in the middle of the sidewalk, I caught my reflection in the window of Burl's, a silhouette floating between his parents. They faced one another across a table. Once the solid embodiments of woman and man, pedestrians and traffic appeared to pass through them.

There were some mornings, seconds before my eyes opened and my senses gathered into consciousness, that the child I was seemed to hover above the bed, and I couldn't tell what form my waking would take—the body of a boy or the body of a girl. Finally stirring, I'd blink against the early light and greet each incarnation as a male with mild surprise. My sex, in other words, didn't seem to be an absolute fact so much as a pleasant, recurring accident.

By the age of eight, I'd experienced this groggy phenomenon several times. Those ethereal moments above my bed made waking up in the tangled blankets, a boy steeped in body heat, all the more astonishing. That this might be an unusual experience never occurred to me; it was one among a flood of sensations I could neither name nor ignore.

And so, shocked as I was when those transvestites passed me in front of Burl's, they confirmed something about which I already had an inkling: the hazy border between the sexes. My father, after all, raised his pinky when he drank from a tea cup, and my mother looked as faded and plain as my father until she fixed her hair and painted her face.

Like most children, I once thought it possible to divide the world into male and female columns. Blue/Pink. Roosters/Hens, Trousers/Skirts. Such divisions were easy, not to mention comforting, for they simplified matter into compatible pairs. But there also existed a vast range of things that didn't fit neatly into either camp: clocks, milk, telephones, grass. There were nights I fell into a fitful sleep while trying to sex the world correctly.

Nothing typified the realms of male and female as clearly as my parents' walk-in closets. Home alone for any length of time, I always found my way inside them. I could stare at my parent's clothes for hours, grateful for the stillness and silence, haunting the very heart of their privacy.

The overhead light in my father's closet was a bare bulb. Whenever I groped for the chain in the dark, it wagged back and forth and resisted my grasp. Once the light clicked on, I saw dozens of ties hanging like stalactites. A monogrammed silk bathrobe sagged from a hook, a gift my father had received on a long-ago birthday and, thinking it fussy, rarely wore. Shirts were cramped together along the length of an aluminum pole, their starched sleeves sticking out as if in a half-hearted gesture of greeting. The medicinal odor of mothballs permeated the boxer shorts that were folded and stacked in a built-in drawer. Immaculate underwear was proof of a tenderness my mother couldn't otherwise express; she may not have touched my father often, but she laundered his boxers with infinite care. Even back then, I suspected that a sense of duty was the final erotic link between them.

Sitting in a neat row on the closet floor were my father's boots and slippers and dress shoes. I'd try on his wing-tips and clomp around, slipping out of them with every step. My wary, unnatural stride made me all the more desperate to affect some authority. I'd whisper orders to imagined lackeys and take my invisible wife in my arms. But no matter how much I wanted them to fit, those shoes were cold and hard as marble.

My mother's shoes were just as uncomfortable, but a lot more fun. From a brightly colored array of pumps and sling-backs, I'd pick a pair with the glee and deliberation of someone choosing a chocolate. Whatever embarrassment I felt was overwhelmed by the exhilaration of being taller in a pair of high heels. Things will look like this someday, I said to myself, gazing out from my new and improved vantage point as if from a crow's nest. Calves elongated, arms akimbo, I gauged each step so I didn't fall over and moved with what might have passed for grace had someone seen me, a possibility I scrupulously avoided by locking the door.

Back and forth I went. The longer I wore a pair of heels, the better my balance. In the periphery of my vision, the shelf of wigs looked like a throng of kindly bystanders. Light streamed down from a high window, causing crystal bottles to glitter, the air ripe with perfume. A make-up mirror above the dressing table invited my self-absorption. Sound was muffled. Time slowed. It seemed as if nothing bad could happen as long as I stayed within those walls.

Though I'd never been discovered in my mother's closet, my parents knew that I was drawn toward girlish things—dolls and jump-rope and jewelry—as well as to the games and preoccupations that were expected of a boy. I'm not sure now if it was my effeminacy itself that bothered them so much as my ability to slide back and forth, without the slightest warning, between male and female mannerisms. After I'd finished building the model of an F-17 bomber, say, I'd sit back to examine my handiwork, pursing my lips in concentration and crossing my legs at the knee.

One day my mother caught me standing in the middle of my bedroom doing an imitation of Mary Injijikian, a dark, over-eager Armenian girl with whom I believed myself to be in love, not only because she was pretty, but because I wanted to be like her.

Collector of effortless A's, Mary seemed to know all the answers in class. Before the teacher had even finished asking a question, Mary would let out a little grunt and practically levitate out of her seat, as if her hand were filled with helium. "Could we please hear from someone else today besides Miss Injijikian," the teacher would say. *Miss Injijikian.* Those were the words I was repeating over and over to myself when my mother caught me. To utter them was rhythmic, delicious, and under their spell I raised my hand and wiggled like Mary. I heard a cough and spun around. My mother froze in the doorway. She clutched the folded sheets to her stomach and turned without saying a word. My sudden flush of shame confused me. Weren't boys supposed to swoon over girls? Hadn't I seen babbling, heartsick men in a dozen movies?

Shortly after the Injijikian incident my parents decided to send me to gymnastics class at The Downtown Athletic Club, a brick relic of a building on Grand Avenue. One of the oldest establishments of its kind in Los Angeles, the club prohibited women from the premises. My parents didn't have to say it aloud: they hoped a fraternal atmosphere would toughen me up and tilt me toward the male side of my nature.

My father drove me downtown so I could sign up for the class, meet the instructor, and get a tour of the place. On the way there, he reminisced about sports. Since he'd grown up in a rough Philadelphia neighborhood, sports consisted of kick-the-can, or rolling a hoop down the street with a stick. The more he talked about his physical prowess, the more convinced I became that my day-dreams and shyness were a disappointment to him.

The hushed lobby of the Athletic Club was paneled in dark wood. A few solitary figures were hidden in wing-chairs. My father and I introduced ourselves to a man at the front desk who seemed unimpressed by our presence. His aloofness unnerved me, which wasn't hard considering that, no matter how my parents put it, I knew their sending me here was a form of disapproval, a way of banishing the part of me they didn't care to know.

A call went out over the intercom for someone to show us around. While we walked, I noticed that the sand in the standing ashtrays had been raked into perfect furrows. The glossy leaves of the potted plants looked as if they'd been polished by hand. The place seemed more like a well-tended hotel than an athletic club. Finally, a stoop-shouldered old man hobbled toward us, his head shrouded in a cloud of white hair. He wore a T-shirt that said *Instructor*, his arms so wrinkled and anemic, I thought I might have misread it. While we followed him to the elevator—it would be easier, he said, than taking the stairs—I readjusted my expectations, which had involved fantasies of a hulking drill-sargent barking orders at a flock of scrawny boys.

We got off the elevator on the second floor. The instructor, mumbling to himself and never turning around to see if we were behind him, showed us where the gymnastics class took place. I'm certain the building was big, but the size of the room must be exaggerated by a trick of memory, because when I envision it, I picture a vast and windowless warehouse. Mats covered the wooden floor. Here and there, in remote and lonely pools of light, stood a pommel horse, a balance beam, and parallel bars. Tiers of bleachers rose into darkness. Unlike the cloistered air of a closet, the room seemed incomplete without a crowd.

Next we visited the dressing room, empty except for a naked, middle-aged man. He sat on a narrow bench and clipped his formidable toenails. Moles dotted his back. He glistened like a fish.

We continued to follow the instructor down an aisle lined with numbered lockers. At the far end, steam billowed from the doorway that led to the showers. Fresh towels stacked on a nearby table made me think of my mother; I knew she liked to have me at home with her—I was often her only companion—and I resented her complicity in the plan to send me here.

The tour ended when the instructor gave me a sign-up sheet. Only a few names preceded mine. They were signatures, or so I imagined, of other soft and wayward sons.

When the day of the first gymnastics class arrived, my mother gave me money and a gym bag (along with a clean towel, she'd packed a banana and a napkin) and sent me to the corner of Hollywood and Western to wait for a bus. The sun was bright, the traffic heavy. While I sat there, an argument raged inside my head, the familiar, battering debate between the wish to be like other boys and the wish to be like myself. Why shouldn't I simply get up and go back home where I'd be left alone to read and think? On the other hand, wouldn't life be easier if I liked athletics, or learned to like them? No sooner did I steel my resolve to get on the bus, than I thought of something better: I could spend the morning wandering through Woolworth's, then tell my parents I'd gone to the class. But would my lie stand up to scrutiny? As I practiced describing phantom gymnastics—*And then we did cartwheels and boy was I dizzy*—I became aware of a car circling the block. It was a large car in whose shaded interior I could barely make out the driver, but I thought it might be the man who owned the local pet store. I'd often gone there on the pretext of looking at the cocker spaniel puppies huddled together in their pen, but I really went to gawk at the owner whose tan chest, in the V of his shirt, was the place I most wanted to rest my head. Every time the man moved, counting stock or writing a receipt, his shirt parted, my mouth went dry, and I smelled the musk of sawdust and dogs.

I found myself hoping that the driver was the man who ran the pet store. I was thrilled by the unlikely possibility that the sight of me, slumped on a bus bench in my T-shirt and shorts, had caused such a man to circle the block. Up to that point in my life, love-making hovered somewhere in the future, an impulse a boy might aspire to, but didn't indulge. And there I was, sitting on a bus bench in the middle of the city, dreaming I could seduce an adult; I showered the owner of the pet store with kisses and, as aquariums bubbled, birds sang, and mice raced in a wire wheel, slipped my hand beneath his shirt. The roar of traffic brought me to my senses. I breathed deeply and blinked against the sun. I crossed my legs at the knee in order to hide an erection. My fantasy left me both drained and changed. The continent of sex had drifted closer.

The car made another round. This time the driver leaned across the passenger seat and peered at me through the window. He was a complete stranger whose gaze filled me with fear. It wasn't the surprise of not recognizing him that frightened me; it was what I did recognize—the unmistakable shame in his expression, and the weary temptation that drove him in circles. Before the car behind him honked, he mouthed "hello" and cocked his head. What now, he seemed to be asking. A bold, unbearable question.

I bolted to my feet, slung the gym bag over my shoulder, and hurried toward home. Now and then I turned around to make sure he wasn't trailing me, both relieved and disappointed when I didn't see his car. Even after I became convinced that he wasn't at my back—my sudden flight had scared him off—I kept turning around to see what was making me so nervous, as if I might spot the source of my discomfort somewhere on the street. I walked faster and faster, trying to outrace myself. Eventually, the bus I was supposed to have taken roared past. Turning the corner, I watched it bob eastward.

Closing the kitchen door behind me, I vowed to never leave home again. I was resolute in this decision without fully understanding why, or what it was I hoped to avoid; I was only aware of the need to hide and a vague notion, fading fast, that my trouble had something to do with sex. Already the mechanism of self-deception was at work. By the time my mother rushed into the kitchen to see why I'd returned so early, the thrill I'd felt while waiting for the bus had given way to indignation.

I poured out the story of the man circling the block and protested, with perhaps too great a passion, my own innocence. "I was just sitting there," I said again and again. I was so determined to deflect suspicion away from myself, and to justify my missing the class, that I portrayed the man as a grizzled pervert who drunkenly veered from lane to lane as he followed me halfway home.

My mother cinched her housecoat. She seemed moved and shocked by what I told her, if a bit incredulous, which prompted me to be more dramatic. "It wouldn't be safe," I insisted, "for me to wait at the bus stop again."

No matter how overwrought my story, I knew my mother wouldn't question it, wouldn't bring the subject up again; sex of any kind, especially sex between a man and a boy, was simply not discussed in our house. The gymnastics class, my parents agreed, was something I could do another time.

And so I spent the remainder of that summer at home with my mother, stirring cake batter, holding the dust pan, helping her fold the sheets. For a while I was proud of myself for engineering a reprieve from The Athletic Club. But as the days wore on, I began to see that my mother had wanted me with her all along, and forcing that to happen wasn't such a feat. Soon a sense of compromise set in; by expressing disgust for the man in the car, I'd expressed disgust for an aspect of myself. Now I had all the time in the world to sit around and contemplate my desire for men. The days grew long and stifling and hot, an endless sentence of self-examination.

Only trips to the pet store offered any respite. Every time I went there, I was too electrified with longing to think about longing in the abstract. The bell tinkled above the door, animals stirred within their cages, and the handsome owner glanced up from his work.

I handed my father the *Herald*. He opened the paper and disappeared behind it. My mother stirred her coffee and sighed. She gazed at the sweltering passersby and probably thought herself lucky. I slid into the vinyl booth and took my place beside my parents.

For a moment, I considered asking them about what had happened on the street, but they would have reacted with censure and alarm, and I sensed there was more to the story than they'd ever be willing to tell me. Men in dresses were only the tip of the iceberg. Who knew what other wonders existed—a boy, for example, who wants to kiss a man—exceptions the world did its best to keep hidden.

It would be years before I heard the word "transvestite," so I struggled to find a word for what I'd seen. "He-she" came to mind, as lilting as "Injijikian." "Burl's" would have been perfect, like "boys" and "girls" spliced together, but I can't claim to have thought of this back then.

I must have looked stricken as I tried to figure it all out, because my mother put down her coffee cup and asked if I was OK. She stopped just short of feeling my forehead. I assured her I was fine, but something within me had shifted, had given way to a heady doubt. When the waitress came and slapped down our check—*Thank You*, it read, *Dine out more often*—I wondered if her lofty hair-do or the breasts on which her name-tag quaked were real. Wax carnations bloomed at every table. Phony wood paneled the walls. Plastic food sat in a display case: fried eggs, a hamburger sandwich, a sundae topped with a garish cherry.

ALLISON ANDERS

I Fall Apart On Planes

I fall apart on planes. I'm not scared of flying, and not always. But sometimes my heart just breaks and I cry and cry. If there's a good woman's melodrama on screen, I cry more. Right now *How To Make An American Quilt* by Jocelyn Morehouse is on. The last time I cried so good was when I watched *The Joy Luck Club* on a plane to Chicago...every aisle had a sniffling woman and the stewardesses came round with Kleenex for all of us. But this plane is full of businessmen and they're either sleeping or working on their laptops. Except the guy sitting next to me—he's a young black guy, who is all hip and funny. I don't think he's a businessman—maybe a musician, or a pro skateboard guy with his own line of skateboards and T-shirts. But he's asleep too. So I'm the only one crying.

I lost someone who was never mine, and I knew the ending was built into the story when I let myself go there. Love rarely chooses to exist when it knows the ending ahead of time. Love has this ridiculous demand of 'forever' that it must believe in order to ignite and flame up inside your cells and make you dizzy and drunk and dumb. Seldom will your heart ever let you get to that first stage if some word of impossibility or finality or rejection has been spoken. Romantic love prefers to believe it has no conditions, but of course—it is the most conditional of all love. I guess what I'm saying is no one chooses a love with conditions built in—blatant, direct, severe. No one would choose a love like that, it chooses you. And for its own reasons.

When I was eight years old I watched my young, divorced, and very beautiful mother chop off all her long dark brown hair. It wasn't just the act of chopping her hair off that made an impression on me, it was the tone in her drained face, and the endless spiral of loss in her deep brown eyes, and the color gone from her raspberry mouth as the locks of hair fell into the sink that told me something very big had happened to her, and that somehow, her life would never be quite the same again. Something had happened. She lost someone who was never really hers.

In 1960, when I was five going on six, my dad walked out for the last time. I don't remember it—though I have an otherwise vivid memory of those early years of my life in Ashland, Kentucky—home of The Judds, Charles Manson, and Chuck Woolery from *Love Connection*. The day my dad left my life we had moved from the holler down on Moore Street to an apartment on 29th Street up over a five-and-dime. I was apparently hysterical, unwilling to listen to reason or promise. My mom kept saying, "He'll be back." But she said to me recalling the incident almost thirty years later—"You knew he was never coming back and you kept saying so over and over again." He walked down the hall and I ran after him and clutched his leg and he dragged me half the way down the stairs attached to his blue jeans by my tiny fingernails. Finally he shook me off and never looked back.

My mother managed to keep that apartment on her wages from Meyers Drugstore across the street. My mother, Alberta Steed-Anders made burgers and vanilla cokes for the soda fountain and Eddie Meyers paid her $40 a week. She, my 2-year-old sister Luanna, and I lived in that one bedroom place with no heat and a stove in the bedroom for cooking. I remember somebody burning some homemade french fries in a blackened skillet one day on that stove. We had a whole bunch of different babysitters—my teenaged cousins Kathy and Carla Click, and Kathy's best friend Brenda Fraley.

My mom was thankful she had managed to save up her S&H Green Stamps for a radio to fill the chilly small rooms in that place. And she also still had her Kay guitar. She sang us to sleep most nights and told us stories to go with some of the songs.

Dottie Roscoe was a girlfriend of my dad's best friend Lee Marshall. They never called Lee Marshall just 'Lee'—he was one of those people that you can't refer to without including their last name too, and Lee Marshall was one of those guys. Dottie was a rich girl from New Jersey. Lee Marshall had met her at college on a football scholarship. My dad got a sports scholarship too, but returned after two days complaining to my mother that he came back cause she was crying when he left. "I was crying," she told me, "because he didn't have any good clothes to wear to college cause we were so poor. And I felt so sorry for him that I started crying. The asshole."

Dottie was a lively girl who could fit in anywhere. For a rich girl she was without pretensions or snobbery, and was as content playing poker and drinking beer with my mom and dad and Lee Marshall in the holler as she might've been doing whatever it was rich girls did in New Jersey. Dottie said her dad was coming to Ashland soon to open an engineering company at Armco Steel, the largest company in our hometown. Armco and Ashland Oil were the two places to work. It was said they kept secret ledgers of grades and behavior on every male child from the time they entered school until graduation. By the time he graduated from Ashland High School and applied for a job at either of these companies, they had already decided years before if he made the grade. This was what my father believed anyway, and if such a ledger existed, there was certainly no doubt in his mind that Bob Anders would not be hired. Dottie was sure that her father would hire everyone when he came to town…she would see to that. But by the time she returned and Mr. Roscoe was hiring, my dad was 3000 miles away and not coming back.

By then, my father was living in Chino, California with his 18-year-old girlfriend Diane who was pregnant and who paid for his divorce. Dottie told my mother she MUST call her father about a job. He was now in Ashland running his company. My mother called, but the first time she met Mr. Roscoe was at a Tupperware party Dottie gave at their mansion on South Bath Avenue.

"He looked like Willem Dafoe," she said, "and the way he dressed and carried himself...I'd never seen anything like it. He dripped money, his shirts were the best shirts, the cufflinks, the suits—there had never been anyone in that town like him, and never would be again, because—well, they don't make men like that anymore. He came into the Tupperware party and Dottie introduced him to me. He took my hand and said something flattering—I don't even remember what...but he didn't leave without saying one special thing to each girl in the room. That's the way he was. You get the picture, he loved women." Mr. Roscoe was a millionaire when being a millionaire meant something.

She failed her first typing test but he gave her the job anyway and she became Mr. Roscoe's private secretary. She made $75 a week, and within a few months she managed to get her sister Jeri a job with him too. Jeri had failed three typing tests. Jeri was my favorite aunt—I looked like her—I had her fair coloring and she told everyone that she considered me part her child cause every time my mother had a labor pain she had one too. She never had a daughter, and would never have one. She was only able to bear one child, Mark, four years before I was born. At the time that my mother got her a job with Mr. Roscoe, Jeri had just been granted a divorce from her husband Bob Fosson on the basis that he had given her gonorrhea three times and the disease had scarred her tubes so badly she could never bear children again.

The two sisters, both divorced from their Bobs, and raising their kids alone on their salaries from Mr. Roscoe, decided to move in together into a big spooky house on Lexington Avenue. We had enough bedrooms and space to all live together—my sister, Mark, and me, and our moms, and there were mysterious blocked-off rooms, and a spooky attic, filled with things like Civil War uniforms, a box of antique guns, and ancient strange, sad photographs. I wasn't too wild about this house, but there we were and I did enjoy this new extended family. Again we had a revolving door of babysitters.

Occasionally, my mamaw would babysit us, before her arthritis confined her to bed. She dazzled us with her astonishing telepathic powers. She read auras around people without even knowing that's what she was doing. And she was the most extraordinarily intuitive person I have ever met. We would sit on the porch with her and she could predict when my mom would be coming around the corner from work. "How many cars, Mamaw?" She tell me to count ten cars—and then my mother would be home. And she was right every time.

Mr. Roscoe received a phone call for my mother in his office one day. It was a creditor. Roscoe figured this out by the discreet way my mother handled the call. After she hung up and was heading back to her desk, Roscoe asked, "How much do you owe him?" "Sixty-seven dollars," she said. "How much could you pay me back each week if I loan you the money right now to pay this guy off?" She figured the best she could promise was $2 a week. It was a deal. And each week, she put two dollars in an envelope and put it on his desk and they never discussed it again.

It took him a year to make his first move on her. "Where do you shop—for clothes?" She shrugged shyly, "Penney's—downtown." He said, "Oh for god's sake not here in Ashland! You can't find decent clothes here! What if I sent you to Cincinnati to buy some nice clothes—how much do you think that would take? And then…we could go out…out to dinner. Not here. Across the river. In Huntington." She said she'd have to think about it. She left his office and went straight to her sister Jeri's desk. An hour later she returned to Roscoe's office and said, "I don't go anywhere without my sister."

Roscoe begrudgingly bankrolled a trip to Cincinnati for both Steed sisters: train tickets, hotel rooms, and a wad of cash for shopping. I'll never forget the tremendous excitement as they prepared to leave. While they were gone, Mark had me wish on a magic rock. I rubbed the rock and thought about what I hoped my mother would bring back for me from her trip. He made a wish too. And so did Luanna.

"We felt *so* fancy!! We had dinner—in a restaurant! We slept in a hotel—I had never slept in a hotel before. And we shopped not only for ourselves but for you kids too. And we got so drunk that we passed out on the train coming back buried under our packages and hat boxes!"

I had asked the magic rock for a red dress—and got it. Luanna had asked for a stuffed bunny—and got it. Mark had asked for some kind of kit and he got it. Later he told me, he had passed our wish list onto our mothers when they called to check up on us.

When my mother told Roscoe she didn't go anywhere without her sister, he thought she just meant Cincinnati. But when the night of their first date came, she and Jeri were waiting, glamourous on his cash. He didn't hesitate, forever the gentleman…he took them both out to dinner in Huntington, West Virginia, and took turns dancing with each sister.

She describes that ride home in the yellow Cadillac across the bridge from West Virginia and back into Kentucky as that delirious high of nights reserved for your twenties—you don't get that again. Things are not without consequences, but the results of our behavior seem manageable, and even more than this, seem to offer a world of possibilities. Sex can lead to love. A date can lead to marriage. After your twenties are gone, even the most die-hard optimists like myself find it hard to return to such unabashed hopefulness.

Imagine the hopes an average twenty-seven-year-old would have had in her head when she knew she had a millionaire wrapped around her finger. But not my mother. She knew Roscoe was never going to marry her. And she didn't want him to. She didn't love him. Her attraction was purely sexual. And they played it out, except fucking—because she refused to sleep with a married man. But she admits they did just about everything else. Their affair was kept secret, of course. Dottie Roscoe never knew that my mother was having a relationship with her father, but she knew he was a womanizer and had many affairs. My aunt Jeri also knew, and often encouraged my mother to sleep with Roscoe and become his mistress, and get herself 'set-up'—why not? But my mother was fairly unambitious, and certainly never had much of a knack for turning her sexual life into a secure financial future: she married poor men. The only thing she accepted from Roscoe was her job security as his secretary, a few small gifts here and there.

My mother continued to date other men while she was having the affair with Mr. Roscoe. She and her sister spent most Saturday nights at the Club Sheridan across the Ohio River in Ironton, Ohio drinking and dancing. Ashland had remained 'dry' since prohibition until just 10 years ago. So everyone had to go across the bridge—either into Ohio or West Virginia—to buy liquor. The Club Sheridan played jazz, blues, and rock 'n' roll. Every Saturday night when the rest of the girls she went to Ashland High School with were getting slapped around by their drunk husbands at country bars, my mom was across the river dancing to live progressive bands, free to come and go as she pleased, to dance with whoever she liked (sometimes she'd boldly dance with black men—so completely unheard of in her own narrow-minded and bigoted community) and she was free to flirt and stay out all night if she wanted with her equally free best friend, sister Jeri.

Burt Nemiroff came to Ashland, Kentucky with the ending built in: he would stay for two years in the Tri-State, work as an engineer for Roscoe, then return home to Philadelphia. His parents were strict Jews who owned a chain of pharmacies in Philadelphia. He was stylish, almost beatnik, with glasses, short hair, and hep clothes. Cute, she says, cute. And he had his priorities—the first thing he asked my mother was where a guy could have some fun and dance. I associated him with The Orlons' song, *Wah-Watusi*. The Orlons exemplified the South Philly sound that was just taking hold of AM radio at that time. And Burt had a sort of pride about this sound, even though his parents would have been plenty upset to find out he had spent any time in the working class district of South Philly. Cause while Jews weren't permitted into the Philadelphia aristocracy and could not live on the Mainline or in fashionable areas like Chestnut Hill, they nonetheless had their own class system, and for upper-middle class Jews, South Philly was the ghetto.

When they first met him, my mother and Jeri tried to fix Burt up with our babysitter Cynthia. Cynthia invited him to Thanksgiving dinner. The date was a bomb—Cynthia thought Burt was a first class drip and he said she was 'not his type.'

After their first few dates at the Club Sheridan, Burt and my mother were sleeping together and in no time at all, they had fallen in love. But his love came with conditions: he could never marry her, because she was not Jewish, she was divorced with two children, and she was from the wrong class. And when his job was up there, he would be leaving without her. What was she thinking? Did she think she would change his mind? That he'd end up staying with her after all, or that he'd take her into his world? Or was she simply not thinking? Deep down, I know the answer, I always knew the answer.

I remember him coming to the house to pick her up for one of their first dates. She was still dolling herself up, or simply making him wait downstairs. While Burt waited for my mother to snap her hose into her garter belt, and spray "White Shoulders" on her skin, my sister Luanna climbed up on his lap, threw her arms around his neck and cooed, "Is you gonna be my Daddy?" Far from scaring him away, we were soon included in many of their dates together: picnics, trips to Carter Caves where we rented peddle boats, Roosevelt

Lake, and even a weekend trip to Virginia Beach, and the Columbus Zoo.

They kept their involvement secret at work, to avoid gossip. And then of course there was Roscoe. She was still seeing him too. Neither man knew about the other. She juggled them farcically. Until Roscoe bought her that car. A brand new car from Chevy, a Corvair.

There is a black and white photo with crinkle-edged borders of my mother and Jeri posed in front of her brand new white Corvair wearing their cashmere coats with fake fur collars. My Aunt Jeri's smiling at the camera. My mother is squinting directly forward, not smiling, with her head cocked to one side. The Corvair had red leather interior and a radio which played music loud as you wanted it. She loved that car, it was her weakness, every other large gift Roscoe had tried to buy her with she had turned down. She'd even turned down the gift of a fur. But the car was a different story, it was practical, it was fast and it was a fashion she understood.

Burt was concerned. For him the car was impractical, well...certainly on her secretary's salary. How could she afford this car? She managed to evade him each time he asked. But one night they were in bed and he persisted in his questions. Her avoidance brought the truth surging up in him. "It's Roscoe! Roscoe bought you that car!!" They fought, he slammed his fist into the wall and she decided to call it quits with the millionaire. She got dressed and left Burt's apartment and drove her car to Roscoe's house and parked it there and walked home. When she got home she called him and said, "Your car is parked in front of your house. It's over."

"Are you out of your mind??!! My wife is here!! What if she sees that car parked downstairs—how do I explain that???" Roscoe promptly got dressed and drove the car to our house and parked it in front, and walked home. My mother on seeing it outside her window, got dressed and drove the car back to his house and walked home. Roscoe called her, "I DON'T WANT THE FUCKING

CAR—I HAVE FIVE CADILLACS—I DON'T NEED A GODDAMNED CHEVY!!" She screamed, "It's over!" He said, "So be smart—keep the car."

He would not have the car back and he drove it to our house one last time, and there it sat. I knew none of this. All I knew was she drove us in the Corvair that Saturday morning and dropped me and Cousin Mark off at the Capitol Theater for a double bill of *40 Lbs. Of Trouble* and *Kid Galahad* the remake—with Elvis and Gig Young, and when she came to pick us up—it was in a rattling and backfiring purple and black '56 Buick! Mark's eyes widened and I winced as my mother waved wildly, smiling.

"He wouldn't take it back, so I sold it and bought that Buick. I was able to pay off some bills and buy you kids some clothes. At least it was over and I didn't have to play games anymore." And then, Jeri started seeing him.

This should have made my mother's life less complicated, but her period was late and she told Burt. They talked and worried and then a week later she was able to give him the happy news that her period had come—it was nothing to worry about. He was so relieved he cried and held her happily. When he said goodnight, without asking her to stay, he kissed her cheek.

On their next date, he held her hand in the movies, and at the end of the evening, he kissed her cheek. On the third date she said, "What is this?" he said, "What is what?" She said, "You're rejecting me and it's cruel." He said, "It's not you." She said, "What is it then if it's not me?" He said, "When I thought you were pregnant, I went to Temple and prayed to God for you not to be pregnant, and I promised if you weren't, I would never touch you again."

It had ended in a way she was never prepared for. You can never be ahead of your fate—you just can't be. You can agree to many things, and you can prepare yourself for a certain ending, but you can never be sure what fate will deal you instead.

Unable to have a platonic relationship with the man she desired with every fiber of her being, my mother quit seeing Burt and yet she had to see him everyday at work. She had quit seeing Roscoe and yet she was still his secretary. She started dating a cheerful drunken gambler named Ralph Barnett. He was fun, she says and, 'a good dancer.' I remember him most for the time I fell out of his Lincoln Continental cruising down Winchester Blvd. I held onto the armrest as my butt dragged on the pavement. I wasn't hurt but it gave poor old Ralph one more reason to drink.

We moved, all five of us, from the scary house on Lexington to a pleasant two-story white house on Bath Avenue and of course Roscoe was always in the background trying to win back my mother's affections, often to my advantage. One day he picked me and my sister Luanna up from my mamaw's apartment on South 29th and took us to Eddie Meyer's drugstore across the street to buy us ice cream cones. We sat at the counter licking our ice cream cones—this was fun enough at first—Luanna and I loved to lean down and look under the counter at the rainbow of colors of gum stuck there—the whole bottom of the counter was covered in once-chewed gum from at least two decades of insolent teenagers. It was cool-looking—even beautiful—and we would talk about our favorite colors of once-chewed gum. Lu preferred the brighter colors of green and banana and pink, while I liked the purples and blues and blacks—forever trying to figure out what exotic flavors they must have been.

After we finished our ice cream cones Mr. Roscoe took us for a stroll through the drugstore, was there anything we wanted? I shrugged. Well, maybe one thing...well maybe this pink vinyl notebook with the ponytailed girls on it—for school, of course. Oh well and there *is* this too, this box called "100 Fun Things To Do" which I've begged my mother to buy me for ages but it costs $6.99 and she says it's mostly paper inside but it has paints and glitter and puzzles and things in it too and I really really want it. But you know what else I really really want? These high heels—blue plastic pretend ones with gold sparkles. Mom says I'll break my neck, but I say she wears her high heels when she goes out on a date with Burt and she never breaks her neck.

Mr. Roscoe drove us home in his yellow Cadillac. My mother stood on the front porch of the house with her hand on her hip, shaking her head as she saw us running toward her loaded down with packages, chocolate all over our faces, and ice cream stains all over our dresses. She smirked at Roscoe as he stood by his car watching the effect this scene may have on her. It could have been the wrong thing to say to mention Burt. But in this case, it seemed to work well for Luanna and me. Maybe he was only planning to buy us one toy each, but the B-word had the magic effect of seducing that bankroll right out of Roscoe's fist—and we bought each and everything we wanted and even things we didn't want, upon his insistence.

One afternoon, she overheard Burt in Roscoe's office. The door was cracked and she busied herself at her desk as she listened. Roscoe was laying people off and my mother knew that. In Burt's case, his job had simply come to an end, sooner than they expected, and he would be sent back to Philadelphia to work. Burt left Roscoe's office, passing through my mother's office to leave but she wasn't there. She was collapsed against the wall in the bathroom in tears.

She called him that night at home. When he answered she said, "When are you leaving?" Her voice was trembling, "When?" He said, "Probably…in a month." She drove to his apartment in her crazy Buick and they sat on his bed kissing and crying, both of them crying. And he must have made another bargain with God, because they decided to have the very best love affair of their lives in that remaining month.

Which they did. To this day, she gets a far away look when she remembers it, but keeps the details to herself. The month passed. Two days before he got on the train back to Philly she couldn't go to his apartment because seeing his bags packed was so painful she lost her breath. And when he left, she stayed crushed and went to bed for months. She had to get up every morning and take us to school, and go to work, and when she came home, she got into her peddle pushers and sweatshirts and barefeet and watched TV on the couch: old films *My Foolish Heart, Johnny Belinda* and her favorite *Ruby Gentry*, and *Alfred Hitchcock Presents* and *One Step Beyond.* She ate food with no pleasure, and a lot of it, and she avoided the phone with a promise to call people back when she could, whenever she woke up again. And then, she hacked off her hair.

It was at night, in the bathroom upstairs under the bare bulb. She didn't cry and it was her passivity juxtaposed with this severe act that was so disturbing, I knew something was really wrong. Had there been energy in the act—anger, hope, sorrow—I could have accepted that, even if it frightened me. But there was a strange surrender that was heavy as tar when she lifted the scissors to her thick hair, and there was that dreary sound, the sound that only a pair of dull shears cutting through a hank of hair makes. Downstairs from the radio sang a tinny, distant Gene Pitney. I expected tears I never got to see on her face. I knew there was something horrible going on. She turned to me and said, "What're you doing out of bed?" I said, "I need a glass of water." She replied, "Get it and get back in bed. It's late."

She stirred only for shock or tragedy—the death of Marilyn Monroe, and the brutal murder on Skyline Drive of Brenda Fraley, my cousin Kathy's best friend and one of our one-time babysitters. She was parked, making-out with her boyfriend in his car. He was shot reaching across the front seat for the glove compartment, she was shot and raped and still alive when she arrived at the hospital. In the glove compartment was their marriage license, they had been secretly married. A guy from the holler was convicted of the murders and sent to prison for ten years. Mr. Fraley sat in his rocking chair on their porch above the street with a chilling smile on his face, staring out at nothing. He had been a very strict father. People wondered. He died shortly after his daughter of unknown causes. The guy who went to prison for her murder swore he didn't do it. My mother managed to get to Brenda's funeral but none of us ever got free of the ghosts her murder left behind.

Now, my mother started going through life again: to baby showers, to funerals, to birthday parties and weddings and school plays. But the tunes on the radio were reminders, sad and eerie...I will always associate Dave Brubeck's *Take Five* with Brenda's death, and *Greenfields* by the Brothers Four with Burt being gone. My mother still played her guitar, her mournful gypsy songs. Eventually she got out of bed and her hair grew back. But her heart and her body never forgot her loss. Women carry memories there. We carry memories like babies.

How many girlfriends of mine have had to get out of bed and go to work in grief like this when a lover has gone for the last time? We cut off our hair, or we let our roots grow out and reveal our real selves, we eat ice cream and mashed potatoes, we sleep, and we watch TV, and we fall asleep with the TV on. Sometimes, we cut ourselves to let the pain out. Or bite our nails down till they bleed. Or chew the skin from our cuticles till they bleed. Maybe we try being wild party girls for a while—fuck a bunch of guys to try and drown it out. But this is the worst of all. With each touch our skin remembers who we loved and how we were betrayed, either by him or by our fate. So we try to escape ourselves. We drive. We drive up the coast. We listen to the radio. We sing loudly and cry as we drive up the coast—such pretty postcards such a pretty beach such a nice life, and we cry. We blame ourselves. We reject our bodies. We blame our desire. We wanted too much and we couldn't help ourselves—we are whorish with desire. We are afraid of what this pain means to be a woman—what is this desire that looks so insane? Maybe we are insane. "Maybe I'm just insane" we say to ourselves.

We fall apart wherever we are. Because if we don't we can't rebuild what is left of us. We fall apart. Because we are too much to hold up...we could never hold up this much—even when we are in the air, defying gravity and swallowed into the mothering comfort of clouds. Clouds which are always, disappointingly, simply air.

First

Ivan's mother stands in the driveway, clutching a gardening trowel and fingering wilted plastic flowers stapled around the brim of her straw hat. Her face is preserved with the painful lamination of a rich woman. She reaches out and adjusts his necktie. It's a loud safari print.

"Don't take your motorcycle," she tells him. "Please. You'll be drinking."

Ivan tosses his leather jacket over the handlebars of his Japanese motorcycle. He wears a gray suit. His father's red Porsche is also parked in the horseshoe-shaped driveway. His mother's brand new '81 Buick Regal, the car Ivan will be driving to his good friend Dougie's wedding reception (although he hasn't admitted it yet), is parked on the street. Her Buick has a handkerchief-sized Confederate flag attached to the antenna. It was sent as a joke from her sister in Ohio. As children, they grew up on a Naval base in Charleston, South Carolina. Thunder thumps the thick air, but the sun still shines. The concussion is like a fat man cannonballing into a pool. Ivan wishes the weather in San Clemente was not always so temperate. He loves lightning and thunder.

"Cars are difficult to drive when I'm drunk," he argues. He fantasized about swatting the sunhat from her head.

"But the police," she persists. "You have long hair."

"They don't give tickets to the terminally ill," he says. "And if they do, I won't pay it."

Ivan's mother feels as if she's entered deep water when his logic favors extreme directions. The only way she can touch bottom is by making physical contact with him. Her hand locks around his belt buckle.

"You know how fatigued you get now," she reminds him. "The drive on your motorcycle will be too much for you."

Ivan tries to step away from her, but she holds tight. As he progressively submerges deeper into his fate, the physical contact from others becomes exasperating. She shoves the trowel into her back pocket, handle down, and grasps his hand. Next door, children run through the sprinklers. Two sisters with identical peach-colored bathing caps kiss each other on the lips once as if saying goodbye, then shoot through the water. Their playmates follow. The family beagle waddles beside the children. He snaps the air each time the spray pelts him, mistaking the sprinkler as an intrusion of their game. Ivan realized he has just become too tired to take his motorcycle.

*   *   *

The Buick's cassette deck blares *I Hate the Rich* by The Dils, and Ivan howls along. The vocalist sounds proudly hysterical, a cross between the Cowardly Lion and a braying ass. As Ivan accelerates down the entrance ramp onto the freeway, a Mercedes convertible carrying two girls sucks up next to him. A brunette wearing a shingled Cleopatra hairstyle grins at him from the passenger seat. Ivan is not familiar with the Buick's main console, so the button for the electric window on the driver's side eludes him. The one he tries first locks all four doors simultaneously. The sound jolts like pinball flippers.

When Ivan glances back over, the Nile queen lifts her blouse and flashes him. Her bean-brown areolas are pimpled like feather-pluck. The Mercedes speeds away, and before Ivan can slide into the left lane to follow, a semi-trailer hauling limestone blocks bars his way.

*   *   *

Ivan shifts back and forth on his bare feet to soothe the burning of the hot asphalt. His new shoes have been pinching. The gas station attendant, a squat ape-armed man whose shirt seems strained, waits impatiently. He peers down and notices a skull and crossbones tattooed on the top of Ivan's left foot.

"My wallet," Ivan offers as an explanation while he vigorously frisks himself, every pocket, for the second time.

The attendant looms treacherously closer, and Ivan suffers a slight spell of fatigue. But he keeps his eyes open to ward off the hovering dizziness. In the distance, droves of rain fall from the bruised bellies of clouds. The downpour appears to rise, an optical illusion that reminds him of how spoked wheels seem to spin backwards as they roll forward.

"What's in the envelope?" the attendant demands. Ivan's equilibrium rushes back to him. A white envelope is on the Buick's front set. It is Ivan's gift to the newlyweds. The attendant reaches inside and grabs the envelope. Ivan half-attempts to snatch it back, but the attendant easily counters him and snorts.

Ivan can do nothing as the attendant tears open the envelope and extracts a crisp fifty dollar bill from the wedding card. The attendant adds the new bill to the outside of a money wad, then counts Ivan's change out, all in ones.

"...thirty-four, thirty-five, thirty-six, thirty-seven." he says. "Now you have a nice day." Ivan replaces the money with the card back in the ruined envelope. It bulges in his hand. He tears the Confederate flag from the antenna and hurls it to the ground as the attendant moves toward another car.

*   *   *

The first drops pop on the windshield like ripe mosquitoes. Most of the cars have their headlights turned on. Ivan leaves his off, even when the rain overcomes the windshield wipers' highest speed. He passes a construction site slowly, and milky puddles form along the roadside where heavy trucks have flattened and kneaded the shoulder. Fifteen minutes later when Ivan pulls into the party center's gravel parking lot, his wipers are no longer necessary.

*   *   *

The gusts still carry the storm's threat. Women in high heels run gawky towards the entrance, like ostriches. They keep their hands over their heads. A Volkswagen bus attempts to saw its way into a narrow space, and Ivan waits. There is tapping at his window, and Ivan whirls and sees his friend Smack. Smack rolls over the hood, an imitation of a Hollywood stuntman, and opens the passenger door and climbs in. A five o'clock shadow shades his scalp. Rows of earrings resembling fishing tackle outline each ear, and like Ivan, he hasn't brought a date.

Smack immediately begins rocking his head violently to the music. He opens the glove compartment, fingers through its contents, and removes two cassette cases. One is the empty of The Dils tape. A squeak escapes from Smack as he holds the other cassette at arms length with two fingers. His eyes are saucered wide in near-sincere panic.

"The Beatles?!" he whispers.

"Don't you know *Helter Skelter?*" Ivan says. He snatches the tape away before Smack destroys it. Smack still considers himself a skinhead.

*   *   *

A few years ago, between tenth and eleventh grades, Ivan spent the entire summer with his aunt and uncle in Cleveland. When he returned to San Clemente that September, his head was shaved. He exposed his friends to slam-dancing and bands like Black Flag and The Crucifucks. On weekends, they drove to The Anti-Club in Los Angeles to hear their favorite local punk bands. In Cleveland, the guys he associated with destroyed and pissed in the interiors of unlocked cars and dropped stolen bowling balls from high places. The most dangerous thing Ivan did with his San Clemente friends was prank-call phone numbers taken from supermarket bulletin boards offering guitar lessons and private nurses. By the next summer, he was already growing his hair long.

*   *   *

Ivan finds a parking space next to a Mercedes exactly like the one driven by the two girls he saw earlier, except that the top is up. He slips his socks and shoes on, and Smack and him step their way over puddles towards the party center.

Smack has borrowed his father's suit. It's not cut for a young man and makes him look like he's going to lose his balance. A policeman cites expensive cars parked illegally in the fire lane along the one-story stucco building. They are there because those spots are closest to the entrance and the fines affordable. Ivan believes the worth of the car should determine the fine. An illegally parked Jaguar should pay more than a Dodge. He told this to his parents once, and they accused him of being a Liberal. Ivan wishes he would have parked along the fire lane too.

"What are you giving Dougie and Denise for their wedding present?" Smack asks. But he isn't really interested in an answer. He wants Ivan to inquire about his gift, which is a free landscaping job up to three-hundred dollars on their first place with a yard. Smack works for his father's landscaping business and plans to do it himself on a day off.

"What if they move to another state?" Ivan asks. Smack hasn't thought of this, and he steps up to his ankle in a puddle.

*   *   *

They move down the receiving line and awkwardly clasp hands with grandparents, sisters, and brothers. Dougie's father shakes his head disapprovingly when they get to him. He hates Smack's shaved head and feels Ivan's long hair is ridiculous and feminine. But he never ignores them.

"Just great to see more of Dougie's cronies," he says.

"Hello Mr. Douglas." Smack is always passive around the man.

"And how are you feeling?" Mr. Douglas badgers Ivan. "I see the chemotherapy hasn't caused your hair to fall out. Yet." Mr. Douglas knows that when that happens, Ivan will have to begin again and go through the medium-length stage that men's hair is supposed to be kept at.

"When Dougie's mother went through chemo, she also retained her hair," Mr. Douglas says. "But her eyebrows and lashes? Gone."

Ivan just smiles. He finds Mr. Douglas' bald head with its long strands of gray combed over to reduce the imagined attention sad. He has always like Dougie's father for not liking Dougie's friends.

*   *   *

Dougie wears no earrings, but the holes are visible. His hair is an inch long. He's grown it out for the wedding pictures and tells Smack and Ivan it's going during the honeymoon.

"I hope they have barbers in Tahiti," Dougie says. He can't stop wringing his hands.

"I thought you wanted to go to Mexico," says Smack.

"Tahiti," states Dougie's wife Denise. She crosses her arms and holds her bouquet upside-down,

"I'm all ready to get my dick wet tonight," Dougie tells his friend. Denise gives him a fermented glance, but Dougie doesn't mean anything concerning her.

Denise once had pink hair and travelled with them to see bands. Now she's an assistant manager at a seafood restaurant and can only dye her hair natural colors. Presently, it's blonde, but so light it's pushing the limit.

Denise offers her mouth to be kissed by Smack, then moves her face to the side as she heartily hugs Ivan. She takes few breaths, and not too deep, as the four talk. Ivan has noticed others do this around him. His sickness is not contagious, but you never know.

*   *   *

Ivan and Smack order beers at the bar, then join the rest of their gang. Ivan is the only one who has abandoned skinhead fashion by growing his hair, but they still whoop greetings and pound him on the back. All of his friends have nicknames except Dougie and himself. There's Smack, Grim One, Hemingway, Skull, Big Time, Fido and State of Alaska. They tried to christen Dougie 'Scab' once, but every time somebody used it, he corrected them. Blood and injuries made him queasy. They finally conceded to Dougie. Ivan retained his name because it was odd enough by itself.

The guys stand near the six-piece ensemble, to the side of the

PA system, catcalling the tuxedoed musicians to play requests. But the songs they holler out are by various punk bands. The saxophonist stops blowing and steps cautiously to the edge of the raised platform stage.

"Come on," he says. "Get serious."

The friends huddle and how. "Get serious!" they mimic. But they don't leave. Even though they resist this kind of music, the bass vibrations from the speakers console them.

"Tequila!" Smack shouts.

Scrawny Fido is sent for a round of Cuervo Gold shots. He hustles off.

"None of us will be sitting together," Hemingway informs Smack and Ivan. "The reception is assigned seating."

The band stops mid-song and the saxophonist instructs the guests to locate their name placards and take their designated places. There is confused clatter and movement of individuals interrupting their booze and conversation. Fido returns during this scramble. His friends have roamed off to find their seats, and he is left holding the nine shots on a round cocktail tray.

* * *

The only familiar person at Ivan's table is the girl from the Mercedes who flashed him. He's not really surprised to see her. Her Egyptian hairdo looks droopy, and he decides she must have gotten rained on before her friend could raise the convertible's top. Ivan is wedged between two elderly ladies, both wearing fuchsias of the same shade, and angry that by being seated so close to each other their extreme gowns have turned farcical. Nobody introduces themselves when Ivan plops down. Servers distribute extravagant salads with shredded radish and carrot, then platters of cheese and deviled eggs. Eggs are one of Ivan's least favorite things. They remind him of old people. He always sees the elderly peeling them, hard-boiled, at the retirement home where his great-grandmother lives. The yolks turn their tongues into pollen-coated stamens. Most of them talk to each other with their mouths full. He dreads visiting his great-grandmother. The weak and tottering agitate him.

"Eggs?" Miss Cleopatra offers Ivan from across the table. His aversion to them is so bad he can only cover his mouth with his napkin.

*   *   *

Two years ago, Ivan's father chartered a boat out of Newport Beach and took him deep-sea fishing for his high school graduation. His mother wanted to pack them a picnic basket.

"Lunch is included in the price," his father told her.

"What will they have?" she asked. Ivan's father was fat, and she worried about him getting enough to eat. Whenever he lost weight, he became more independent.

"Who knows, but I'm sure it will be adequate."

Ivan's mother packed a picnic basket for her two boys anyways. They left early in the morning while it was still dark. At a stop light, Ivan's father opened the basket. Inside were baloney sandwiches, cans of root beer, Musketeer bars, and hard-boiled eggs. His father tossed everything out the window, one at a time, as they drove along. He seemed to enjoy himself. Ivan never knew this about his father, although he couldn't specify what it was he had discovered.

*   *   *

Ivan accidentally dumps his beer. Some of the guests throw in their napkins to sop up the spill. Neither woman in fuchsia does. An older gentleman has an extra vodka and grapefruit that he got before sitting down so he wouldn't run out during dinner, and he offers it to Ivan. Ivan thanks him and rolls his empty beer bottle under the table. The man chuckles.

"That's littering," a woman in fuchsia says.

"It's not possible to litter inside," explains Ivan.

"Oh yes it is," the woman claims. She believes that the problem with the young is that they are lazy and destructive and have changed the rules and definitions to accommodate those characteristics. Too crafty for their own good, she feels.

"Nature is being ruined," she tells the guests around the table.

"This has nothing to do with nature," says the older gentleman. "It's a Goddamn wedding."

*   *   *

Ivan and Cleopatra dance to a slow song. She is one of the bride's cousins and lives in a guest house on the edge of an orange grove in Ojai. She laughs easily at his jokes, but he doesn't feel all that funny. He wonders if Denise has informed her about his sickness. Too bad it's not something exotic, something that people can talk about and shake their heads in amusement and maybe envy after he is dead.

Dougie also dances. One of the women in fuchsia is his partner, and she's rooster-proud to be with the groom. Every time Ivan goes by, Dougie pinches him in the ass and blurts out 'Bang!'

The summer Ivan spent in Cleveland almost ended tragically. He had been downtown late one night with a few guys releasing garbage dumpsters down hills. They usually didn't roll far before crashing into cars parked along the side of the street. Suddenly, a Cadillac hearse zoomed by, gunfire blaring from its half-open tinted windows. Ivan was the only one to field a bullet. It hit him low in the right buttock. The sting felt like a match had been lit inside his flesh. Later, he'd tell people the bullet had entered his upper thigh. Being shot in the ass was comical, but the leg was a legitimate wound. The slug was never removed. X-rays showed it to be of a smaller caliber, and the scar tissue caused by extraction would be more damaging than allowing it to remain. Ever since that night, he's felt special, marked.

*   *   *

Denise's cousin knows about Ivan. Three different relatives whispered it earlier, each hoping to be the first to inform her. But she just became more intrigued. Now she sits with Ivan outside on a stone bench supported by miniature imitation Doric columns, kissing. His hands press where her velvet blouse covers her breasts. Red and blue spotlights hidden in the crabgrass light the palm trees. Vigorous flowers surrounded with thick growth define the crushed shell pathway. Couples stroll by occasionally, holding drinks, off to find seats for themselves.

The girl stops kissing Ivan and realizes that maybe his feelings are hurt.

"I'm sorry about what I said earlier."

Ivan tugs her hair, teasingly. She told him while they were dancing that she didn't believe in a god or the soul. They just seemed like fairy tales to her. But Ivan believes. He explained that if we knew how to look, we would see thousands of souls in the air, like a blizzard of ash. They're always around. Don't ask him how he knows, he just does. Common sense.

*   *   *

"There he is," Smack says. Big Time is with him. They trudge purposefully towards Ivan and the girl and do not nudge or joke with each other.

Ivan rises from the bench. He tells Cleopatra this shouldn't take too long. She seems puzzled by the abrupt shift in him. The three leave her.

*   *   *

A man stands outside the bathroom door, uncertain whether to be angry or not. He really needs to use the toilet and wants to know what's going on in there anyway. Smack knocks, and the door cracks open. He enters with Big Time and Ivan and the door closes. Then Smack pops his head back out and grins at the man.

"I'd be careful if I were you," Smack warns. "Drugs may be involved in here."

The man backs up. Smack enjoys the scarecrow effect the word 'drugs' has sometimes. He barks happily and lets the door close.

Everyone is in there. Dougie has his back to the mirrors. The counter is puddled from people washing their hands in the oval sinks. There is a wet blot low on the back of Dougie's tuxedo jacket from sitting momentarily on the counter. Skull and Grim One slide the garbage container and block the door so nobody can interrupt.

Smack pulls a ceramic bread plate from his jacket pocket, and the mood becomes sepulchral and ceremonial. He balances it in his palm.

"Set everything on the plate," he tells Dougie. "And I don't want anything touching my skin."

Everyone laughs, then grows silent when Dougie unzips his pants and pulls himself out. He is uncircumsized. He pretends that he's going to dab Smack's hand, and the group howls.

"Come on, get serious," Smack commands.

Dougie pushes his hips forward, and Smack brings the plate up until dick and balls are resting on the shiny white surface.

"Chilly," Dougie whispers.

Nobody knows exactly how to proceed, so Smack, realizing that the momentum must not be interrupted, takes the initiative.

"Because you're the first of us, Dougie," he intones, leaning over close to the plate. "Like we all agreed." Then he purses his lips and lets a stream of spit drop smoothly, like syrup, onto Dougie's parts. Smack wipes his mouth with his free hand.

Ivan steps forward, and Dougie smiles nervously at him. His hips are still rotated frontwards. Ivan has wondered all day if he will be excluded, that maybe his participation is bad luck. But nobody stops him. He holds his hair back, bends down, and spits a small sneeze of spray.

"That's two," says Smack. "Who's next?"

It becomes more relaxed as each takes his turn. Hemingway makes the sign of the cross before he goes. "Not so long down there," Dougie tells Fido, and that really gets them roaring. Someone taps at the door, but they pound back and dare anybody to enter. State of Alaska is the last to spit. When he finishes, Smack removes the plate, and Dougie instantly places paper towels on himself to clean off.

"Only a wipe," Smack says. "No washing. That's holy stuff."

They wait for Dougie to finish. He tucks his shirt in and zips and buckles his pants. Smack hands him a small hoop earring, and Dougie stares close in the mirror as he attaches it to his left lobe. Grim One goes to unblock the door.

"Do me," Ivan urges. He motions for the garbage container to be left. "I want you to do me too." He unzips his pants.

"But it was for the first one of us only," Smack explains. He runs water over the plate as if to emphasize his statement.

"Exactly!" Ivan says.

They wait. Smack dries the plate with a paper towel and looks at Dougie. It is clearly their decision. Nobody offers anything. Dougie shrugs, then nods.

"Pull it out," Smack tells Ivan.

Ivan lets his pants and underwear fall to his knees. His skin is sectioned by tan-line and buffed like citrus peel. The friends shrink close, whistling and clapping.

"No pubic hair!" someone cries.

"Bald as an egg!" says another friend.
Gone with the treatment that didn't cure him.
Smack moves first with the plate.

Mountain

You can't explain it. But that's just how people behave. Some say it's in their nature. Some claim the devil made them do it. A few dare say that God abandoned them and pushed them over the edge. If your faith is strong enough, you could move mountains. If you close your eyes and wish upon a star, dreams will come true. She believed this.

She told me that on the night they escaped, the ocean was like the sky, dark and translucent, and shimmering as if with floating candles burning so strong no storm or wind could blow them out. She kept describing how warm the sand was and how softly the breeze caressed her body. She was annoyed, though, that the boy saviors were loud and talking nonsense, and grunting like boars. *And all night long, too,* she said. *All night long. All night long.*

"Don't drink too much or we'll run out before we reach dry land." She remembered the captain saying on the boat. *But he was wrong,* she insisted, *there's water everywhere.*

The boys, she told me again, *the boys, they were so loud and hollering and all that.*

She remembered the captain yelling. "Our savior's here! Our savior's here!" And then everyone on the boat chanting after him, "Our savior's here! Our savior's here!" But she revealed that there were eight saviors on a small boat who led them to a nearby island. She said that it was so dark, she could barely see the island, except that its shore was pale as neon white and looking like it was foaming at the mouth. She said the eight boys kept laughing and pushing each other around. She told me they used their guns and blades to make everyone walk off the boat onto the shore and sit on the warm sand. "Sit still!" they yelled. "Sit still!" *They were rude and loud,* she said.

They searched the boat's cargo and threw some things overboard, she recalled. *And all the while laughing so loud, the trees rattled.* "Sit still!" they yelled, "Sit!" *They weren't speaking Vietnamese,* she said, *but I understood everything they were saying.* She described how quickly the moon rose high above as the soft sand glowed pale blue when the boy saviors separated the men and boys from the women and girls. She said they kept screaming and yelling at everybody, and ordering all jewelry and watches be removed and dropped in a burlap sack. "Shut up!" they scoffed. "Nobody talk! Nobody cry!" They laughed again and tied the men and boys together by their ankles. "No noise!" they demanded. They shot their guns in the air and ordered the women and girls to remove all their clothes and undergarments. She said that soon, there was a mound of panties, slips and bras. "Nobody cry!" they repeated. The saviors then promised to set them free with fresh supplies of food and water and directions to the nearest refugee site if they would all cooperate. It was then that the noise really began. She said they started picking out some of the women and doing things she had not seen before. A couple of the saviors stood guard and repeatedly beat the men, forcing them to watch the scene unfolding on the moon-lit stage. An old priest began saying his prayers out loud and was clubbed until rivers of red flowed out his ears. She sobbed and said she closed her eyes but the moon pierced right through them. She then covered her ears, but *those boys,* she cried, *those boys, they kept making all that noise and talking nonsense and grunting so loud.* She told me, again, how warm the sand was and how soft the breeze hugged her but that the boys kept up their noise. "Nobody cry!" they yelled again, "Nobody make a sound!" *But they made all the noise,* she insisted, *they and the waves foaming at the mouth, they made all the noise!* She said that she closed her eyes again but kept seeing the shimmering mound of silk bras and slips and panties, and the silhouettes of the boy saviors doing silly things. *I forced my eyes tighter,* she uttered, *and covered them with my hands.* She said that after a long time under the protection of her eyelids, she imagined a faint image of a snow-capped mountain glowing in the moonlight. She confessed, *I'd never seen snow before except in magazines and in American and French movies. The snow-capped mountain shimmered, she whispered, white as unspun silk. And the noises,* she continued, *the boy saviors made those noises all night long.*

Ya Heard It Here First

My friends, the days of leather and latex have ended. Nose rings? Last Year! Cock rings are tired. Dungeons closing down. Perverts and the voyeuristic public are hungry for something new. And so they've turned their eyes and tastes south. It is the real result of NAFTA: Mexican Wrestling Fetish Wear!

They meet in shady little clubs with rings in the center of them. Dressed like overweight superheroes. Theirs is a brutal dance. Where sex only occurs after numerous takedowns. A prize served up to the victor like a solid gold belt. They call each other little pet names like El Satano, Todo El Mundo, and Sabado Gigante. One of the most popular themes is to design your costume like Spiderman's. Or Ultraman. Part of the fun at these sex parties is never knowing exactly who's behind the mask. Anonymous sex. Yet it's safe sex, since there are never actually any fluids exchanged. Wrestling combines the thrill of S&M with the added support of spandex. So it was really no surprise when we began to see those new boutiques sprouting up in trendy urban neighborhoods, South Street, Soho, the lower Haight, Seattle. Stores which only sell Mexican wrestling lingerie and fetish wear. Glossy fashion magazines will spread it out to Middle America, *Entertainment Tonight's* titillating expose will beam it to culturally elitist perverts everywhere and soon there'll be wrestling matches going on in every bedroom in America.

"It had been a really cool hardcore scene when it started out in the inner cities, one that created some truly historic outfits and matches, but by the time it got mainstreamed out to the suburbs all the costumes had this watered down generic American Gladiators Fetish Wear look to them and you could order them from just about any Fredrick's of Hollywood catalogue."

—Jean Paul Gaultier pronouncing the "El Santo Look" dead in *Details* magazine.

All his statement did was cause more eyes to look south.

Like all good subcultures this one has its drug of choice: steroids. Shooting up raw testosterone has become a real epidemic with Mexican Wrestling Fetish Wear enthusiasts. If you're not into girls with chest hair then maybe you've picked the wrong sexual sport. Stick to masturbation you little girly man! Paunchy studs with nombres like El Gordo Gonad will tell you that nothing gets them hotter than a woman who looks like a Russian Shot-putter.

So it's time to liberate yourself from the dungeon. Those genital rings been weighing you down? Cast them off and get hip to the new kink. Nobody does it like Mexican Wrestlers. It's a steroid thing. There's no bigger turn-on than the smell of sweaty spandex. The little threats and bragging like, "Meet me at the Cow Palace on October 13 and I'll rip your face off in front of ten thousand fans," these are the sweet nothings that love is made of. So throw away those handcuffs, toss off that gas mask, pick either gender and pin me to the mat.

NANCY KRUSOE

Who I'll Run Away With

Mrs. Hermenes is lying in the street. It's Mrs. Hermenes with a man lying on top of her. He moves a little, wiggles a little this way and that, up and down, stays around, doesn't leave when he's done, stays just as if she's invited him to stay there on top of her in the street where I am walking to my boyfriend's house.

This isn't the street I usually take. I'm not here by choice but because it's a school night and I'm late. Who would choose to be on a street such as this where a person you know could be dying? I'm not sure what is happening because Mrs. Hermenes isn't moving, isn't yelling, is lying very still, but I know it's her by that turquoise dress of hers that I can see a little bit of sticking out; even running I can see the colors of her dress that I love.

Mrs. Hermenes is too young and beautiful to be called Mrs. Hermenes; it's a mistake, just like my being here is a mistake. It's because of her husband, Mr. Hermenes, that she's called Mrs. Hermenes, and where is this husband who always is looking out for Mrs. Hermenes in such a way as to make it impossible for her to be called anything but Mrs. Hermenes? Where is he now that his wife is lying on her back in the street with another man lying on top of her?

Another man? Maybe this is Mr. Hermenes. How would I know from where I am if it is Mr. Hermenes? I'd have to go over and ask his name. I'd have to stand right there beside them and say, Mrs. Hermenes, is this your husband? But I'm running away as fast as I can to Al's house because I have to be home early tonight—my mother will be waiting. I'm running and I'm crying: Mrs. Hermenes, Mrs. Hermenes, how I love you—please don't be hurt. I go to my boyfriend's house for help because what could I do by myself? I am thirteen and sometimes I feel it.

The first time I saw Mrs. Hermenes, she scared me because she said look at me, Lucy, when such a thing isn't polite at my house. I am forbidden to look but I did look, and now I can't stop, and what does that mean? It means I am more than I was but not enough to know who I am. I'm part of Mrs. Hermenes now and part of my mother and part of myself. Mrs. Hermenes is dark, sort of olive, really brown, and sometimes she wears her turquoise dress with white wavy rivers running through its blue to her knees where it ends and splits up her thigh in front as if buttons had been called for on this dress—would have been there on anyone else's but hers.

Hello, Lucy, Al says. He kisses me and I try to tell him what I've seen—if only I knew what I'd seen I could tell him, I think—and he waits, standing in the doorway of his house, while I try to make sense, try to get Al to go with me to rescue my friend who he doesn't know. If you come with me, maybe we can help Mrs. Hermenes, maybe it's not too late, I say. Come now. Hurry. Al is big. Hurry, Al, hurry.

What kind of man is Mr. Hermenes? He's young but older than Al, who's twenty-two. He's not a friend of anyone I know. My mother says Mr. Hermenes is a man she wouldn't want to tangle with. What does she mean? I think of the man in the street entangled with Mrs. Hermenes, and I am scared.

Al gets his jacket. He gets his tennis shoes, no socks. Am I hurrying enough? he says.

Faster, Al, I say. She could be dead before we get there. Hurry, Al. If Al takes steps any longer than he's taking, I can't keep up with him—Al is a giant.

When we get to the street where she is, Mrs. Hermenes is dancing. She is up and dancing in the street, and Al stares in wonder. I look and wonder, too. It's staged, I say. They've made this up so I won't believe my eyes. It's not real, it doesn't exist, they've made her do this. Al's my friend, and I think I can say these things to a friend, although I see his face and there's something wrong with the way he's looking at me. If there were two moons in the sky, would you believe it? I ask him. What does Al see that I don't see?

Mrs. Hermenes is swaying between the walls of tall dark buildings, and her body is what Al sees. I look, too. Her face is in the dark, almost invisible in the yellow moonlight. For sure she isn't smiling; that much I can tell you, but her body is swinging and the turquoise dress is sliding on her hips like soft warm butter. I want to touch her but I stand very still. Without wanting to I am humming. It's more like a cluck—noises come out of my body and they're mine. I am making music for her dance. I say to myself it's a dream, then Al says what d'you think? He's red in the face—red on an icy blue night. Of course, the way she's dancing, I say, of course something is wrong.

Mrs. Hermenes, I call out, wishing she had disappeared, wishing we hadn't found her. Are you all right?

Come dance with me, she says, and I am surprised it's really a voice.

This street has hazel lights. It has lights even though what it lights is a yellow ugly narrow street with too many trash cans and it stinks. I don't know how my street smells—it must have an odor, but to me it's just home. Al's house has a smell, and I think of it as the smell of the people who had the house before him because it doesn't smell like Al at all. This street smells like garbage in your mouth like it will never wash off.

Mrs. Hermenes, whoever she is, walks up to us, all swish of silky turquoise and rivers running fast. Big sunny Al lights up. He's my daddy-lover-brother rolled into one.

What happened to you? I ask. This is how it was, she says, I was walking home when a man came up to me and whispered in my ear. Then he did this: she pushes her tongue into my mouth where it stays for a long time. I'm doubly confused, but I ask: Did he force you to? Did he hurt you? I kissed him, she says.

I have Al at my side, and he's jumping like a fish. I tell him to get lost, but his eyes are glued to the scene—Al cannot go.

But I don't understand, I say at last, relieved to say what I meant all along, even though it isn't much of anything. Who was this man? Are you the same Mrs. Hermenes I saw? What is what and why're you here like this in this yellow ugly street? Did you die? Can I believe this is you? But there is something to this thirteen-doesn't-know-it-all business, as my mother says, but who listens to her? It's not as simple in my head as her words would seem to tell me. What I saw was not what I thought I saw because I didn't really see. I'm not sure what I saw, but I'm sure there is more. And I want to go home now. I don't want to be late because my mother will ask me questions, and whenever that happens I'm split inside.

I have two parents, but one of them is gone. My father is a sailor and he lives overseas. He was already gone when I was born, and he has never come home. Missing in action, he sails all over the world, and this means my mother is alone. What she says about this aloneness is, I am not sure, Lucy, men may not be the answer. That's what she says. And a navy man—you can't count on a navy man. What thirteen-year-old doesn't know that? I say to her. You think you know it all, but you know nothing, she says.

Don't I know it's true—my innocence is a long, long story, the story of my life. Are you content to make a joke of your life? she says.

When I repeat these conversations to Al, he loves me more. What man doesn't love a bad young girl? My boyfriend Al is an

Eskimo, and Aleut from Alaska living in L.A. in the desert which he's crazy about because he's too young for Alaska. He says Alaska makes you old. He says his name is Alonzo. I accuse him of making it up and making up the igloos, too, but he assures me I can ask his parents if all of it is true, but I'll never meet Al's parents—my mother will never let me go to Alaska with Al. My father sailed off and he didn't come back. You think I'm crazy? she says. Al thinks she is; I don't. Are you like a navy man? I ask him, and he's sure he must be. After all, growing up in the Bering Sea, living in an igloo on ice, after all he must be a navy man, too.

And so I knew where Al stands which is more that I can say for Mrs. Hermenes, who I don't know now if I ever have known. She touches my hair which has curled in fright. Ok, I have too many feelings tonight. I want to go home, home to Al's house, his sweet blue house which I love; I love its path from the front door to the bedroom, the way it's crooked and nothing in it is straight, not a window or a chair or a door. Take me home, I tell him. We shouldn't be here. I'm a child anyway, pretending to know what I don't know. But even as I'm saying this, I'm crying, and it's Mrs. Hermenes I'm crying for. I want to turn around, take it all back.

There's another boy in my life besides Al. Of course Al doesn't know, and still I have a curfew and school and a mother. If I had a father, too, I could never get away with this because he'd take up too much of my time. My mother isn't so demanding. The kinds of things she worries about are exercise and cholesterol and, because I look healthy, she thinks I am good, too. Or else she doesn't want to look beneath my healthy glow. I say to her sometime we'll go do something together. We'll go to the beach or a dance or something, and she's eager to go because her life is dull, very monotonous, and I'm her only child. You might wonder why she hasn't married again—I have never ever seen my father—but she says, Why bother? Oh well, it is a bother, I say.

Why bother! What sort of mother is she? Sometimes I wonder if she even enjoys her life or if her life disappeared. When I run away with Mrs. Hermenes, it's going to break my mother's heart.

There have been lots of times in my life when I saw something and then forgot it or else someone had to tell me what I'd seen, but tonight isn't one of those times. This is so different I can't say what it is and I can't ask Al to explain it because he doesn't know. This is what I know:

1. I thought my friend, Mrs. Hermenes, was being raped and killed in front of my eyes, but what I saw I didn't see because what happened next couldn't have happened next. No one saw it but me, and I don't know what I saw.

2. Thinking something's so doesn't make it so.

3. Mrs. Hermenes was dancing in the yellow moonlight like nothing happened to her in this street tonight.

4. You have to watch closely to know what you see, and even then you don't know—even then they can change it. There is no way to hold things in place.

5. In the yellow moonlight, Mrs. Hermenes became someone else or else I did—either way, I'm changed. By seeing or not, am I not already changed?

At Al's house, inside his crooked blue house, I cry for a long time. I am too sad to talk. Al holds me in his lap like a baby with awful long legs, and he tells me it will be all right. I pretend that we're married and have just lost a baby—maybe I've had a miscarriage or an abortion. Maybe I've lost his baby and can't ever have another. When I pretend this while Al is holding me, something very funny happens inside me: it feels like I am not me anymore, nothing will ever happen to me again. This is a good deep feeling, a feeling of cosmic relief.

Al wonders if he looks like my dad and I tell him for sure he does. He laughs hard because he knows I am lying. I know what I've seen, I say, and I've seen his face in yours.

In bed I tell Al that the face of he man on top of Mrs. Hermenes was the color of the light in the street. How do I know

this since he didn't turn around? Al asks me that. This is my pic-
ture, Al. How do I know what I know? Do you do so much better?
When Al makes love to me, I'm like a big salt block being licked.
When you are licked, you disappear.

The thing about my mother is she loves holidays, especially
the cooking ones. On family holidays she cooks for days and invites
everyone we know to our house to eat—that's about twenty people.
Sometime I will invite Mrs. Hermenes and Al. My mother lost two
babies, but she doesn't like to talk about them. She makes them
sound like a big secret. I don't know if their father was my father.
Sometimes I find her dancing by herself at home in the dark. Her
favorite music is sixties pop, and now she says it's coming back so
my father must be heading home, too. She likes to masturbate in
the shower. She doesn't know I caught her and if I asked, she'd
admit it, but I won't ask because what would I do with all that honesty. I can't stand her loneliness. I feel trapped because she's so
right-there-waiting-for-me-always. Al says she has wasted her life,
but what does Al know? He goes out with a child. Big deal, Eskimo
boy with skin so beautiful I eat it.

When I found her again, I asked Mrs. Hermenes how come
she was never the same. She said: My name is Papina and I come
from a very good family. My mother lives in Peru. She has eleven
children so she can't travel. See the world, she says to me. Sure, I
say. It's easy to see the world; all you need is money, clothes, lan-
guages, style and good looks. So she sells her chickens to send me
out into the world—maybe around the world. Nothing's impossible. Take this, she says, and she gives me her old wedding gown. Oh
no, I say, although I know I will take it. It seems like a burden crossing the border in a stained white wedding gown, but it worked. I
arrived in L.A. on my wedding day. I told everyone I saw. They
thought I was sad and confused, addled a little, but this was my
mother's plan for me to be the Helpless Border-Crossing Bride.
When I was already here and wearing my mother's wedding gown

all the time people got to know me as the Virgin Bride, and they decided I was a stunned altar bride, you know, stood up at the altar and grieving and never undressing again. For two years I lived like this until I met Tony, so I married him in my mother's white wedding gown and then I took it off.

Her story makes me happy. She shows me a picture of her in her mother's wedding dress, and it's signed with love from someone I've never heard of, and I wonder how many of her there are.

I would've gone anywhere with Tony, she says. We could have gone around the world on love, but Tony has a job. He's the night clerk at 7-Eleven and he's the Pinball King. He's already been shot twice, but nobody beats Tony at pinball. How can I leave when I'm so good? he says. And so we never go around the world—we stay here while he makes his reputation. We wait until he loses at pinball. When that day comes, we will go.

This goes on for pages and pages—Mrs. Hermenes and her endless story. And she has sisters, too, who also have stories about the dangers of crossing the border. North American men, Latin men, men and more men. I go once a week to see Mrs. Hermenes and she tells me more, and I tell her more about me. Her husband has a big black doberman who guards us. He has no name, and his ears and tail are long. Except for his growl, you wouldn't know he was a Doberman. My friendship with Mrs. Hermenes—it's like having another boyfriend. Even Al seems surplus sometimes.

A few questions I have:

1. Why didn't Mr. Hermenes give his dog a name?

2. Why doesn't my mother seem real to me? Does she have a real life? Can I become like Mrs. Hermenes?

3. My mother loves me, but so what? What does it matter if she sees through me? Who is she seeing and who's looking?

4. What does it mean to live in a world where you are forbidden to look? I am forbidden to look: I am a girl.

5. I think my father is the answer to some of my questions, but how will I ever know him?

My father interviews me:
Q. What is your dream, Lucy?
A. To be safe.
Q. To be safe from what?
A. Fear.
Q. How does your fear manifest itself?
A. Like dying in a war. My doorbell rings and it's you. Then I'm dead and I can't come back again. It's you and you take me away. You have guns and you shoot me. There's always someone following you. They shoot me, too.
Q. If you could leave, where would you go?
A. To the equator. Things might be different there.
Q. There's more death at the equator—more violence in the heat. I know, I've been there.
A. Maybe I could go to the North Pole—find you in the ice.
Q. What do you do when you're frightened?
A. I stare at myself. If I'm the moment of looking, what does it mean that the image keeps splitting? I am the object of my own looking. I am the gaze and the gazed at—I am my double. Where am I when I am not looking? Where do I exist when I turn my eyes away? When I looked away, Mrs. Hermenes split, and when I looked again, she's already become someone else, but what had I become? I became the moment of not seeing. I became the event that occurred that was lost to me forever. Mrs. Hermenes, how I miss you!
Q. Is Mrs. Hermenes lost forever?
A. I have her stories. I have her words and her presence here in my words.
Q. Did you write this story because you were afraid?
A. Yes, I was afraid. I am still afraid. My fright is bigger than my words.

Papina says: My sister Angela had no wedding gown to wear across the border. My mother was desperate so she went to my Aunt Sophia for help so Angela could cross over. Aunt Sophia said maybe Angela could go as a saint. Aunt Sophia's husband, my uncle who is large and ugly, went to the church and asked for interference for a cure. If Angela had a cure, she could go over.

What kind of cure can you get from the church? I asked.

A cure-all. An apostle's cure. To look upon my Aunt Sophia is a cure. Maybe Angela could have such a power.

Did it work?

Angela crossed over and joined a rock band, but then she got married and now she has a baby.

I imagine that Angela looks like Mrs. Hermenes, that she, too, has long brown legs and walks like a Quechuan queen.

I ask my mother, What do you think is the most important thing in the world?

She thinks. She hums la la, as if her unadmitted dream is stuck in a pop song like it's finger-lickin' good.

Mother, why are you singing now?

Okay, it's you, she says.

No, mother. I can't be your object of desire. I desire Mrs. Hermenes. She asks me why I desire her. Because, I say, she is many in one; she's many and I am like her. I will fall in love with Mrs. Hermenes. Love letters will pile up at her door from me.

Mrs. Hermenes and I talk about the night I didn't see what happened. He put his tongue in your throat and said kiss me sounds so much like kill me that I can't switch it. He wanted you to kill him, I say. It's a language problem I can't get over.

He didn't have a gun that I could see, she says. What was I going to kill him with? He wasn't as bad as some.

Nevertheless! You didn't agree to do it. The way she looks at me, I falter. I don't understand.

What have you ever agreed to? she asks. What have you ever been asked?

Al, ask me a question. Ask me anything. Ask me if I like to fuck you. Al, ask me if I am who you think I am, Al, ask. Ask me the distance to the moon, Al, ask me!

My mother and I talk. Another thing about my mother is she's always available. What I want to know is did he ask you—my father, I mean—were you ever asked? What have you ever agreed to?

She says: It goes back so much farther, Lucy. It is so much more complicated than you think and there's no end to it.

Al says: What good are questions? I read your mind already. Sure, Al.

Mrs. Hermenes says: No one ever asks me.

I am asking, I say. Will you take me away with you?

What good does it do to ask if it's the wrong question, even the wrong kind of question? If you aren't asked, do you exist? I associate myself with what I can't ask, with what I can't ever have asked.

My mother says she was a tom-girl and she climbed trees all day as if it's something that will dazzle me. Her misjudgement of me is sublime. I can slide right through the holes in her thinking. OK, Mother, what else did you do? Were you a good girl, too? Were you licked, too?

I think my mother has disappeared. I think this one's an impersonator. She has this past that can't be said to be a past and a present that isn't a present and I am her future. And who am I? Maybe my father doesn't exist, either. Maybe without asking, he fucked her and left. Maybe he's only a memory: am I only a memory, too? If I met him, would he remember my mother? I have only one story about him, this one: he had killed some people, maybe lots of them, and it was in the war—some war. Does that make him a killer forever?

My mother says to me: Of course he's not a killer.

Maybe he's still killing, I say. Maybe he didn't stop. Maybe that's why he never comes back.

Oh no, she says. He never came back because he was already married. He would have loved you if he'd known you.

So, my daddy's wife is the great big secret. She called to her sailor across the sea to come back to her while love letters arrived from everywhere for my father from the women he'd loved and killed. But I have Al, my Eskimo boy, my hero, my big Aleutian loose sunny boy. With Al, I'm any girl I want to be.

For my mother, I am her unforgettable love, her future dimension, her imaginary life, her look-out on life. We are filtered through each other: I make her up and she's sweet, so so sweetly she wants me. She's not real, nor am I. We are comfort, we anger, we are slime filth death in a moment of delirium. Men in our lives: mother is a one-man woman, I'm not. When mother stops looking, I will be gone. I will be the vanished truth of her past.

Papina says: Once I was out in the ocean and I ran into a man who said he knew me. I was in the water—swimming in the ocean—and he was alone in a boat. He was all alone. His wife had left him and his children had left him.

Why had they left him? I ask.

They had left because he stank. Or he drank. I don't remember which.

Was he crying?

Yes, he cried. Quietly. Over the edge of his little boat, his tears fell.

Like gentle raindrops?

Yes, he cried like a good slow rain. He cried to be rid of his tears. But more kept coming. He couldn't find the end. That's where I came in.

You stopped his tears?

No, I made him cry even more. I was worse he said than his wife. He said I broke his heart in one instant whereas she had taken many years.

Maybe this man was my father, I say. He sails all over the world. For fourteen years, he has sailed without stopping. Imagine that.

He might have been your father. Then, he was crying for you.

Some of the questions I will ask my father are:

Did you know my mother was pregnant?

Did you know about me?

How many people did you kill?

Do women swim out to your boat?

Should I swim out to you?

I ask myself should I swim out to him where the ocean is everywhere around and easily ease my body into the water where I am like a bird? I mean I can swim and sing. Should I go to the man who is my father who doesn't know me, and I am only the moment of asking, when he has bombed my world? Should he be the one who travels forever while I am the one who waits? He dropped the bomb and I'm not kidding. And if my mother had told me my daddy bombed the world, would I have waited so long for him?

Of course, I can blame my mother who taught me how to wait. There's nothing more like prison than waiting, and while you wait you think these thoughts: will he like me, am I pretty enough, am I smart enough, am I tough enough, too tough, too much too little too big too tall too many arms too many toes, am I going to be able to talk when I see him, will he listen, will he be wild and rugged and never say a word just leave—he'll leave and I'll leave. His only answer has been silence.

Will there be other women swimming around his boat, mermaids who beg for his favors, murmuring to him to take them into the boat where they will die of love, happy to be there, seen by the man who bombed the world? Daddy's women—such a great big secret.

Instead, here's where I jump: I swim into the white wavy rivers of Mrs. Hermenes where everything is always more than it seems, where there's more to see than meets the eye, and I am my mother's future.

The Holocaust Museum

The housewife in toreador pants had been squinting from the moment he walked in; when Horvitz introduced him, she went nuts.

"Chet Stoddard who had the talk show?"

"That's right." Oh Christ, he thought. Why hadn't he used an alias?

"I knew it!"

"Isn't that something," said the husband.

"Great memory," said Chet with a Dick Clark smile.

"He doesn't tell me *anything*, this guy." Horvitz smiled too but a little awkwardly. He didn't like surprises, especially at the beginning of a pitch.

"That was a good show. We *watched* that show, didn't we, Kenny?"

"Yes, we did," said Kenny, matter-of-fact. "You were one of the first guys to jump into the audience."

"That's right," said Chet. "With the long microphones. They called 'em shotgun mikes."

"Shotgun mikes!" Kenny effused, turning to his wife. "I remember that."

"We're not going to be on a talk show, are we?"

"Not even an infomercial," said Horvitz, taking over the reins.
"Not today, I hope," said Marion. "I'm having a bad hair day."
ViatiCorps helped the terminally ill cash in life insurance, pro-
viding the option of accelerated benefits. The debt-ridden former
personality dropped by for an interview, then signed on as an "independent seller's advocate" trainee. Kenny and Marion Stovall were
glad to have a nominal public figure in the house—somehow, it
made the investment more of an adventure, and less of a risk.

"How did you become involved, Chet?" That was the dentist.

"Well, I do a lot of fund-raising," he lied. "Walkathons, benefits. I met Stu at the carnival."

"For Children with AIDS," said Horvitz. "They had a tremendous amount of celebrities this time around. Tom Hanks and his
wife Rita always make an appearance. They're good people. Jerry
Seinfeld, Marcia Clark, Jay Leno." He turned to Chet. "There's
someone who'll give you a run for your money."

Chet rolled with the punch. "He's got a helluva car collection.
I was an unlucky man this year—got trapped in a ring-toss booth
with Sharon Stone. It was sheer hell." The dentist asked if the star
wore panties and was promptly swatted by his wife. "Let's just say
that with or without, she arouses some fairly basic instincts."
Everyone laughed as Marion went for coffee.

"Anyway," said Horvitz, "Chet liked what we were doing and
wanted to come along to see how this thing works, on a personal
level."

"I hope that's not too much of an intrusion," Chet said diffi-
dently.

"Hell, no." said Kenny, " but I warn you: by the time you leave
here, I *will* be your dentist."

"Kenny, stop it!" cried Marion, from the kitchen.

"You have to promise to bring in a photo for my Wall of
Stars."

"It's a deal."

Horvitz dug in. "Kenny, your profession certainly hasn't been untouched by this terrible disease and its attendant controversies."

"I hate to say that's true."

"As you know, there's a lot of lip service given to 'awareness.' What's wonderful about ViatiCorp—and its database of professionals like yourselves—is that you and Marion can do something concrete, something tangible to ease human suffering."

"That's what's so appealing," said Marion, bringing in the tray. She looked to her husband, then added: "To me."

"How exactly does it work?"

"Simplicity itself. I have a client who's perfect to wet your feet with."

Horvitz reached for his satchel and Chet passed it on. He sorted through documents, grousing about life as a "great paper chase." Then he found what he was looking for: a Polaroid of a wispy-haired man in his forties. Chet knew the picture had been taken by a nurse who supplied ViatiCorps with leads on the dying, for a percentage.

"He's a costume designer. Has a T-cell count of twenty-two."

Marion looked pained as she examined the photo. "Is that very bad?"

"It's not great."

"What's a normal count, Stu?" asked the dentist, with alacrity.

"It's a bit arbitrary but as a guide or indicator, that's about all we have. The government defines full-blown AIDS as anything under a hundred T-cells." Marion screwed her eyes and nodded. "You and I may have six or seven hundred. Funny thing is, you can have nine hundred and still be on your way out."

Ken shook his head. "That's insidious."

Marion tucked now shoeless feet underneath her and studied the photo. Chet noted a passing resemblance to Sally Field. "What's his name?"

"Philip Dagrom. He's actually fairly well known for what he

does. He was working on *Blue Matrix* up until a month or so ago. I saw him on Friday—he's pretty much clinically depressed."

"Who wouldn't be?" said the dentist.

"He doesn't *look* all that terrible," said Marion, grimly fascinated. "Don't they usually have those spots? What are they called?"

"Kaposi's sarcoma. Phil's had everything *but* KS. Now, he's losing his sight."

"Real sci-fi stuff, isn't it?" Chet chimed in.

"It is diabolical, believe me." said Horvitz. They made a fairly decent tag team. "But Phil's a fighter. We're still looking at an expectancy of three to six months—don't quote me now!"

"Was he an addict?"

"No, no. A hemophiliac—also gay."

"Wow," said Marion. "Double whammy time."

"I've worked on hemophiliacs."

"I always wanted to know," said Chet, "how you fill a cavity in that situation."

"Very carefully!" laughed the dentist. "What kind of insurance does he have?"

"A two hundred thousand-dollar policy. We can get it for maybe sixty cents on the dollar. You become eighty percent beneficiaries, with ViatiCorps retaining twenty."

"Receivable upon his death, of course."

"That is correct. And subject to federal tax, not state."

"Why did he wait until now?" asked Ken. "Pretty soon, he won't be able to enjoy himself."

"That's the risk they take. Maybe he didn't need the money—until now. Or maybe he was just in denial. You have to understand there's a finality involved in the selling of a policy."

Marion bounced up. "I've got *great* pastries from Mäni's, sugar-free—muffins, too. Chet?"

"Love some."

"Then follow."

Chet brought his coffee with him. On the way, he amended his observation. He told her she looked like a young Mary Tyler Moore and Marion seemed to like that.

Back in the living room, the dentist was concerned. "Stu...if we do the deal, what happens if he lives a full twelve months—or more?"

"It's an inexact science, but I have a pretty good gut. We'll also furnish a doctor's opinion so you know we're not whistling in the dark. Let's say, for argument's sake, he lives a year instead of six months. You'd still be earning twenty-three percent on your money."

The dentist nodded. "That's better than CDs."

Chet chose a chocolate croissant while Marion poured a refill. She asked if he wanted sugar and he said, "Just dip your little finger in there." Marion blushed; all in good fun. Gotta keep a hand in, Chet thought.

"Soupy Sales used to come on your show all the time," she said.

"He was marvelous," said Chet. "An early genius of the medium, like Ernie Kovacs."

"And those pie fights! Weren't those crazy days?"

"They certainly were. Good days."

They walked back to the living room and Marion replenished the cups. Horvitz was explaining how the couple could go in on a pool if they were leery of forking over the full amount.

"What will Mr. Dagrom do with the money, Stu?" she asked. Her husband was tucking into a bear claw. "If we buy the policy and give him the cash?"

"I understand he wants to take a cruise. I think he'd like to die in Greece. He evidently used to travel there quite a bit."

The dentist grew pensive. "I know this is a pretty big hypothetical, Stu, but let's say—for argument's sake—that out of the blue, a cure is found."

Marion was mildly embarrassed. "I don't think we have to worry about that, honey." She looked toward Stu. "I mean, I don't mean to be a pessimist."

"I'm glad you asked," Horvitz said. "It's a good question, ask anything, that's why we're here—put it all on the table, so there aren't many surprises." The advocate clasped hands together as if in prayer then placed them to his lips. "Even if a cure were found, and that's highly unlikely"—a glance at Marion—"from everything we know…the people we're dealing with are just too sick to be helped." His logic was irrefutable; the room responded with a moment of silent gravity. "What I'd really like to get you in on," he said, emptying a second pink packet into his coffee, "is an IV drug-user. Once you hand them the money, they tend to shoot it straight into their arms. Dramatically shortens expectancy."

The dentist's wife was an exception. Not too many people recognized him anymore and that was a blessing.

He used to look like his letterman homeboy from Wayne State, Chad Everett. Chet 'n' Chad, gridiron buds. People thought they were brothers. They came to Hollywood and got jobs parking cars at the Luau on Rodeo Drive. Those were prehistoric days, when the street had a leafy small-town charm—nineteen sixty-two. A twenty-four hour coffee shop at the corner of the Beverly Wilshire was always good for star-gazing: Broderick "Ten-Four" Crawford and Phil Silvers, Nick Adams and Frank Sutton (Sarge from *Gomer Pyle*). One night after work Chet smoked some reefer, walked to the hotel and plunked himself down in a booth where Tony Curtis was holding court. No one seemed to care. He chatted up a redhead, the roommate of Curtis's girl. Her name was Lavinia Welch and she was a secretary at the Morris Agency around the corner. Her father, a writer for Bob Hope, was a client there. She was nineteen years old.

They started dating and Lavinia pushed him on auditions. He won bit parts in *The Sons of Katie Elder* and *Follow Me, Boys!* and a recurring role on TV's *Rawhide*. Lavinia wanted to marry but Chet was still sowing wild oats. When she caught him in bed with her roommate, they split up. He spent days and nights drinking and playing pool at Barney's Beanery, back when the place still had a FAGGOTS STAY OUT sign nailed above the door. The barflies, especially showbiz fringers, knew Chet from his television work and accorded him real-actor status. He moved nearby so he wouldn't have to drive—he'd been busted twice for DUI. That was okay too because all the sluts and fine ladies liked driving him home.

His career foundered—cut from *The Wild Bunch*, Chet never worked as a film actor again. He crawled back to Lavinia and after they married, the father-in-law helped buy them a house in a new development called Mount Olympus. That was fitting because Lavinia—new husband and new digs, high above the glittering city—really did feel like a God in Heaven. He remembered a time long ago, the first day of summer: Lavinia threw her dad a surprise party on his birthday. Chet felt free and easy, out from under. Things hadn't turned out the way he'd expected, but they never did, not for anyone. From the backyard, the Hollywood sign looked impossibly, hilariously near. Jack Cassidy and Shirley Jones were there and the TV producer Saul Frake. At dusk, Chet and Jack smoked a roach by the pool and everyone played charades. When the game was over, Chet launched into a *Tonight Show* improv, sitting on the diving board introducing Jack as his first guest. The actor had just finished shooting *Bunny O'Hare* and Chet asked if there was any truth to his "reputed long-term affair with Ernie Borgnine." Saul Frake laughed so hard he broke a blood vessel in his eye.

Frake called two weeks later, wanting to know if Chet would be interested in hosting a talk show. He thought it was one of Cassidy's pranks, but Saul paid for a test and Jack was gracious enough to replay their expurgated poolside shenanigans for the camera. Saul convinced the network boys they had something special and they bit—four months later, *The Chet Stoddard Show* debuted. That first week, guests included Bobby Rydell and Judy Carne, the cast of *Don't Bother Me I Can't Cope,* Dionne Warwick and Karen Valentine, the ubiquitous Joey Bishop, dancer Larry Kert, a Lloyd's of London man who insured anything, the Ace Trucking Company comedy troupe and Eartha Kitt. *Medical Center's* Chad Everett dropped by and they cut up old times with clubby, pre-gonzo repartee, a Rat Pack of two. Chet was quick and telegenic, but after eighteen months the show fizzled. By then, he'd already bought a Cobra for the hooker who supplied him with coke. At the final taping, he announced Molly's birth, then flew to Vegas and lost sixty thousand dollars in forty minutes. When Lavinia came to get him, he fractured her skull with a chair during a black-out at the Sands.

They divorced. He stayed in town to be close to his daughter. Somewhere around nineteen seventy-nine, he free-based himself into a heart attack. When Chet recovered, he returned to Michigan (those were the go-go years of detox) and found his Twelve-Step niche, becoming a paid counselor and proselytizer for the cause.

Now, he had returned to the city that once held so much promise—and somehow still did—to buy and sell the bones of the dead.

That night, he went trolling for HIVs at a Narcotics Anonymous meeting in Van Nuys. Horvitz said those were good places for leads. The ones restricted to sero-positives were easy to crash—no one asked questions. Chet watched and listened, attuned to money woes. Not everyone had life insurance. Finding out who did was tricky, especially if you weren't infected yourself; one didn't want to be tagged a policy-chaser. Sussing out candidates was dicey all around. Though he used an alias, eventually some trivial pursuiter was bound to know him as Chet Stoddard, boob-tube relic. Winding up on the "Where Are They Now?" page of a tabloid wasn't a pleasant prospect. ONE-TIME TALKER FULL-TIME HAWKER: ADVANCES $$ TO WALKING DEAD. The meeting was lower-scale then Chet would have wished. Lots of bad news bears: sour prison faces, weepy dementia heads, remorseful crack bingers and the usual quota of self-important alcoholics—smug vampires who felt less hopeless hanging with the pozzies. Whenever they stood to speak, you could feel the room's fatal contempt. Around mid-meeting, Chet realized there was a halfway house next door and that explained it; a pissy, policy-poor crowd if ever he'd seen one, hard-core wraiths who rode the RTD to get their methadone. Still, you never knew when that stuntman (Aetna) or production designer (Prudential) might stand and share. Expect the unexpected, Horvitz always said.

Luckily, he remembered the party. Someone started a group for heteros with AIDs and tonight they were having a shindig. Chet fished in the glove compartment for a flyer given him by one of his Viatical co-workers: Oakhurst Drive, south three-hundreds. That was Beverly Hills, over by Olympic—Persian World. No mansions but sure as hell no halfway houses, either. Sounded promising.

The modest two-story home was probably in the eight hundred thousand range. The canape-eaters were nicely dressed, to be sure, and none had the Look except one—a swarthy, charismatic man with thick Yves St. Laurent glasses, a stylish cane supporting sinewy legs and a telltale girth that betrayed (to the trained eye) a set of diapers. Emblazoned across his T-shirt was: I SURVIVED THE HOLOCAUST MUSEUM. He was holding court, in the middle of one of those comically anarchic HIV riffs featuring Mothers in Denial, Sado-Healthcare Worker Mayhem, Brides in Dementia on Their Wedding Days and other assorted gruesomely hilarious phantasmagoria. A black-haired boy ran twittering circles around him, mummifying the monologist with imaginary streams, like a maypole.

Chet was about to knock at the bathroom door when a woman in a crazy miniskirt emerged.

"This is the hour of lead," she said, looking straight in his eye. "Remembered, if outlived, as freezing persons recollect the snow..." He smiled and she went on, very dramatic, "First, chill: then, stupor—then, the letting go." She held an arm toward the toilet, like Vanna White. "You're free to wash up now. I am through vomiting."

He found her in the backyard a few minutes later. Her name was Aubrey and this was her house.

"How long have you known?" she asked, out of nowhere.

How long have you... His mind stuttered: she assumed he was HIV-positive. Chet scrambled up the slick rock of her question— the Question of all Questions, it seemed—trying not to fall into the swallowing sea. "About six months."

"You're a virgin."

"You?"

"Seven years, eight come May. What do you do?"

"I work at the Holocaust Museum." It was supposed to be a kind of joke.

"No shit, the Wiesenthal? What do you do there?"

"Acquisitions."

"Well, that makes you the perfect host—for this party, I mean." She nodded toward the diapered man, expostulating poolside. "Did you see Ziggy's shirt?"

"Pretty fuckin' funny."

"You're not going to sue, are you?"

She was swept away by new arrivals and Chet milled around, waiting for her to get free. He'd used his real name and was glad about that. After a while he decided to leave, thinking the time they had in the yard was as good as it would get—tonight. On the way out, she slipped a card into his shirt pocket. He didn't look until he was in the car.

Trysts & Confabulations

Aubrey Anne Turtletaub
(310) 279-1722

The dentist and his wife finally took the viatical plunge. When Horvitz brought the cashier's check to the dying costume designer, Chet went along.

The bungalow on Cynthia Street had a Grecian facade. An Abyssinian slept through its sunny porch sentinel. Ryan, Philip's roommate, showed them in. The house was clean and bare, low-budget minimalist. In the living room were a few Noguchi lamps, a tulip in a tall vase and the requisite Mapplethorpe photo book. It sat on a low boomerang table like a stage prop.

Philip lay in a hospital bed, neck arched back, eyes closed, mustachy open mouth. A male nurse smiled at the visitors, lowering the volume of *The Flying Dutchman*. *The closest he'll get to Greece,* Chet thought, *is inside a fucking urn.* The lids fluttered and Philip coughed; Ryan handed him a glass, guiding the straw to his mouth.

"I knew you were awake," said the roommate. "He always pretends to sleep."

"The Great Pretender," Philip muttered, clearing his throat while lifting himself on sharp elbows.

"Stu's here," Ryan said, pitched a little louder. "Looks like you won the Lotto."

Philip smiled broadly. Horvitz asked how he was doing. The lucky policy seller coughed while Ryan answered for him.

"Not so good."

"Not so good," echoed Philip, rheumily.

"Yesterday was better."

He closed his eyes as the roiling clouds of a coughing jag loomed then passed, chased by merciful winds. "Yesterday was *definitely* better." Cued by Ryan, the others laughed. "As David Bailey said,"—eyes opening again—"there is nothing uglier than the sight of four men in a car. Well. Maybe four men with Kaposi in a car."

"Forgive him," said Ryan, with mocking affection. "He slips in and out of dementia."

"Why, pastor! You *must* try Dementia, the new altar boy—I've been slipping in and out all day!"

"Now listen, my son—"

They went on like that until more cough clouds overtook their cabaret. "He might have pneumonia," said Ryan, sotto voce. The elder viatical rep removed an envelope from his attaché. Upon Philip's convulsive recovery, the roommate placed it in hand.

"Mr. Horvitz brought us a little check."

"Checks and balances," said Philip, with that mustached smile; it made Chet forlorn. He fingered the paper. "Well, this is glorious. We must call the limousine company, at once."

"When do you leave on your voyage?" asked Horvitz.

"Friday," said the roommate, somewhat skeptically.

"Will you manage?" Chet thought his boss's grave, stagy modulation had belied the euphemism.

"Better believe we'll manage," said the plucky invalid.

"Big boys don't die," Ryan said.

"And white men don't jump—but boy, do they Gump."

"So wish Jason and his Argonaut well."

Just before dessert, Aubrey Turtletaub took a fistful of pills from a Kleenex. She pressed each to her lips as if to divine a codeword before letting it pass—admitting them one by one, with slow, steady intimacy while Chet confessed. Well, half confessed, because there was no way he was going to discuss his short-lived career as a rising viatical settlement advocate.

Chet told her he knew the party was for positives only, but hadn't been deterred. Aubrey smiled mordantly and called him a "singles night bottom-feeder." Shamefaced, he apologized for misleading her on his HIV status. It's just that he got so flustered when she asked, *How long have you known?*

"How many years did you say you've been sober?"

"Four, going on five." That was the truth.

"People tend to get squirrely around that fifth chip," she said. "I know I did."

"I still feel like a jerk."

"You just didn't want to disappoint."

"Maybe. It gets a little twisted. You did dazzle me, though—I guess that was part of it."

Aubrey smiled; she liked that. "Sure you're not one of *those?*"

"What do you mean?"

"Oh, there was a chick who hung around forever—we finally had to tell her to fuck off. She was *desperate* to test positive, had no life. A *huge* chick—five-two, two-fifty. She was a *wall*. Her old man taught jumping. Parachuting. He was pretty strange himself. She started taking his AZT when he died—I mean *before, before* he died! She was always asking people for their Zovirax, so we finally said, *Here, bitch—take it.* Everyone has shitloads of Zovirax. And she's *still* testing negative."

Chet eyed the last of the pills. "They *do* look sort of appetizing. Mind if I—"

"Go right ahead," she said, without missing a beat. "This one puts hair on your liver."

On the way back to Oakhurst, they drove to Roxbury Park. He'd been to AA clubhouse meetings there. Aubrey pointed to an apartment building with a Frank Gehry penthouse floating above the trees, a tiled post-modern elysium. They walked in darkness and sat on a bench in front of the lawn where the retirees did their Sunday-bowling.

"I was married. He was a lawyer. We weren't rich, but he did okay. You know, the Tom Hayden type, public-interest. We tried having kids, for six years—nothing. That turned out to be a good thing though, I guess. It ended. He has two now, boy and a girl. Then I met this guy through my brother. I wasn't really looking. My brother works in film, does *rather* well. Anyway, this guy was an editor and I wound up apprenticing. It felt good. I never really had a vocation—God, that sounds dumb! 'Vocation.' White-trashy. But I *liked* editing—that sounds dumb too, I know. I guess what I *really* liked was the idea of cutting something together, having to make sense of something, be in that kind of control. *Some* kind of control. I decided I was going to 'edit' my life. Hey, why not? Naturally, I fell in love with the man who was teaching me. Women are like that." She laughed. "Jake—the editor, that was his name—he was a sweet man and I was needy, to put it mildly. Sexually, I was *starved*, not to mention emotionally. I mean, at this point if it wasn't for the fertility stuff—having a kid became an *obsession*—I don't think my husband (the lawyer) would have ever *touched* me. And most of the ways we tried, he didn't *have* to! I mean, it was bad. I got pretty out there for a while. Anyway, we divorced. I got pregnant right away with Jake—of course, right? He was *ecstatic*—I mean, Jake was. Am I confusing you? I look back and...Jake used to sweat at night, I mean sweat *a lot*. I thought it was just the sex—he was *so* attracted to me. There was never a question about that...and I just wasn't thinking in any other terms. This was a good, gentle man. Never used drugs. Zephyr was negative—that's our son—so *something* went right. Jake got sick a few months after Zeph was born. Six months later, he died. Wanna see something?"

Aubrey searched her pocketbook while the wind gusted the trees outside the designer aerie. She stuck a snapshot in his hand. "Isn't he beautiful?"

"I saw him at the party."

"My American Zephyr—we named him after a train, you know."

When Chet got home, there was a message from Horvitz. He turned off the machine; he would listen in the morning. Then he'd call and quit—death takes a holiday. He fell asleep and dreamed Aubrey was a guest on the old talk show. The theme was "People Who Have Recovered from AIDS."

He awoke around six, lonely and bloated. The damp morning paper was stuck in the hedge. Chet sorted out the sections he wouldn't read—he always tossed the classifieds and the sports. Must be a redwood a year.

He made himself a cappuccino and retrieved the personals. It was surprising to find *Women Seeking Women* and *Men Seeking Men* in the stodgy *L.A. Times*—he felt like Rip Van Winkle. A 900 number let you hear the voice of the person who placed the ad. Chet skimmed the messages as a goof, listening to the singsong sixty seconds allotted to lure Mister Right. All the women were attractive professionals who liked long walks on the beach and "lots of hugs, and other things too"; Vanessa Williams and Helen Hunt lookalikes searching for their "knight in shining Armani"—sensuous, spiritual, funloving, non-smoking Mensans in pursuit of politically incorrect, financially secure family-oriented men "willing to lie about how we met." One or two even said they had beautiful daughters and it sounded to Chet like some kind of bonus burger come-on, insurance against rejection.

His eyes floated down:

TERM, ILL-DJF redhead seeking 40ish SJM for Bach & Bagels brunch, Topanga hikes and hugs. Must cry at Schindler's (and laugh at Letterman's) List; picnic under stars at Bowl with wine, cheese and long-stemmed kisses. RU the 1?

He punched in the code number, booting up the cheerful voice: "Hi! I'm Marcie and I want to thank you for calling. I'm a 44-year-old woman, attractive and outgoing. I have cancer—there, I said it! I like to be up front with my illness. But I can do just about everything a woman can do, and I'll be around for a long time because I'm *very strong.* Gee, this is hard! Here goes: I'm looking for a man to share my life with, someone who likes cuddles and long kisses, with a (hopefully) wicked sense of humor. I like symphonies, cineplexes and City Walk, and *love* to read: Cormac McCarthy, Anne Tyler, and *anyone* who's won the Booker...though I'm not above slumming on the Via Rodeo with Jackie Collins (I draw the line at Joan). If I had a motto, it'd be: 'Girls just want to have fun.' Tell me yours—"

He left his number and a fake name after the tone.

IMMEDIATE CASH for the Terminally Ill

We are committed to advising terminally ill people who seek financial assistance by selling their life insurance policy.

The transaction is quick, easy and confidential. See new places, see old faces. Do something you've always wanted to do. Take care of business—or pleasure.

LIVING WELL IS THE BEST REVENGE

We know the effect of stress on the immune system and do everything we can to minimize your effort.

Generally, the viatical companies pay between 40%-80% of policy face amount, paid in a lump sum by wire transfer or bank check. The purchase price is based upon size of policy, cost of ongoing premiums, life expectancy, etc. and must meet the following criteria:

- 6 mo. to 4 year life expectancy
- policy face value from $10,000 to $3,000,000
  (lower/higher amounts are considered)
- policy is beyond the contestability period of –

He sat in the outer office, scanning a ViatiCorps brochure. Horvitz appeared behind the girl at the desk, waving him back.

"I'm sorry you're leaving, but I understand. It's not for everyone."

"And I thought show business was depressing."

"Thinking of giving the talkers another shot?"

"Too many out there right now."

"Every time I pick up *TV Guide*, there's a new one. Where do they find these people?" He took an envelope from a drawer, handing it to Chet. "Your paycheck and…a partial commission from the 'dentist' deal."

"I appreciate that, Stu."

"Not at all. Keep in touch. If you change your mind, the door is open."

"I'll call you."

"By the way, Phil Dagrom just died. The costume designer."

"I'm not surprised."

"You know, he got much better—after we gave him the money. Happens all the time: pressure eases, spirits rise, they get better. And Ryan—the roommate?"

"What about him?"

Horvitz smiled like a maitre d' with no more tables. "He ran off with the money."

"You're kidding."

"With a lover. They get on a plane to Paris."

"Oh Jesus."

"And poor Philip dies forty-eight hours later."

"Did you tell the dentist that?"

Did Chet think he had no finesse? "I told the dentist Mr. Dagrom died in Crete, in his roommate's arms, while the sun went down on a ruin. Hey! Isn't that what Jackie O called it when she gave Onassis a blow job? Going down on a ruin?"

Aubrey was subdued. He was desperate to touch her, kiss her. The timing was bad, she said. She'd been to UCLA that day for tests. Something was funny with her eyes. They dilated the pupils and made her scan a grid—she was certain it was CMV. If the virus was confirmed, she'd have to take medicine each day through a shunt in her chest. She was forthright and resolved except when it came to Zephyr. She didn't want the boy to see her around the house with a fucking permanent tube.

Chet laid her shaking body down. She wet his face with tears and sex and searched his eyes with the drama of the inchoately blind. He pulled off the condom but Aubrey made him put on another. She came in great, shuddering waves, and when Chet let himself go he hated that his come couldn't find hers, turning stickily onto itself, sheer pornography; he wanted to give her his best, a viscous magic bullet—to fuck her to life as she'd been fucked to early death. Once outside, he tore off latex and quickly wrapped their bodies in the white sheets, as if to preserve and protect—to cleanse—through an improvised classicism of the bedroom.

Zephyr and the sitter were asleep on the couch when they came in. The girl quietly gathered her things while Aubrey lifted the unconscious child in her arms. She trudged upstairs and tucked him in, then called to Chet from the landing. They went right to bed. It was a long time since Chet had a sleepover. He hoped he wouldn't snore or cry out from a dream.

His last thoughts were of the treasonous roommate: Ryan the apostate, Ryan the cockatrice, *à table* at a swanky bistro, say, Le Voltaire, beneath what was once the master's house—supping on *canard aux cerises*, awaiting his lover's return from the urinal.

Wish Jason and his Argonaut well...

"Hello, is this Victor?"

"Who's calling?"

"Marcie—from the ad in the *Times.*"

Chet wanted to say he was just out the door but the words didn't come.

"Hi, Marcie. This is Victor."

"You don't sound like you."

"Don't be disappointed. I give better voicemail."

Marcie laughed softly. "Well, it's good to finally connect. Did you get my message?"

"You know, I did," Chet said glibly, survival instincts returning. "And I apologize for not calling you back. I was away and neglected to take your number with me."

"Someplace fun, I hope."

"Palm Springs."

"Ooh, I love it there—lucky you."

"Friend has a place at the Desert Princess."

"That's a good friend to have."

"We play golf and generally drink ourselves stupid."

"I wanted to thank you for calling. I know my message is a little *unusual...*"

"Not at all," said Mr. Slick. "I was touched by it." He pulled the ad from his daybook. "It was courageous. I admire your candor."

"Gets me in trouble sometimes. I guess a lot of people are turned off by that—honesty. I figure I'm already operating at a disadvantage. But people do tend to get intimidated and I'm glad you didn't."

Instead of saying, "The ridiculous thing is, since I left that message an old love came back into my life," Chet asked what kind of response she'd gotten.

"I wasn't exactly flooded with calls."

"Is that right?"

"There were a few—some nutcases. You don't sound too crazy."

"I've been known to get a little out of hand."

Her laugh was musical and appealing. "Some of these people were *way* outta hand. I never met with any of them, thank God. Do you mind if I call you Vic?"

"Not at all."

"I'm always giving people nicknames. I don't know why."

"How about Vicks Vapo Rub?"

She laughed again, really loosening up. "My mother used to *paint* me with that stuff. Have you answered ads before, Vic? I'm sorry—that sounded like a survey question, didn't it?"

"That's all right, Marcie. Oh, just once or twice."

"So what made you call *me?*"

"I don't know. I'm going through a lonesome time; you seemed a little lonely yourself." He sounded so spot-on authentic that it was killing him. "When I heard your voice, I thought, I'd like to get to know that person."

"That's sweet. Lonesome doves...did you like that show?"

"I *loved* that show."

"Oh. me too. I just eat up Robert Duvall. He's the sexiest man alive."

"Now, what about you? Have you met people this way?"

"Once. About a year and a half ago."

"What happened?"

"Fell in love!"

"How great."

"Aren't women silly?"

"You broke up."

"He died."

"Oh shit. I'm sorry. Was he ill? Is that how you—"

"Huh uh. He was fine when we met. We had a great time, How old are you?"

"Show me yours and I'll show you mine."

The tinkly laugh. "*Thir-ties...*"

"Fifties." He scanned the ad: *DWJF redhead seeking 40ish SJM for*—"Whoops. Too old, huh."

"No!" she said, unconvincingly. Somehow he didn't feel up to being blown off by someone who was terminal. "I find honesty *very* attractive. Besides, I have a real affinity for the fifties."

"That's good, 'cause I have a nostalgia for the thirties." They laughed together. "It said 'redhead.' Just how red are you?"

"Very. And I'm red all over."

"Like a fire truck?"

"Four alarm."

"Somebody better put you out."

"He better have a long hose."

"Never had a complaint."

"I'm sorry. That was terrible."

"You got my siren going now."

"I'll have to pull over, then."

"It's the law."

Her voice lost its jokey tone as she got down to business. "Did you want to get together, Vic?"

"Absolutely."

"There's one more thing I should tell you." Here's the part she says she shits in a bag. "I just wanted to tell you up front I'm a big woman—generously proportioned. Do you have a problem with that?"

"I'm a fireman, remember? When there's smoke, we enter all manner of structure."

"You know, I think I like you."

"Do I need to bring my ladder?"

"Just your hose—and maybe some rope."

"Now you've got my attention."

The laugh again—smokey, this time.

"Victor," she said, suddenly serious, "aren't you going to ask what's wrong with me?"

"We can talk about it when we see each other." Then, a little sly: "Think you can hold on until then?"

Aubrey wouldn't let him come to the hospital. When he called, she gasped like someone who'd just run a marathon. "*How! are you! can't! talk! call! back! how! are! you! do! ing! can't!*—" Diapered Ziggy occasionally picked up the phone and that's how Chet got his information.

She had a horrible rash, he said, a side effect of the drug taken intravenously for her eyes. And she was out of breath like that because she probably had bronchitis—the docs had ruled out PCP, a viral pneumonia. The minute he got her home, Ziggy was gonna do his alternative thing: ayurvedic eyedrops and hydrogen peroxide baths, ganoderma, schisandra and white atractylodes, ligustrum and licorice. Toad's breath and baby-tooth, if he had to.

Chet felt her weight on him at night. He carried her during the day, too—like the fat lady he read about in *Star* who strapped on her invalid husband before morning chores. Why this mawkish preoccupation, this neediness, this nostalgia for what they nearly were? Why now, why *this* woman—merely because she was dying? How obscene. Even as Chet told himself he loved her, the question cuffed his ear: how was it he hadn't forced a visit? He hated hospitals, spent too much time there recovering from too many battles lost. Days of infamy. He remembered the blur of visiting hours with a shudder, friends and flunkies come to view the perpetrator in his habitat. Aubrey was different that way—she wasn't cowardly, spiteful or ashamed; she wasn't a neurotic with a death wish. There was the thoughtful moment Chet reasoned that she'd want her privacy but after a week this delicacy showed its color of fraud. He went to bars and flirted instead, nursing drinks like a jilted man, telling himself lies about love's labors lost.

He kept calling her room—Chet knew she wouldn't answer—
and Ziggy didn't seem to mind picking up. Ziggy didn't judge.
They scheduled a spinal tap because Aubrey had lost some muscle
coordination. The doctors wanted to check for cryptococcal menin-
gitis, a fungal infection that swelled the brain. It was shoptalk for
Ziggy, inventory and nothing more. Voices subdued, they lolly-
gagged on the phone like teenagers with crushes on Death—guides
to the Holocaust Museum.

Marcie had seven or eight siamese that hung around in cliche
poses, like a cartoon for cat-lovers. She looked like a cartoon herself, with twinkly eyes, faultless fields of skin and a luxuriant head
of soft, orange hair. Chet couldn't imagine what kind of cancer left
someone so fat and sassy.

Before they went out, she wanted him to see her 8 X 10's—
Marcie in a negligee, "surprised" by the camera; Marcie as a nasty
meter maid, citation book in hand; Marcie pushing a whole shopping cart of detergent; Marcie as a *Saturday Night Live* bumble bee;
Marcie as some kind of crazed Valkyrie diva. A separate page listed talents ("Lambada, Net surfing and shopping. Some dialects")
and credits: *The Golden Girls, Burke's Law*, a Comedy Store Belly
Room stint, a *Larry Springer Show* whose theme was ample ladies.

The Nu-Art was showing an old French film about a woman
whose husband kills her lover in a duel. At the end, when
wifemistress died of grief, Marcie got teary-eyed. They had dinner
at Trader Vic's and Marcie drank Scorpions and talked about her
ex, a skydiver dead of AIDS. All in all, a real dream date.

The bit about her husband's parachuting school had a familiar
ring but Chet didn't connect it to anything until he opened the
bathroom cabinet and saw the AZT and nystatin, arithromycin,
ethambutol and bottles of Zovirax prescribed to different names—
including *aubrey a turtletaub*. Suddenly, he felt lost and depressed,
like an acrobat sacked from a dreary circus; outside the tent, the fat

lady waited, unsung. Where could he go, dressed up like a harlequin as he was? He padded his face with cold water, heard the dirty waves lap the decayed piles of forgotten pier, foam caught in bark like spittle. He dried himself with a tiny, embroidered towel while Marcie put on the Eagles—*Get Over It* blared stupidly from the speakers. She was standing there as he opened the door, ready to change places. On her way in, Marcie said, "Know what I'm gonna call you? Trader Vic's Vapo Rub."

What was she going to do in there? Better get on the phone if it's Number Two—a real circus elephant-type dump. Call 911 Roto-Rooter. Chet stifled a laugh. She was rummaging around, he could hear it through the tinny diatribe: *Get over it!* Maybe she'd just hose herself off then hop in the tub for a douche. The phrase 'manatee's ablutions' came to mind, and stuck. Chet cackled again then shook it off because it frightened him, welling up from too deep a place. He saw her in the tub again and quaked, choking off a howl. Get over it... He made his mind a blank but the instant Marcie appeared, he laughed out loud at the sight of her. She was uncomprehending but still friendly and Chet said it was a joke he'd heard, too vulgar to repeat.

"We've been avoiding something."

"No, we haven't," he said.

"I thought we should talk about it. Then we can just put it away."

"Sounds like a plan." The hysteria had passed. He felt cool and cocksure as a country star.

"I didn't bring it up at dinner, because you just seemed—I didn't think you wanted me to get into it..."

"Not true, darlin'. Not true at all."

"Some people are put off by my honesty."

"Well, you've said that—but not I, m'lady. I'm fearless Trader Vic."

"I believe that." She paused, as if to regroup. Chet tried making his mind blank again to avoid the treacherous shoals of hilarity looming off-prow. "What I have," she said gravely, "is relatively rare." He forced himself to think of the briny piles again, mind flitting about the room like a panicky bird; the piles became telephone poles and Chet a lineman, climbing rusty rungs impaled in the timber, bleeding with sap. "They call it hairy cell leukemia."

Chet belched a laugh, dizzying: a cork of snot blew from his nose, then he sprung up rigid, dissociative stare struck toward ceiling, lips white and quivering, barely holding on, pretending something was lodged in his throat.

"What's the matter? Vic? What is it?

> *hairy cell*
> *hairy cell*
> > *hairycellhairycell*

Trembling head to toe, he felt the strange ostentatious liberation of the exhibitionist.

"I'm sorry—please—I can't—" Marcie looked so weird and wounded.

> *hairy cell*
> *hairy cell*
> *hairy cell*

Letting everything go now, vamping, tittering, weeping -

> manatee

An explosion, stertorous laugh now hideous and unashamed like some beer-farting stag party lummox, backing to the door while Marcie rubber-necked, Trader Victor Mature excused himself, he'd call her tomorrow *hairy cell* he was sorry, he said, something wrong with him tonight, friend in hospital with AIDS, too much death, sorry he was acting like this, so *stupid*

Manatee. Hairy cell. Manatee
the stupid *joke*, nothing to do with her, he said—

hairy cell!

manatee!

hairy
hairy
hairy
hairy
hairy

yanking the door open, feverish, howling, pounding the road with his Fryes, running into the night elated like an arsonist from a burning disco.

He phoned the hospital in Sherman Oaks but Aubrey wasn't there. He drove by the Oakhurst house for almost a week, at different hours of day and night. There were no lights and nothing stirred. Chet revisited some NA/HIV meetings and was able to track Ziggy down.

The garden apartment was just south of Sunset, by the Virgin Megastore. The "infected faggot" cordially asked him in—that's what Ziggy liked to call himself. A burly volunteer from one of the AIDS organizations was just leaving. When he was gone, the shut-in held forth from the center of the living room in trademark stand-up despot mode.

"Why do they send me this straight guy who can't clean? I'm sorry, but the straight guys do *not* know how to clean a kitchen floor. He comes and he sits, with his Ziplock'd tuna sandwich and his little apple. *A polished little apple!* My ultimate horror is that when I'm bedridden, this motherfucker's gonna sit there and read aloud from Marianne Williamson! I mean, what is he *doing* here?"

"I've been trying to get hold of Aubrey."

"She's in a world of shit."

"What's happening?"

"She's toxo: toxoplasmosis. Attack of the Brain Parasites."

"Oh Jesus."

"*Totally* crazy and half paralyzed and that ain't all. Her brother got rid of her."

"What are you talking about?"

"She took a fucking *bite* out of him! Isn't that the most fabulous thing you ever heard? Very Anne Rice—and lemme tell you, he is the biggest, *meanest* cunt on the planet. Zev Turtletaub, the producer, ever heard? He of the Shelley Winters-sized arms, zee very grandest of Grand Wazoos. Zev's the one who introduced her to husband Jake—Jake was Zev's lover. Zev knew Jake was sick, and never told her! Jake was doing him in the hospital while Aubrey was giving birth. Well, our Miss Aubrey gave him a lovely going-away shove—now he's on the funicular to Dementia Street and Diarrhea Way as we speak!" Chet reached for a Marlboro and lit up, his first in eighteen months. "I know, 'cause I was *there*, right after it happened—before the parasites turned her into Sybil." Ziggy started to cackle. "She said she was trying for his *neck*, but he backed up and fell or something and hit his head. So she *jumps* on him and takes a chunk from his arm—then she *barfs* into his mouth! Oh God! Don't you just love it?"

The phone rang and Ziggy networked awhile. Whoever it was needed advice on whether to sue a hospital, healthcare worker, insurance company or possibly the government over some incident Chet couldn't discern. As far as Ziggy knew, the details—petty, real or imagined—didn't matter. It was *attitude* that counted. Attitude was agitprop; attitude was sacred; attitude was all. Today, "attitude" decreed that *someone* needed to be sued.

He hung up. "See, she was worried he was going to take Zephyr after she was gone. She didn't like that idea at all."

"Where is he?"

"Long gone. Underground railway. Vee haff ways."

"But where?"

Ziggy's jaw moved around, itching to blab. But the loquacious gadfly was mum.

"Gone in sixty seconds."

Chet went to Circuit City and bought himself one of those little satellite dishes—a gift to himself. He surfed until he got to T3. The screen read:

'THE FOXXXY CHANNEL'—ADULT MOVIES
ALL DAY—THEATER 10

Rating: NR
Cost: $ 6.00
(plus applicable taxes)

Started at: 4:30 A.M.
Time Left: 3:15:26
(Press ENTER to purchase program)
(Otherwise change channel)

When the show came on, a number of things were happening. A hostess was interviewing a comedian called the Jokeman. At the same time, half-nude girls struck lascivious poses on ratty motel-yellow couches; folks at home could dial a 900 number to access live on-camera one-on-ones with their favorites. The robo-nymphos pouted, preened and gyrated on the auction block, tweaking their nipples with red-lacquered pincers, snarling and working their tongues like the village idiot in a Monty Python sketch. It was amazing to Chet that this could be someone's idea of a hard-on. The medley format was surreal: in a decathlon of carnival burlesque, the Jokeman ran his crude shtick while hopped-up yeomanettes, in varied states of bullshit arousal, feigned underworld versions of mirth.

The camera discovered the girl at the end of the couch, and Chet got a start: it was his daughter. JABBA, her *nom de porn*, flashed on-screen in orange neon letters, like a game show's secret clue. She winked at the camera and crowed: "Jabba Dabba do!"

The last time he saw Molly was Thanksgiving Day, a few years back. She was on bail for possession and soliciting. He took her to the Sepulveda Velvet Turtle for turkey and all the trimmings. After, they saw Lavinia at the unkempt Mount Olympus place—what a mistake. Sixty pounds overweight and housebound with a stress fracture. Molly nodded out in her old room while Chet endured his ex's harangues and sophistic recriminations. It was two hours before they got out of there. He dropped Molly at a motel somewhere on La Brea.

The sweaty Jokeman stood before the camera like a boxer in a cheap interactive game. "A wife goes to her husband and says, 'I don't have any tits. I want you to buy me some tits.' Husband says, 'We can't afford it.' Wife starts crying. '*I want you to buy me tits.*' Husband says, 'Tell you what. Here's what you do. Get some toilet paper and rub it between your chest, okay? Wife says, 'What'll *that* do?' Husband says, 'Well, it sure worked on your *ass!*'"

The camera panned to the couch where Molly, hand inside panties, busied herself with the garish chores of simulated masturbation. She still managed to catch the punch line and laugh, a bad actress rehearsing for bedlam.

It was cold in the house. Chet found two dusty Placidyls

zipped into a weathered shaving kit. He swallowed them and got into bed.

His thoughts turned to Aubrey's boy. He wished they were on the road together—why not? He always wanted a son. Where would they go? Taos, maybe, or Santa Fe. Some big beautiful place with chapparal. Orphans from the plague, they'd be, riders on the storm. He'd find work on a big spread belonging to Hollywood-types who remembered him from the glory days. Saul Frake maybe had a ranch somewhere in Wyoming...Moab or Ketchum or Sedona—herds of bison à la Ted Turner. Or Chad Everett: an absentee landlord situation. Live in the caretaker's house. Take Zephyr everywhere, tutor him at home. There were laws about that—a boy didn't have to go to school if a parent taught him right. Part of the Homestead Act. Together, they'd learn the way of the Hopi and celebrate winter solstice, whittling *tithu* for prayer and protection from rough things. They would honor his mother—

Chet grew warm as the pills did their work. Tears lowered him like a soft rope into sleep. Holding fast as he fell, he begged his daughter's forgiveness. His sorrow had no bottom and mercifully, upon his awakening, could not be recalled to extinguish the hopes of this savage new morning.

PETER PLATE

The Devil's Quadrant

This is an anecdote, just a trifling about San Francisco. The way things work, this story may or may not be real; but we can always take solace in knowing this was an anecdote told at a perfect hour. The truth will not matter, since there isn't any, because as with everything else in the city, the facts have been stolen and rearranged.

These are the demographics and they point out where we are going.

In this story the landscape displays itself, starting with the sometimes bright, but often tarnished colors of 16th and Valencia streets in the Mission district. In the middle of the chi-chi cafes, the crack hippies, the cute, kitsch-inspired second hand stores, the speed vegans, the homeless guys and their shopping carts, a solitary man is sitting, hunching over on a bench at the Muni bus stop.

He is thinking about the summer of 1966. It was a season for change, the month of August to be exact. The man at the stop is reminiscing under questioning, of interrogatives posed to him from me, about a police officer he once shot.

It was a few weeks before the murder of sixteen-year-old Peanut Johnson in the Bayview district by a San Franciscan cop. It was a section in our tale where little was getting better, and it was fast becoming a time to destroy, to set fire to what was unhealthy, and to start over.

Riots ensued, fanning out from Third and Palou, spreading to the Fillmore. Martial law was declared; National Guard soldiers patrolled the neighborhoods. Three weeks after this, the Diggers began to feed homeless people in the panhandle of Golden Gate park. The world was turning quicker.

In the second chapter to the story, the man at the bus stop has reached the munificent age of forty-nine but he looks about seventy-five. His profile: tall and gaunt with piercing gray eyes that are murky or clear, depending on the amount of medication traveling through his bloodstream. But in between every opportunistic infection on the planet plaguing his body, he's got this thing about smiling at the most painful subjects.

"That's right," he says, wheezing. "I shot that cop right there on Albion street. He didn't have his badge on, but I had a gun," he grins.

He points up the street with a long finger. I know what he's talking about. The story could be left alone as a fragment, as something to tease the minds of readers, or to be employed as most words are, as a pause or as punctuation for circumstances that have become forgettable. Albion is just another typical block in the neighborhood, tree-lined, populated by nickel bag dealers, but apart from the geography, another factor has entered the passage of events.

"Listen to this," I say to him.

His name is John Bigarani. He was a well known police officer who gained prominence by repeatedly arresting and beating the poet Bob Kaufman in North Beach during the late 1950s. Bob Kaufman was a labor organizer from Louisiana and Texas, a black man and a jew, who was, arguably, the finest poet to arise from the propaganda campaign known as the beat generation.

"You're fucking with me," the man at the bus stop comments.

"I don't know much about poetry, but I didn't like cops, and that Bigarani, he was a bastard of a cop. The way he cracked heads open at the San Francisco State student strike a couple years after I shot him, man, it was breathtaking," he cackles. "But when I shot him, he didn't have his badge on. And when I got caught, I had to serve seven years in Soledad State prison."

With this incident, the story turns a page, or jumps several chapters ahead, not heeding the logical order of sequence, but rather, choosing its own destination at random, as to imply that nothing can be taken for granted anymore.

Among other things, it's possible to say the injuries Bob Kaufman suffered at the hands of John Bigarani resulted in permanent damage to his spirit and health. Some years later, the writer passed away. The policeman is still living (but the poet is hardly remembered).

That's a common refrain to any chronicle about this town; a narrative which accretes pieces, spewing them out like vomit from a drunk's open toothless mouth when too much has been taken in.

When we put two and two together, when we do our arithmetic like we learned in California's public schools: it seems that only in San Francisco, could a man presently expiring from AIDS, avenge a poet by shooting a cop, at the edge of the Valencia street housing projects in the summer time.

It's one of the angles we can look at the situation from, in an epic of unacknowledged debts. The names of the innocent have not been changed to protect the guilty. For the purposes of confidentiality, the man at the bus stop is called Paul Stevens, a community worker with the Mission Rebels on the day he put down John Bigarani.

I had the pleasure of meeting him on the sixth floor of the city prison. I was handcuffed to a bench near the holding cell, and he was sitting next to me. Several county sheriffs were discussing whether to kick the crap out of me or not.

Perky as hell, the gray-haired man on the bench introduced himself to me by whispering: "Relax. These assholes aren't jackshit." And I believed him.

Here is where the dialogue of Paul Stevens and myself began; it was the balmy evening of the Dan White riot on May 21st in 1979.

Some memories do not bear repeating; other recollections must be turned into ciphers that have hope and meaning for the living.

The story will emerge from when McAllister street went up in the flames of eleven burning police cars. Every window to San Francisco's city hall was broken; only the public library escaped harm.

For books are important; they possess the fiction that is always changing, and the stories themselves tell us: the city looks quite attractive when it's smoking. More accurate, less precious; untranslatable, and unable to present itself as a backdrop for tourists taking pictures

"Remember? The police picked me up on Castro street," Paul Stevens quips. "I was a nurse, and I was wearing my surgical smock. But when I stepped out of a taxi cab, and I saw cops attacking people in the street, I started throwing rocks. So what were you busted for?" he asks me.

"For torching a cop car," I reply.

This is where the anecdote could possibly stop. We could save our places with a book marker for the next time. It will be the journey of a thousand jail cells, and the less we imagine what this is like, the better off we feel.

At this very moment, Paul Stevens sits at the Muni stop when the weather is good; he stays in bed when the temperatures are low. The conclusion to the story will become a dream, hastily planned, irrevocable.

"This is my last year," he informs me. "The doctors can do so much. Chemotherapy can only take you so far. Do you know what I mean?"

Where he is heading to, that's where this story will take us. He announces his own departure from life while gazing at the exhausted drift of traffic on Valencia street. Born in a Catholic orphanage, the city is Paul's body, and he has worn it well.

"But it doesn't matter," he says, shaking his head. "It doesn't fucking matter."

I stare at his face, and I see the last days of Bob Kaufman. I glance at 16th street, at the mojados, the pretty college students, the winos, and the police station down the block, to see a river with Paul Stevens' name floating on its surface. I look to myself and I know these episodes were borrowed, fabricated, deformed.

What are the choices? There aren't any. From here, we can only go back to the beginning again, because no story can end without an act of freedom, not in San Francisco.

DICK HEBDIGE

Home. Alone.

Like many relatively recent immigrants, I live stretched and doubled up if not actively divided across disparate places, spaces, scales and times in ways that aren't readily reducible to a single representable 'experience' or coherent 'point of view.' It is, in fact, precisely in the in-between, in the empty gaps that hold those places, spaces, scales and times apart that the desire both to move and to stay put, the yearning for identity and home is continuously provoked and re-engendered. However, certain facts, even biographically inflected ones, are irrefutable. For instance...

The author lives in the fastness of Ventura county in southern California, amid antique orange groves in the foothills flanking the Santa Clara Valley at the end of a road that pulls up off the 126, a two-lane blacktop highway, then snakes off abruptly through a small town where most of the inhabitants speak Spanish and the average per capita income in 1994 levelled out a little over $8000 a year. Citrus production and processing are the main sources of employment though the town is also used as a location by the film and TV industries, its down-at-heel rural ambience appealing in particular to the makers of horror movies, westerns and small-town dramas set between the '30s and the '50s.

As he wrote this essay, he liked to think of pints of orange juice packaged at the Sunkist plant, half a mile away on Main Street, sitting in refrigerators in londonberlinstockholmparisfrance, places he had visited in person years before in what sometimes seemed like someone else's lifetime. He liked to think of the town where he now lived figuring as a spooky backdrop in an episode of HBO's *Tales of the Crypt* though he never got to see the episode in question as the local TV company doesn't run a cable out this far. When he wrote at night he was occasionally distracted by the mewling of coyotes squabbling close by in a pack, or, in the afternoons, by the circus antics, visible through the window above his desk, performed in his backyard by witless rabbits and gangs of nervous quail. One misty early morning in November he met a sick one-eyed owl that came, unannounced like an augur in some ancient myth, to die in the driveway.

One evening in the summer while sitting outside his house with a friend gazing up in silence at the canopy of stars, he heard automatic gunfire and the next day learned that two men, one a young Asian from British Columbia, the other a Chicano in his 40s from a neighboring town had been found dead outside the elementary school, shot in the back, executed gangland style. "L.A." his neighbors said, returning the crime to what everyone agreed was its proper point of origin, "it's just an hour's drive away." Later that same day he found bear prints in the groves behind his house pressed into the mud of the freshly irrigated soil with the preternatural clarity of an illustration in a backpacker's handbook.

He became obsessed with tracing the itineraries of other strangers from distant places who had passed close to where he now lived: the Spanish friars heading north on the Camino Real who traded with local Indians and recorded the first North American earthquake documented by Europeans in the mountains adjacent to this town...the Scandinavian millionaire philanthropist who, in the early 1900s, tried without success to found a Christian utopia, another New Canaan here in this idyllic setting...Helen Hunt Jackson, the Massachusetts writer who used the historic Rancho Camulos, two miles to the east as the setting for her Spanish mission novel, *Ramona*, the book boosters used for 50 years to sell the Southlands to romantically inclined retirees...Charles Manson and his Family, packed into their necromantic bus headed south on the 101, thirty miles to the west, en route to the Spahn Ranch, in the Simi Valley, detained, then released in 1968 by the sheriffs in nearby Oxnard...Bobby Beausoleil, Lucifer in Kenneth Anger's 1966 cult movie, *Lucifer Rising*, another charismatic drifter convicted three years later of the Gary Hinman killing travelling with *his* "family" on the same road in the opposite direction, headed for the remnants of the hippy scene on Haight.

He traced with one finger on a map the surging liquid passage, more lethal yet by far, of the wall of mud and water that swept down the Santa Clara river on the night of March 12, 1928 when the St. Francis Dam, designed by William *Chinatown* Mulholland collapsed beneath the weight of the 11.4 billion gallons backed up in the reservoir just above Castaic. He followed with his finger on paper the journey undertaken by this water, 'stolen' in a series of dubious buy-outs from the now dessicated Owens Valley by a cartel of wealthy southern California businessmen and siphoned 240 miles to feed speculative property development in northern L.A. county—a 60 mile deluge that left 1,200 demolished houses and at least 450 corpses in its wake. He read how one four-room house was lifted off its foundations to float a mile downstream, how, when the owners finally caught up with their newly mobile home resting on a mudbank, they found everything intact, the lamps still standing upright on the living room tables. Sometimes he would cross the road to the graveyard opposite the house he rented and he would read the names engraved on the single headstone erected in memory of the Savala family, swept westwards to Ventura and the ocean that night almost 70 years ago, the first names of four females—mothers, daughters, granddaughters—listed with their birthdates on one side of the stone, the names and birthdates of three males lined up on the other. So many birthdates spread out across the decades converging on a single Doomsday number.

"...home—the last safe place in a city that is already scary enough—no longer feels safe."
—*L.A. TIMES*, January 19, 1994

After the half-minute temblor of January 17, 1994, centered 30 miles away in Northridge, the author squatted in the darkness among the wreckage in his home and listened to the stock-taking on the radio news: 51 dead; 114,000 buildings damaged or destroyed, 13 freeways seriously hit, 2 trailer parks gutted in fires sparked by severed gas lines; 147,000 gallons of crude from a punctured pipe line leaked into the Santa Clara river; 150,000 households in rural Idaho without electricity as the entire west coast grid from Nevada to Alberta, Canada came crashing down in 30 shaking seconds. He read that the $12 billion price tag made this, financially at least, the greatest natural disaster in the history of the United States. He read that the *New York Times* had run an editorial suggesting, he hoped with some degree of irony, that the disaster was divinely ordained and in the *Weekly World News* he learned that 17 demons had been released from Hell (they were sighted emerging out of fissures in the freeways and lining up for food stamps) in a quake that had been upgraded on the Richter scale, according to this same journalist, from the original estimate of 6.6 to 6.66...

Occasionally he would sit at the town's one bar and over a beer he'd debate the New World Order with a beekeeper in a baseball cap who outflanked him at every turn on points of political history, described himself as a "libertarian conservative who can't stand liberals or militias" and who insisted, using detailed constitutional and etymological arguments derived from ancient Greek, that "America is a republic, not a democracy..."

He spent one Christmas alone, in self-inflicted solitary, detached at last after several years in exile from most of the moorings that had tied him to his old life back in Britain, and like some latter-day Scrooge, he found himself assailed, of course, by all the ghosts and distant objects he'd mislaid or thrown away to escape to this place. On Christmas day he picked up the phone and called one of his oldest friends in London, the widow of his other oldest friend and he was shocked as always, thanks to fiber-optic technology, by the 'fact' she sounded close enough to touch (for some reason he preferred to imagine her living in another quaint, yet inaccessible dimension, at the edges of some lost horizon he called the distant past where everything abandoned is stored yet subject to decay, like food in a malfunctioning refrigerator, like crackling voice recordings on perishable wax discs).

Instead she's right here next to me, her voice crisp and light and girlish, thrown back twenty years by the shock of this call and she takes the phone into another room so we can talk unimpeded without being overheard by her new family. Within minutes we're talking old times, old friends and it all feels so effortless leaning back two decades into the old understandings, the shared and private language, the sweet weight of intimacy and closeness recollected where you move in unison in the tiny gaps that separate each breath along a single string of words that draws one party in towards the other down the line. It feels so comfortable and right to talk here and now in the present tense across 6,000 miles and an eight-hour time difference, then pause to wait inside a silence, wait for it to break without having to worry about what's coming next, confident in the knowledge—possibly fallacious—that the person on the other end is riding every nuance right alongside you and that everything is flowing unimpeded back and forth along the telepathic circuitry set up all those years ago in all those hours spent sitting together in the same apartment where she's sitting now, in the hours that passed as we sat there listening to music, smoking, making cups of tea, dissecting who said what to whom with what effect earlier that evening in the pub, watching the grey London dawn come up, slow and still, over the rain-wet rooftops of the houses opposite.

Suddenly it's time to leave home again and come back here to where I live and as I replace the receiver I catch myself, reflected in the mirror by the mantlepiece, face cracked open in the goofy, oafish adolescent grin I recognize from ancient schoolboy portraits in the family photo album. Imperceptibly, old London wraps me in its foggy aura and I move about the sunlit California kitchen with the costermonger swagger of a juvenile extra in *Oliver!*, the musical. My accent has slipped so far back down towards its 1950s cockney origin that the attendant at the Arco station, where I stop several hours later to buy gas, cannot understand a single word I'm saying.

Biographies

DAVE ALVIN is a songwriter, guitarist and singer who grew up in Downey, California when there were still orange groves. In 1979 he founded the legendary roots-rock band, The Blasters, he was later a member of the influential punk band X. Since 1987 he has concentrated on his own solo albums as well as producing other artists. Alvin studied writing at Long Beach State with Richard Lee, Elliot Fried and Gerald Locklin. He has written two books, *Nana, Big Joe and the Fourth of July*, and the 1995 Incommunicado release, *Any Rough Times Are Now Behind You*.

ALLISON ANDERS was raised in rural Kentucky, spent much of her youth running away from home and hitchhiking around the United States. She credits these experiences with inspiring her cinematic creations as a filmmaker. Her work includes *Border Radio*, co-directed with Dean Lent and Kurt Voss (1989), *Gas Food Lodging* (1992), *Mi Vida Loca* (1994), *Four Rooms*, co-directed with Alex Rockwell, Robert Rodriquez and Quentin Tarantino (1995) and the upcoming *Grace of My Heart*. Allison attended UCLA film school where she won the Nichols Fellowship from the Academy of Motion Picture Arts and Sciences for her screenplay *Lost Highway*. In 1995 she was awarded a MacArthur Fellowship. Ms. Anders has three children. Her eldest, Tiffany, lives in Seattle, her daughter Devon and son Ruben live with their mom in Topanga Canyon.

RON ATHEY has lived in Los Angeles since 1963. He began his performance career in 1981, a collaboration with Rozz Williams called *Premature Ejaculation*, which was violent and short-lived. Since 1992, Ron Athey & Co. have toured *Martyrs & Saints* and *4 Scenes In A Harsh Life* in the US, UK, Europe and Mexico City. By day, he works as Assistant-to-the-Editor of the *L.A. Weekly* in addition to writing about arts and culture. His writing has also appeared in the *Village Voice*, *Details*, *Ben is Dead*, *Provocateur*, *Steam* and *Infected Faggot Perspectives*. Athey is still writing *Gifts of the Spirit*, a collection of short stories and recollections based on his training to be a Pentacostal minister, the accompanying perversions and aftermath, for which he received the 1994 PEN Center award for HIV/AIDS Writers. In 1996, in addition to a solo visual arts show at ACME Gallery in Santa Monica, Ron Athey & Co. will be extensively touring Europe and Brazil with *Deliverance*, his new performance piece which was commissioned by the Institute of Contemporary Art, Live Arts Department, London.

DANIEL CANO was born in Santa Monica. He grew up on the westside of Los Angeles and attended Santa Monica High School. After returning from Vietnam in 1969, where he received the Purple Heart, he completed studies at Santa Monica College, CSU Dominguez Hills, and the universities of Madrid and Granada, Spain. He has held administrative positions at UCLA, UC Davis and CSU Dominguez Hills. He began writing fiction in 1970. His first novel *Pepe Rios* (Arte Publico Press) was published in 1991. *Shifting Loyalties* (Arte Publico Press) was published in 1995. He is currently working on a sequel to *Pepe Rios* and he teaches at Santa Monica College, where he is an Associate Professor of English.

BERNARD COOPER is the author of *Maps To Anywhere,* and *A Year of Rhymes* (both from Penguin). *Burl's* is from *Truth Serum,* a recent collection of memoirs from Houghton Mifflin. Cooper received the 1991 PEN/Ernest Hemingway Award and a 1995 O. Henry Prize. His work has been widely anthologized, including *The Best American Essays of 1988, The Best American Essays of 1995, The Oxford Book of Literature On Aging,* and *The Penguin Book of Gay Short Stories,* and in many publications including *Harper's Magazine, The Paris Review* and *The Los Angeles Times Magazine.*

DR. VAGINAL DAVIS was born in Los Angeles as a result of the fornication of an unwed 46-year-old Creole woman and a 21-year-old Mexican man under a table during a Ray Charles concert at the Hollywood Palladium in the early 1960s. Miss Davis grew up disadvantaged, yet spirited in the housing projects of East LA, South Central and Watts. She began her career as a child, performing in the streets as a public nuisance. During the punk and post-punk era she became notorious in the seminal art and music scenes with her many concept bands, The Afro Sisters, Cholita (the female Menudo), black fag, and PME, which just recorded their debut LP, *The White to be Angry,* recorded by Steve Albini. Her published work includes the stories *Myself Sexual (Discontents: An Anthology of New Queer Writers,* 1992 Amethyst Press), *Monstar (Good To Go: An Anthology of West Coast Writers,* 1994, Zero Hour Press) *The Pioneering Periodicals, Fertile LaToya Jackson* and *Shrimp: The Magazine for Licking and Sucking Bigger and Better Feet.* As an award-winning Blacktress, she can be seen in the PBS mini-series *Tales of the City, Hustler White,* as well as her own underground experimental films. She is currently working on a semi-autobiographical novel called *Mary Magdalene.*

BOB FLANAGAN is the author of several books of poetry and prose, including *The Wedding of Everything, Slave Sonnets,* and the infamous *Fuck Journal,* which was destroyed by its printer in India out of fear of reprisals by Indian customs agents. Selections from his current work in progress, *The Book of Medicine,* appear in numerous journals and anthologies, including *High Risk* (Dutton/Plume) and *Best American Erotica, 1993.* In collaboration with his partner Sheree Rose, Bob Flanagan's performances have shocked and inspired audiences from coast to coast. Their most recent work, *Visiting Hours,* an installation at the Santa Monica Museum of Art, dealt with Bob's lifelong battle with cystic fibrosis and its influence on his sexuality. The installation subsequently traveled to New York and Boston. *Bob Flanagan: Supermasochist,* a book of interviews with Bob and photographs by Sheree Rose, was published in 1993 by Re/Search Publications. Bob Flanagan succumbed to his disease as heroically as he lived on January 4, 1996—nine days after his forty-third birthday. *Sick,* a feature-length documentary directed by Kirby Dick, in collaboration with Bob Flanagan and Sheree Rose will be completed in Spring, 1996.

DICK HEBDIGE is the author of three books, *Subculture: The Meaning of Style, Cut 'n'Mix: Culture, Identity and Caribbean Music* and *Hiding in the Light: On Images and Things.* Born and raised in London, Britain he emigrated to the USA in 1992 and is currently Dean of Critical Studies and Director of the MFA Writing Program at California Institute of the Arts.

JIM KALIN wrestled varsity at 158 lbs for Ohio State University, where he graduated with a degree in Public Relations/Advertising. He has written for *Venice* magazine and has had fiction published in the *Santa Monica Review,* the *Agincourt Irregular,* and *Columbus Singles Scene.* He presently tends bar in Hollywood and has just completed his first novel, *One Worm.*

PAM KIPP is a photographer and filmmaker who currently attends Cal Arts. From San Diego, she began writing at thirteen and hasn't stopped since. She has been published in the underground literary press and cites as influences Wonder Woman, Miss Piggy and Princess Leia. Her work often deals with the excesses of consumer culture of the '70s and '80s.

NANCY KRUSOE is an L.A. writer most recently published in *The Northridge Review, 13th Moon* (excerpts from a collaborative novel written with Jan Ramjerdi), and in *The Best American Short Stories, 1994.* She is currently teaching and working on a novel.

JON LONGHI is the author of several popular short story collections: *Bricks and Anchors, Zucchini and other Stories,* and *The Rise and Fall of Third Leg.* Among his fans is legendary comix artist R. Crumb, who referred to Longhi as "a Bukowski for the '90s." He has read his stories at literary festivals including LtEruption in Portland, Oregon, rock concerts, including the 1992 & 1994 Lollapalooza Festivals, public libraries, college campuses, bookstores, cafes and bars. He resides in San Francisco.

PHONG NGUYEN is a former refugee. Due to the economy, he still lives with his parents in Orange County, plus, no one cooks better than Mom and no one cracks jokes better than Dad. Phong will be the one taking care of them in their old age. He is being pressured to get married and have kids before the age of 30. Phong writes and makes Super 8 films no one has seen.

QUINCY PEARSON was born and raised in Riverside, California before she escaped to Los Angeles. She builds dollhouses out of cardboard and paints knife-wielding devil girls, while working stupid, low-paying retail jobs. She has been published in several underground literary concerns and also publishes her own zines, *Imaginary Friend* and *My Private Life,* and has played in several failed punk bands. She now resides in Silverlake with six cats, one dog, five roommates and a ghost. A recent Cal Arts graduate, she is currently working on a novel, *The Day Jerry Garcia Died.*

PETER PLATE is the author of several novels, including *One Foot Off the Gutter.* He taught himself to write fiction during eight years spent squatting in abandoned buildings. He began performing his work in dive bars and underground clubs during the punk era of the mid-'80s, which has left him with a distinct performance style. He lives in San Francisco, whose extremes of wealth and poverty are interwoven with American myth and history in his unique writing. His new novel *Snitch Factory* is forthcoming on Incommunicado.

JILL ST. JACQUES is an escapee from the Black Ice Fiction Collec-tive, where she alone practiced narrative. He has also been published in *Fiction International, Sensitive Skin, Nobodaddies, Avant Pop: Fiction for a Daydream Nation, Cups,* and *Errant Bodies.* He has also performed his work at Beyond Baroque and LACE in Los Angeles; The Whore Academy in Helsinki; and at Southern Exposure in San Francisco. He lives in Val Verde, California.

DIANE SHERRY CASE is an actress who started writing a few years ago. Her stories have been published in *American Fiction, Best Short Stories by Emerging Writers, Caffeine, Potpourri, Strictly Fiction,* and *The Distillery, Artistic Spirits of the South.* She lives in Santa Monica with her husband, musician Peter Case, and their two young daughters. She has just finished her first novel entitled *Elephant Milk.*

JERRY STAHL's narcotic autobiography *Permanent Midnight* was published by Warner Books. His column *Bad Liver* appears in the *L.A. Reader.* Another column, *A Year To Live,* runs in *Bikini.* His work also appears in British and American *Esquire, Buzz, Raygun* and a variety of other places.

CAROL TREADWELL (or Ms. Treadwell) was born in 1968 in Oakland, California. During her youth, she was raised in a series of 17 separate residences, almost all of which fell within the city limits of either Oakland or Berkeley, California. She graduated from Berkeley High School in 1986 and, after some hedging, followed her parents' wishes and graduated from UC Berkeley in 1991 (with a degree in studio art). Ever since then, much to her pleasure and betterment, she has lived in the Los Angeles metropolitan area. She has published articles in *Yolk* magazine and the *Los Angeles Times.* The only previous publication of her fiction has been in *Stilts,* a zine put out periodically by her revered older sister Elizabeth (also Treadwell). She is currently a student in the Writing Program at Cal Arts.

BRUCE WAGNER wrote *Force Majeure* (Random House, 1991) and *I'm Losing You* (1996). In 1993, he created the critically acclaimed miniseries *Wild Palms.* He has directed a number of volumes of Carlos Castaneda's *Tensegrity* series. He currently lives in Los Angeles, where he writes for films.

BENJAMIN WEISSMAN is an artist and writer living one mile from Dodger Stadium. This year and last he exhibited drawings and paintings at Galerie Krinzinger in Vienna and at the Christopher Grimes Gallery in Santa Monica. He is the author of a story collection entitled *Dear Dead Person* (High Risk Books/Serpent's Tail). He teaches writing and is a Graduate Advisor in the Department of Fine Art at Art Center College of Design. His writing has appeared in *Artforum, Bomb, L.A. Times Book Review* and *The Village Voice Literary Supplement.* He is completing a new book of stories and is also at work with artist Paul McCarthy on a 365 page daybook about a year in the life of a strange kid.

BANA WITT is a former sex slave, software librarian, rock singer and jeweler. Her first two books of poems, *Compass in An Armored Car* and *Eight for Artie (Poems for Pornographer Artie Mitchell)* were followed by a collection of vivid autobiographical short stories, *Mobius Stripper,* published by Manic D Press. She writes and performs her work in San Francisco where she manages to keep walking past open windows.

SANDRA ZANE travels the triangle of San Diego, Loma Linda (birthplace), and Los Angeles on a regular basis. Her Hakka nomadic roots find her in no place and all places at the same time. Currently receiving a MFA in Poetry from SDSU, she's also working on a novel about southland Asian gangs.

About the Editor

NICOLE PANTER was raised in Palm Springs, California. She managed the notorious punk band the Germs in the mid/late '70s; in the early '80s she was in the original cast of *Pee Wee's Playhouse*. She spent 1984-90 on the run, living in Mexico, Haiti, London, India and Nepal. Missing the desert in spring and the smell of night-blooming jasmine in the summer, she finally returned to Southern California and began writing fiction. Her work has been published in *The New Censorship, Clutch, Fuel, L.A. Reader, Chiron Review, Long Shot, Haight Ashbury Literary Journal, Poison Ivy, Rock She Wrote: Women Write About Rock, Pop, and Rap,* and many more. In 1994, Incommunicado published her first book, *Mr. Right On & Other Stories*. She is currently working on her first novel, *Swap Meet*. She teaches writing at Cal Arts and lives near the Pacific Ocean with several vicious dogs.

ACKNOWLEDGEMENT OF COPYRIGHT

A Prayer For Los Angeles ©1995 by Dave Alvin. Originally published in *Any Rough Times Are Now Behind You: Selected Poems and Stories, 1979-1995* by Dave Alvin (Incommunicado, 1995).

Spa-Tel ©1994 by Diane Sherry Case. Originally published in *Caffeine*.

Just Another River in Egypt ©1996 by Jill St. Jacques.

My First Thousand Years in San Bernardino ©1996 by Quincy Pearson.

The Comedy Writer ©1994 by Nicole Panter. Originally published in the *Los Angeles Reader*, December 1994.

Kill Your Darling ©1996 by Pam Kipp.

Dead President's Son ©1996 by Vaginal Davis.

Gifts of the Spirit ©1996 by Ron Athey.

Suzanne ©1996 by Carol Treadwell.

Giving Up the Ghost ©1995 by Daniel Cano. Originally published in *Shifting Loyalties* by Daniel Cano (Arte Publico Press, University of Houston, 1995).

Highway 1 ©1992 by Bana Witt. Originally published in *Mobius Stripper* by Bana Witt (Manic D Press, 1992).

Twins ©1996 by Benjamin Weissman.

Traveling ©1996 by Sandra Zane.

The Age of Love ©1996 by Jerry Stahl.

Pain Journal ©1996 by Bob Flanagan.

Burl's ©1994 by Bernard Cooper. Originally published in the *Los Angeles Times Magazine*, November 1994.

I Fall Apart On Planes ©1996 by Allison Anders.

First ©1996 by Jim Kalin.

Mountain ©1996 by Phong Nguyen.

Ya Heard It Here First ©1996 by Jon Longhi.

Who I'll Run Away With ©1993 by Nancy Krusoe. Originally published in a slightly different form in American Writing, V. 7, 1993.

The Holocaust Museum ©1996 by Bruce Wagner. This excerpt from the novel *I'm Losing You* (Villard Books, 1996), contains material added by the author for this anthology.

The Devil's Quadrant ©1996 by Peter Plate.

Home. Alone. ©1996 by Dick Hebdige is an excerpt from '*on tumbleweed and body bags: remembering america*' catalogue essay for the first biannual exhibition of international art entitled *Longing and Belonging: from the Faraway Nearby* sponsored by SITE Santa Fe (Santa Fe, New Mexico, 1996).

incommunicado

INCOMMUNICADO PRESS ☆ SAN DIEGO

STEVE ABEE ☆ KING PLANET 150 pages, $12.

DAVE ALVIN ☆ ANY ROUGH TIMES ARE NOW BEHIND YOU 164 pages, $12.

ELISABETH A. BELILE ☆ POLISHING THE BAYONET 150 pages, $12.

IRIS BERRY ☆ TWO BLOCKS EAST OF VINE 108 pages, $11.

BETH BORRUS ☆ FAST DIVORCE BANKRUPTCY 142 pages, $12.

PLEASANT GEHMAN ☆ PRINCESS OF HOLLYWOOD 152 pages, $12.

PLEASANT GEHMAN ☆ SEÑORITA SIN 110 pages, $11.

R. COLE HEINOWITZ ☆ DAILY CHIMERA 124 pages, $12.

HELL ON WHEELS ☆ ED. BY GREG JACOBS 148 pages, $15.

JIMMY JAZZ ☆ THE SUB 108 pages, $11.

NICOLE PANTER ☆ MR. RIGHT ON AND OTHER STORIES 110 pages, $11.

PETER PLATE ☆ ONE FOOT OFF THE GUTTER 200 pages, $13.

UNNATURAL DISASTERS ☆ ED. BY NICOLE PANTER 250 pages, $15.

☆ SPOKEN WORD CDS: GYNOMITE—FEARLESS FEMINIST PORN, $14.
EXPLODED VIEWS—A SAN DIEGO SPOKEN WORD COMPILATION, $14.

☆ COMING SOON:

SCREAM WHEN YOU BURN ☆ ED. BY ROB COHEN

DAHLIA & RUDE ☆ ARMED TO THE TEETH WITH LIPSTICK

PETER PLATE ☆ SNITCH FACTORY

AVAILABLE AT BOOKSTORES NATIONALLY OR ORDER DIRECT: INCOMMUNICADO, P.O. BOX 99090 SAN DIEGO CA 92169. INCLUDE $3 SHIPPING FOR 1,2, OR 3 ITEMS, $5 FOR 4 OR MORE. MAKE CHECKS PAYABLE TO ROCKPRESS. FOR CREDIT CARD ORDERS CALL 619-234-9400. WRITE FOR FREE CATALOG OR VISIT OUR WEBSITE: http://www.tumyeto.com/incom/ DISTRIBUTED TO THE TRADE BY CONSORTIUM BOOK SALES.